GYPSY HEART

A NOVEL BY

DEE COHOON-MADORE

DEELIGHTFUL READING

Original Copyright 2014
Revised Edition 2019
Self-published by Dee Cohoon-Madore
Digby, NS, Canada

Visit DEELIGHTFUL READING on the web at
http://deelightfulreading.com

e-mail: dee@deelightfulreading.com

Gypsy Heart, the novel, is fictional. Any similarity to actual
persons is completely coincidental.

Gypsy Heart (paperback) = ISBN 978-0-9869507-3-5
Gypsy Heart (e-book) = ISBN 978-0-9869507-4-2

Cover Designed by Cedar Springs

About the Author

As someone with a youthful spirit, Dee is happily retired in the beautiful village of Digby, Nova Scotia, Canada. The quiet freedom of the seaside setting allows her to escape into endless hours of writing.

Her dysfunctional family was a very sad and unhappy place during childhood, but the resulting poverty in her youth was no deterrent to her resolve to eventually raise two beautiful children and become an entrepreneurial success.

After her business days, she remarried and started to seriously focus on her writing. Dee's first novel Gifted came out of a dream she had one night. Once published, she started recording countless thoughts as they popped into her head in notebooks and on endless scraps of paper. With what seemed like endless material, her next effort was published as an eBook; Tidbits, Tips & Treasures is a self-help book meant to have something for everyone.

Now, her latest effort Gypsy Heart is a revised release of her third book. Updated, it is now available on Amazon, as well as her own website, deelighfulreading.com. GH, as she refers to it, follows on the heels of The Grand Manor, Timeless Love, Secrets in Kanyon Ridge and another updated release of Gifted in Kanyon Beach.

Ideas still flow, and she has now turned her attention to her next adventure, JOY.

Having six novels, to her credit now, Dee hopes that you will share your thoughts with her. Leave a comment on her website at deelightfulreading.com or email her directly at dee@cedarsprings.cc. She reads and replies personally to every bit of correspondence that arrives so, don't be shy.

Dee thanks everyone for their love and support, and hopes you enjoy reading her works as much as she enjoys writing them.

Dedicated to:

My God, who is my source of words, and without
His constant presence in my life, this book
would not have been written.
His guidance and everlasting love,
have led me to this place of
Peace, Tranquility and Creativity I now enjoy.

Acknowledgements

For the many hours spent re-reading Gypsy Heart for this revised copy, I would like to express my sincere thanks and gratitude to my friend Joan Marshall and my 'go to' guy at Cedar Springs for the countless hours you both have dedicated to this book.

Thank you both so much, for always being there for me throughout my edits and re-edits. 'A true friend is one without an agenda... just friendship,' and this is the kind of friendship you have always given me. Thank you for the many hours you have both spent helping me to edit my book when you had so much else to keep you busy. You were always just a phone call or text message away.

Finally, I wish to thank my readers who have always encouraged me to continue writing. Your support is never taken for granted.

My life consists of two kinds of Time
The Time when I am with you
And the Time when I am waiting
To be with you again

Words from my friend and mentor – GAZ

Prologue

The lives of Bradley and Anna Lake resembled a runaway train looking for a place to derail. A couple of young lovers, who didn't know the first thing about love, jumped at the chance for happiness. But what they thought they were searching for, would soon come to a sad end. With the birth of each child, it widened the already growing gap between them. When baby number two, three and four came along not only did the space grow but so did the tension in an already unstable home.

... And then there was Gia, Georgia Emily-Anne Lake, an innocent child who was born smack dab in the middle of chaos, jealousy and abuse and into a torment that would follow her throughout her lifetime.

In her book, Gia goes through her life from her past to present, repeatedly, in order to help rid herself of the torment from where it all began. Back to the time when life got complicated, and her happiness was stolen from her, robbing her of a normal childhood, adolescence and her entire adult life. This journey takes her back in time to try to erase the demons that have haunted her since childhood.

The Present

Georgia Lake and her husband, Lane Walters, have spent their winters in Florida as snowbirds for the past several years. It had been a blessing to be able to escape the cold and usually harsh Canadian winters.

As it became hotter in Florida, they knew it was time to pack up and make the four-day trip back home. It had been a long and tiring trip, but it felt good to be back to the waterfront property in Nova Scotia.

Missing the Florida sunshine, she knew it would soon warm up although it seemed to take forever. Spring had arrived, but signs of winter still lingered and was visible.

Deciding to take up writing, after marrying Lane, she chose to write under her own name. Always having had an interest in writing, she dabbled in poetry, short stories and children's stories but had never had anything come out of it except the pleasure it gave her to finish something.

Already an accomplished novelist of two books, she had decided to write another novel, and this was the perfect time to begin logging her notes that she had written while in Florida. She had done a lot of soul-searching by reaching into the deepest crevices of her past and put it all down on paper.

She could never find time to sit and type them up, but once she got her feet back on Canadian soil, it set the mood again.

She planned to write a semi-autobiographical novel, a more personal journey to track, trace and erase the demons that have haunted her since childhood. She felt ready to start typing up the written thoughts from reams of paper notes, for when she was ready to actually put her book together. She also made a few notes on what she must do to complete her book once she was home.

~

Settling in after the long drive home, it had finally warmed up enough to sit outside in her favorite sun faded, red canvas chair. Sitting in the warmth, of an early spring sun, she thought, 'it doesn't get much better than this,' as she felt the delightful spray of sun touch her skin. Along with her laptop, she brought a notebook and a pencil, but she just sat there with the cover closed thinking about her novel notes but was in no rush to begin. For a few minutes, she just wanted to enjoy being home again.

Off in the distance, she saw a lone sailboat drifting lazily along with the breeze, and she imagined it wouldn't be long before other sailors would be taking their boats out of winter storage too. 'This is definitely the warmest day since we returned, and it feels so good to be back,' she thought.

The breeze off the water was still a little sharp at times, so she wrapped her sweater tighter around her body, laid her head back against the chair and smiled as the afternoon sun touched her face. She had always been aware of the damage the sun can do to her delicate skin, so she didn't spend a lot of time in it unless clothing, a hat and sunscreen protected her. Being fair skinned and a redhead, she burned quite easily.

A sudden gust whipped her hair around, but she didn't care because it was finally warm enough to sit out without being bundled up in heavy clothing. She sensed it would be a good day as another gentle breeze blew in from the Bay of Fundy. The lone sailboat, the first one she had seen so far, held her attention until it disappeared from view.

Resting her head against her chair, she closed her eyes and listened intently to the sounds around her. 'Yes, it really doesn't get much better than this.' Faintly, car horns pierced her solitude and she thought there must be a wedding at the Baptist church on Main Street. It was a perfectly beautiful day for a spring wedding. She, herself, had been married several years ago in the spring. It was a day very similar to this one except hers had been in late May and this was mid-April.

Shouting children caused her to raise her head and shade her eyes against the sun as she saw three young boys climbing up the bank from the beach below. The wind carried their laughter and chatter to where she sat. Watching them for a few minutes, they soon disappeared in search of new adventures... it seemed as if her life had been nothing but adventures. Closing her eyes again, she began to think about many of her own memories. One, in particular, was of how much she hated the darkness and the older she got, the more noticeable it became. Damn him for that. Damn him for everything he had caused her to be afraid of. Damn him for making her entire life seem empty and lonely. Parents... weren't they supposed to make their children feel safe? Never, in her entire life, had she ever felt safe.

Men especially were the most frightening creatures to her. Never trusting them, made every relationship she'd ever had, end in failure. Her mind began to slip back to that unhappy and scary time. Remembering how she hated those nocturnal peregrinations her mind took when night fell. Although they were inevitable, she could not bring herself to enjoy the solitude that nights could bring. She could not stop herself from taking the journey back there, even in the middle of the day.

In order to clear her mind, of the rubble, that had collected there over the years, she remembered a few facts told to her by her mother years ago. About some of the early years of her own tormented life and how she had come to meet Gia's father. For her story to make sense to her, she had to begin with her mother's words.

Opening her laptop to a clean blank page, her fingers hovered over the keyboard, in hesitation. With one single tap, she was ready to begin to transfer her notes.

She knew it would not be easy, but if she wanted her next book to be successful, she had to allow her mind to go through and take the journey. Her first step began as she flipped her notepad open to page one and thought about her mother, Anna.

Bradley and Anna

(The Early Years)

They had met when Anna was barely sixteen, and Bradley was nearly twenty-six. Gia remembered stories over the years that were told of their past lives and from what she had gathered, the relationship had been doomed from the very beginning... because...

Bradley's mother had died when he was only eight months old. His father had been overseas, leaving him and his sister Hannah, orphaned. Hannah was only a few years older than Bradley and she, too, was still only a wee child. Trying to care for her baby brother, she had been much too young and too inexperienced to carry such a burden. Bradley hadn't had anyone except his sister, and she was neither old enough to be a parent or a mentor, but she was all he'd had.

Their father had been serving overseas and had already lost two other sons to typhoid fever. Since there had been no one nearby to help him, they were both 'farmed out' to different relatives who were either too old to take care of two young children or did not have extra money to support them. They ended up with an elderly great aunt who did the best she could with help from Hannah. Their father had sent money home when he could, and it had helped his aunt with the expense of having two extra mouths to feed.

Bradley had no one to teach him the life skills that he needed to have a relationship with other people. He was spoiled mostly to make up for being motherless and any child being raised without a mother was pitiful.

Anna's father had been a drunkard and a rum-runner in the United States until he was caught and had been deported back to his homeland.

Anna was the middle of three daughters. The oldest sister had been born with a heart defect and had needed special care. So, under the doctor's orders, she had been advised to rest as much as possible. It meant that she had been unable to help out around the house like a normal child. She had no chores, no responsibilities of any kind, just rest.

The youngest sister, known as 'the baby,' was spoiled rotten. She had used every possible angle to get out of doing chores and housework. She had her daddy wrapped around her little finger from the time she was born. It had become Anna's responsibility to do the chores that her oldest sister had been unable to do, and the youngest had been too spoiled and lazy to even think about getting her hands dirty. So, Anna had been the one that was picked on and he had mentally, physically, and sexually abused her. She was the one who carried water, filled the wood box, cleaned the barn and tended the animals and when it was not done properly, and to her father's liking, she was beaten into doing it his way. Life was not good for Anna, and she began to search for a way out.

Anna was attractive with long auburn hair and eyes the color of dark chocolate. She was a few months away from her sixteenth birthday when a job opportunity came up outside of her hometown. It had been the perfect excuse for her to leave home and she had anxiously accepted the position and left.

As the wheels of fate would have it, Anna had met Bradley Lake when she showed up for work in his hometown. He was tall, slim, had a great personality and had been quite likeable. His kindness towards her had been what she had been craving from her father. She had finally met someone who had shown a 'sweet' side. That was something she was unfamiliar with but exactly what he had to offer. However, there were consequences when an inexperienced youth confuses kindness with love. In her mind, it had to be love since it had been the only bit of human kindness she had ever known. When he'd offered her a warm spirit and genuine desire, she had grabbed on to it for dear life. She thought it had to be the love she had been searching for but had never found. Consequently, she had been searching for something she would likely never find.

Their relationship had been an accident waiting for a place to happen. She had been looking for a love she'd never had from her father and Bradley, he was looking for the mother's love he had been deprived of as a child. So, there it was, an even swap and a dangerous combination.

Shortly after they met, she had become pregnant, and they were married on a cold December day. Bradley had been a 'Mr. Do Nothing' lazy sort who could not or would not hold on to a job. Whenever a job opportunity would come up, he had looked for reasons why he couldn't take it, and when he did take it he would find reasons why he couldn't keep it. He just didn't want to work, and that was that.

Several years later and producing as many children, life was not great. Having several kids in the house was taking Anna farther and farther away from him. He didn't want the responsibility of children, but they were the end result of his passion for his wife. Brad had always been a selfish loner and had spent a lot of his time walking on the beaches or in the woods. Most times, he had escaped to those places just to be alone. He had never wanted to take one of the children with him to give them an outing; he had been too selfish for that, so he would venture out alone and wanted nothing to do with dragging kids along.

Responsibility not being his forte, he hadn't been a good father, and he simply didn't want to be one. After several years of marriage, and several offspring, he had begun to resent the fact that there were so many children in the house and under foot. He had loved Anna the only way he had known how to, but he'd wanted her for himself. As the birth of each new baby came, it was one more person for Anna to care for, and it had taken her attention away from him. It had seemed that Anna got pregnant every time he hung his pants on the bedpost.

He'd always had someone taking care of him so when Anna came along, he had fully intended for her to take over. The irony of it all was that now he was expected to care for a woman and a brood of kids. Brad had no patience with the children he didn't want, couldn't love and didn't know how to make them feel safe. He had only managed to make them all feel as if they were in his way. He'd resented each one; he had no favorites, he had just seemed to hate them all, especially his fifth child, Gia, (Gee-ya) a nickname for Georgia.

Bradley and Anna had separated shortly after Gia was born. They'd been separated for three years causing the longest gap between births, so Gia was the one baby that Anna could actually enjoy. They bonded from the beginning and Anna spent a lot of time with her. When Gia was born fifth in line, the oldest child had been only six, so there had been no time in between births to spend with any one child long enough to form a strong bond like that of Anna and Gia.

When Gia turned three, her parents had gotten back together, and in no time another baby was born and one more person for Bradley to abuse and resent. Even though there had been a new baby in the house, the bond and the closeness had remained between Gia and her mother, causing jealousy on Bradley's part. He hated the bond that Anna had with her daughter.

Turning into a mean-spirited sod, Brad could not stand the fact that there were so many little people standing between him and Anna. Having a sadistic nature, he had all his children scared to death of him. He had gotten enjoyment out of it when he realized he could control them with fear.

There were times when he had tried to be a dad, and he would play and romp around the living room. Bradley, having no social skills with children, had not learned how to play or to interact with them. He was rough, not realizing his own strength, and sometimes they had thought it was intentional so that he could make them cry. Nearly every time he had played with them, they would end up bawling, and usually he had not given up until he had most of them, if not all, in tears. He had not considered them as real people but instead, they were royal pains in his ass just having them around. Although he was rough and sadistic, he did not know or care about, the pain he was causing. If you are giving it, then you cannot feel it until someone gives it back to you. In hindsight, Gia felt he hadn't left this world guilt free and that, in itself, was her revenge.

They'd heard, "shut up, or I'll give you something to cry for," so many times that they all learned how to stifle their emotions, and no one wanted him to play or to be around them. It was always a tossup between the joy of having a dad to play with them and knowing the end result, so they avoided him completely.

When someone had done something that deserved punishment, no one dared admit to it. If they had told the truth or had come forward, it still caused them all to get the strap for not squealing on the one who was guilty. They soon learned to lie about everything because the truth had never won them any prizes, so they learned at the beginning that there was no fairness in their home either. They all saw and quickly understood his sadistic side when it came to his children. He seemed to take great joy in bringing them to tears. Yet in the eyes of friends and neighbors, he was the greatest thing since sliced bread was invented, but he was not that shining star in his own children's eyes.

He wanted them out of his sight as early as possible and so every night at six o'clock they were sent to bed. In the summertime, while all their friends were still outside playing, they were in their beds and expected to go to sleep with the sun still shining high in the sky.

Each night Gia and her older sisters, Megan and Molly, would cuddle under the covers in the double bed and giggle and laugh and tell each other what they wanted to be when they grew up, and they played the quilt patch game to pass the time. The 'quilt patch game' was invented by them. They would each choose a favorite patch from the quilt that covered their heads, and they would point at a pretty square and say, 'I want a dress made out of this someday,' and when they each had a turn, they would choose another patch until the entire quilt was done. Even while their heads were under the covers, it was still daylight.

Little did they know that 'father dearest' had been standing at the bottom of the stairwell listening. Then when he heard a snicker or a stifled giggle, his voice roared up through the walls for them to shut up and go to sleep. They would desperately try to whisper as quietly as they possibly could, but he was always listening and waiting for an opportunity to scream at them. When he had gotten tired of yelling, they would hear his foot thump on the first step, and the belt buckle would rattle at the same time. They had heard the slick 'swoosh' of the one movement sound of the belt being whipped from the loops and then fear set in.

The siblings could never understand how or why a mother could sit downstairs with her sewing needle, darning needle or her ironing and ignore the fact that her children were being abused and tortured by a lunatic. It made no sense to them, and a little bit of resentment grew between all of them after each episode, especially towards their mother, because there had been no one else there to protect them and she did not. They only had each other, and so the deception, lies and mistrust began for Gia whenever someone new entered her life. The walls she had put in place began when she was a small child, and she trusted no one and believed that everyone lied to her. So far, no one had proved her wrong.

Gia figured that neither parent had been taught about love, neither one had gotten the love they needed and deserved, nor did they know how to give it. The only thing Bradley had known was abandonment, and Anna had been familiar only with abuse. Were they even capable of showing love or had this been the only way they had known, and the rest had to be learned? Since neither one had had parents to love them, teach them or show them, then how were they really supposed to know how to love a child; then again, was that not supposed to come naturally to parents? The first instinct parents should have, is to not want their children to be treated as they had been and work toward changing that.

The only logical explanation was that they had been two dysfunctional people who had come from dysfunctional families with dysfunctional family values. Neither had any concept about family, love, relationships or a normal home life. They did not have respect for each other and therefore had absolutely none for their children. Gia often wondered if it had been impossible for them to know how to be kind and loving parents because, to her knowledge, they never were.

Gia had remembered only sporadic parts of her childhood. Suppression is a wonderful thing. Snippets of her young life were few and far between, but there were a few things that came to mind. She remembered that she and her siblings were made to play outside more than they were allowed to play inside. Kids were meant to be 'seen and not heard,' but in this case, it was 'not seen' also. There was no communication in the house.

They were not allowed to have an opinion. They had no right to speak because they thought children were obviously born without brains. There were orders, and they were to be followed, or they paid the consequences. Those consequences were to go to bed without supper, or a slap-up-side of the head. His belt could easily be torn from the belt loops and a leather strap hung by the sink for shaving purposes, or a kindling lay in the warming oven nearby, all just waiting for an opportunity to be used.

When they were very young, treats and snacks were not heard of. Anna was a great cook, bread maker and baker. Gia and her siblings would come home from school, hungry as bear cubs, and the smell of homemade bread hit them in the face as soon as they walked in the house. They were not allowed to have a slice no matter how much they begged, or whined, that they were hungry. It did not matter to her.

"You'll wait 'til supper!" she'd snap. "If you eat now, you'll ruin your meal! Now get outside and play!" Each of them could have eaten a loaf of bread and still would have been hungry after the scant portion they would get for supper.

At the table, if they asked for another piece of bread, Brad would scream at them and call them names like pigs or gluttons. They were afraid to ask for more, so they learned, very quickly, to leave the table hungry. He cursed and swore at them for being 'gluttons' and 'eating too much' but after they were fast asleep, with growling bellies, he would go into the pantry and eat everything that was left over from supper.

When Anna baked cookies, she would use a recipe for three dozen cookies, but she would get six dozen out of it. When they were baked and on a cookie rack to cool, they were no bigger around than a quarter. Gia, in her mind's eye, can still see her mother with the cookie jar under her arm, passing out one little cookie to each kid and then putting the cookie jar back in the pantry. That would be the last time they would see that particular batch of more than five dozen cookies. Brad would eat the rest of them once the kids were safely upstairs in their beds.

When they were fortunate enough to see a cake on the counter, they knew it was their dessert. But the slice was so thinly cut it would fall apart on their plate. There would be over half a cake left from the scant pieces served and never seen again. There was never anything left over for school lunches the next day. No fruit, nothing sweet except for a molasses sandwich wrapped up in a piece of waxed paper. From breakfast, which was usually a bowl of oatmeal, cream of wheat or Red River cereal, to the molasses sandwich at noon and home in the afternoon... hunger had already set in.

If they reached for anything on the table, Brad was like 'Quick Draw McGraw' with his knife at the ready to rap them on the knuckles. They were not allowed to have a knife at their place at the table. Either Brad or Anna would spread their bread and Anna prepared their plates by serving them their portions, buttering their vegetables and cutting their meat up as if they were all toddlers. To say they were selfish was an understatement. It was all about them. It seemed they were both in the running for first place. He begrudged them every bite and Anna did not care if they ever had a full belly. They made sure, though, that they, themselves, were well fed and they could snack any time of the day or night.

There had been no happy conversations at meal times to share what happened that day. There were no words spoken at the table except to pass something and many times, they left the table still hungry. Nobody cared, so, 'shut up, eat and disappear', became the motto in their house. Times were not good in the Lake household that Gia could ever remember.

Once, from one of Brad's solo trips to the beach, he'd found a huge piece of dried beige-brown beach sponge with numerous arms and legs. Brad snuck it home and kept it under the sink and out of sight from the kids. One day, and a rare time when life was normal in the house, he had to 'upset the apple cart' so to speak, with his fear tactics. He had pulled that scary looking thing out from under the sink and held it over his head shaking it into the air and letting out a scream. Each child stood stark still, paralyzed with fear, and he was in his glory.

"This is called a Bugger-Boo!" he shouted, shaking it at them. "When you are bad, this thing will get you, so you'd better behave yourselves!" Grimacing, everyone all took a step backwards, pulling their necks back as far as they could to avoid it touching their faces. As he shook it at them the 'arms and legs' were flying all over the place, and they figured, if one had touched them, they would be sucked up by it and disappear forever. She remembered how mean and yes, even cruel, adults could be when it came to the trickery that scared the life and soul out of children, while finding sheer joy and entertainment in it.

Anna had turned her back, so no one would see her grinning from ear to ear and enjoying the fact that her children were scared out of their minds. She could not hide the thrill it had given her, but they all saw her shoulders moving up and down in a fit of laughter. From then on, whenever anybody had done anything wrong, the threat of the 'Bugger-Boo' was front and center.

She remembered another time when there were several kids around the kitchen table doing school homework, and a couple of preschoolers were playing on the floor when the back door was flung open with a bang! There, in the doorway, stood this horrible looking 'thing' wearing a long trench coat. It had big bulging eyes and a long elephant trunk-like nose. Both the noise from the door being slammed open, the sight in the doorway along with a loud roar, sent the kids into a panic mode. Fear gripped them all as they froze in silence. This 'thing' walked with two stiff legs, arms raised and had taken a few slow motion, robotic-type steps towards the middle of the kitchen. In a deep, scary voice it growled, "I am Trace-Leg, and I have come to get you!" The entire kitchen filled up with screaming, crying kids while Anna stood there laughing and pointing at them like they were all idiots for being afraid.

As it turned out, it had been Anna's youngest sister who was there for a visit and had found a gas mask, goggles and trench coat in the old attached garage and thought it would be fun to dress up and scare the young one. Again, an adult had taken the opportunity to scare the daylights out of innocent children. So... where was the trust factor supposed to begin? When they couldn't trust the adults in their family, then who they to trust? That concept set in quickly for Gia even as a young child.

~

Her mother had ears like a hawk. By the time Gia was in high school, her mother had a habit of napping every afternoon. Getting home from school, the house was usually quiet, and her mother was lying down. The world had to stop so she could sleep. One day Gia opened the refrigerator door, and as soon as her hand pulled it open, her mother roared from the back bedroom. "Don't touch that milk in there, that's for my tea!"

To this day Gia has difficulty drinking a glass of milk.

Another time during one of the infamous naps, Gia turned the television on to watch the Guiding Light and The Secret Storm. Once again came a roar from the bedroom.

"Turn that TV down, I'm trying to sleep!" Gia turned the TV down so low that she had to sit on the floor with her ear pressed up against the speaker to hear what they were saying. It didn't matter though because, again, came the roar from the end of the hall.

"I told you to turn that damned TV down, you're an ungrateful little pup! Don't you have any consideration for other people!?"

By that time Gia had the TV off and had gone to her room. Nothing would ever please her mother, and it had to be 'her way or no way.'

They had gotten a table hockey game for Christmas one year. Gia's mother and 'stepfather' played the game all the time. Then one afternoon, at naptime, Gia and one of the siblings decided they would learn how to play. Excitement grew as they spun the men around the game to shoot or prevent the puck from crossing the goal line. They would give little squeals of delight as the game progressed and as they pulled the men down the 'ice' the sliding of the rods was heard as far down as the back bedroom.

"Stop that noise out there! Get away from that game! Don't you know how noisy that is when I'm trying to sleep!" The game had to stop, and so did the world, and no conversations were heard so that 'Mommy Dearest' could have her nap.

~

The Lake family moved around a lot from house to house like gypsies and Gia did not remember being in one place for longer than a year and sometimes less. Their furnishings were sparse, and there had always been a barrel in the kitchen. Wherever the barrel was pulled out from its spot, a move was in the air. It held their few pots and pans, dishes and glassware for the move. She remembered helping to carry furniture from one place to another and running through a big empty house wondering which room she and her sisters were going to sleep in that night. The other old houses they had lived in were either being torn down, sold or her mother heard of another place that was cheaper to rent, but there was always a reason to move. In one neighborhood alone, she remembered living in six different houses, and that was not counting the many times they had moved back to her grandparent's home to live in the ell.

They liked it when they were living in the ell. Except for her family, no one, to Gia's knowledge, had ever lived there. That seemed to be the stopover until something else became available. They were not in one place long enough to set down roots and call it home. Many times, they would wake up in one house and were told to go to another house after school and her mother would spend the day looking for someone to move their belongings. It was like magic when they arrived 'home' from school. Everything was unpacked; beds were set up and made as if they had always lived there.

~

She didn't remember her grandparents as being anything except Christians. The stories had come from her mother's memories from her own childhood. Their grandfather had changed his life around completely from a drunken rumrunner to an over the top religious fanatic. From Gia's earliest memories of them, both grandparents were strict 'God-fearing' people and made their grandchildren afraid of God. They all loved their Grandma and Grandpa and enjoyed spending time with them, but unlike her friend's grandparents, the Lake kids were not spoiled by theirs. They were good to them although they were strict and if Gia and her siblings listened to them, and did what they were told, then life was good. They were made to go to church whether they wanted to go or not. The minister preached about unconditional love that God had for everyone and how His only Son loved us so much that He sacrificed His own life. "Jesus loves you, Gia," she remembered her Grampa saying. It might have been comforting, had she known what love was.

They were scared straight by their grandfather's strict comments about God and how He saw everything they did. The smallest things, like lipstick and nail polish, brought down a flurry of condemnation. Their biggest fear was disappointing their grandfather and listening to his rants. He told them they'd go to Hell if they wore nail polish or lipstick. He would point his finger at them and tell them that if they were meant to have red lips and painted fingernails, they would have been born with them. He told them it was the work of the devil and if you play with the devil, you will end up in Hell with him. Gia and her siblings lived in fear, not only from their parents and grandparents but they added God to the mix as well.

Broken Promises and Disappointments

There were many disappointments in Gia's young life; one right after another until she learned to mistrust everything that was told to her.

One warm, summer day, an uncle came for a visit. The uncle and Gia's parents were sitting on the veranda chatting, drinking water from mason jars and watching the children play in the front yard. Gia and her sisters were on the lawn playing jump rope with an old piece of rope they had retrieved from a neighbor's dump. When Gia had had her turn, she ran up on the veranda, and her uncle promptly pulled her onto his lap. Spreading his legs wide apart, he insisted she sit close to his body so that she was nearly sitting on his hip.

"How would you like it if I buy you a brand-new skipping rope?" he asked. Instantly imagining herself having a shiny plastic skip rope, she beamed. Seeing her excitement, he pulled her thigh even closer and promised to buy her one of her very own. Gia was beside herself with anticipation, and he took advantage of it by stroking her back and down her thigh. She was unable to remember anyone ever rubbing her back, and although it felt good, she felt uncomfortable. Relief came when her sisters called her to take her turn. Thinking there would likely be a price to pay, it was just as well that the promise was never followed up.

Another time when he took the opportunity to pull her onto his lap, he stroked her long hair that hung down her back. "You have beautiful hair, Gia, and one day soon," he said, "I'm going to take you to a hairdresser and pay her to give you a real pretty hair-do, would you like that?"

"Oh, yes, I would!" she said clapping her hands while envisioning sitting in a real hairdresser's chair. Gia thought of nothing else other than the fact that she was going to sit in a beauty shop and have someone do her hair! A trip to the hairdresser never happened either. She had been taken in yet again by his promises.

Another broken promise came when he told her he wanted to take her to town and buy her pretty clothes and shoes for school. "How would you like to have a new pair of saddle shoes," he asked as he pulled her close, "or how about white bucks?"

Letting her guard down again, she was absolutely thrilled that he had chosen her to take shopping for new stuff for school. He had made her feel special because he had chosen her over the other sisters, but the shopping trip never came either. Every time he came to visit, she thought he was there to take her shopping. He promised to take her to a circus that had come to town, and another time, to a nice dinner at the restaurant in town. In the moment the promises were made, she felt like a princess awaiting the ball, but the carriage never arrived to pick her up.

There were many other visits over the years but not one of the promises was ever brought up and there was never a reason why the promises were broken nor was there ever an apology. There were always people around when he made the promises, but no one had asked him why he made promises he had no intentions on keeping. They allowed him to continue to disappoint her time after time.

Disappointment had become second nature to her, and her young heart had been broken so many times that it felt natural by now. Why he had chosen her, to make broken promises to, she did not know. She later came to realize that all he wanted from her was to snuggle close enough to feel her leg against his crotch. What other reason could there have been for a man to make promises to a child who had never had anything except hand-me-downs and heartache? Therefore, every promise, that was ever made, gave her hope that something special could actually happen to her, only to be let down repeatedly.

Family members made promises that also never saw the light of day. It was always 'you do for me, and I'll give you' promises, but whatever she'd do for them, it was never reciprocated. They used her, and they didn't care about her disappointment. She wanted so badly to feel a part of something that she allowed herself to be used in hopes that someone would actually like her for who she was and not only for what she could do for them.

She was well acquainted with the phrase 'alone in a crowd' because she had never felt any differently for as long as she could remember. She had enough broken promises and disappointments to last a lifetime. From a very young age, with every broken promise, it cut deeper into her heart until she believed that everybody was a liar.

On a sunny winter afternoon when Gia was six or seven years old, the neighborhood kids gathered for a skating day. The pond was a good walk into the woods, and since her brothers and sisters were going, she wanted to go along too. She would do almost anything just to be acknowledged as 'one of the crowd,' and even though she hated the cold she was willing to stay out in it to be a part of the skating team. They had all helped to clear off the pond so that skating could begin. Gia and her sisters had one pair of old second-hand skates that were to be shared, but Gia had known that she didn't stand a snowball's chance in Hell of getting a turn on the pond, so she busied herself with other things while the others skated.

After the skating party was over, once again she was forgotten as everyone gathered up their belongings to head home. They seemed to have forgotten she was even there, and they left her behind to find her own way home through the woods. It was as if she had been invisible to them. Not one person, family or friend, called to tell her that they were leaving. When she realized the pond was not abuzz, she turned just as she saw that everyone had headed for the path in the woods. She had to run through the snow to keep them in her sight so that she could get safely out of the woods.

She had felt the same way in the one-room schoolhouse packed with kids of all ages and every grade. She never did anything special enough to stand out, and she was never called upon to read aloud. She tried very hard to be special for someone, anyone, but it didn't happen.

She remembered how she absolutely hated the cold. Winter had never been her favorite time of year. The long walks to school were very difficult for her, and she had never, ever been dressed warm enough. The hand-me-down clothes she'd had to wear hadn't been heavy enough to keep her warm, and her worn hand-me-down boots had little protection against the cold making her feet instantly cold when they hit the snow. Many times, on her walks to school, she would cry from being so cold. Older school chums would carry her on their shoulders and although she was still cold, it kept her feet up off the freezing ground.

After tearing the old school down, the students were bused to the high school. School friends didn't remember, or didn't care, to save her a seat with them in the cafeteria, and she sat alone and listened to them giggle and laugh. Her heart was broken, but she didn't let it show, as fear set in that they might be laughing at her. She still felt like a deserted rat, so she sat alone pushing a sandwich down past the lump in her throat and pretended everything was perfectly fine.

She remembered the scant Christmases they'd had. There had been very little money for anything during the early years. The same was true at Christmas. It was not a difficult concept to figure out why there was barely anything under the sparsely trimmed tree. She supposed her parents had done the best they could, with what they had, but when you are a child and still believed in Santa Claus, it was not easy to accept that even Santa was a disappointment like everything else in her life.

They hung their stockings up on Christmas Eve, but they were not the pretty red ones trimmed in white faux fur. Their Christmas stockings were their father's wool socks with an orange jammed down in the toe, a barley toy candy, a ribbon candy and a few pieces of hard tack, all of which were covered with wool from the sock. Those were the Christmases that she remembered, without fondness. She still dreaded that particular time of year. There had not been a time during her young life where she felt the creature comforts of love, security or protection.

Present

These memories have haunted her since childhood. She had to go back there in order to deal with her issues, but for now she just hit 'save' on her pages and closed the laptop. 'That's enough for today,' she thought as she tried to shake off the thoughts of yesteryear. They'd held her captive over her life, and both her thoughts and her actions had brought her to this point. She took the pencil, that she had pushed into the back of her hair and drew a line through the finished pages in the notebook, indicating they were typed and done.

Gia, deep into her past, was forced back to the waterfront by a voice. "Hey, you, where were you just now?" Lane asked bringing her back from her memories and handing her a mug of hot tea. "It looked as if you were miles from here."

"It's more like years past from here, instead of miles, Lane," Gia replied, smiled and thanked him for the tea and cupped both hands around the mug feeling the warmth. "I've decided to start copying my notes over to the laptop today, and it takes me to places I'd rather forget and although the notes have already been written it's still difficult to go through them again."

He figured by the expression on her face that she had been somewhere unpleasant. He'd seen the expression many times while she sat in the lanai, in Florida, and wrote page after page of notes. He knew it was not an easy process for her, but he thought once it had been written down it would help but there it was again, the expression of pain. "Yes," he said, "I'm sure it is and a word of advice if I may, take your time and don't dwell on it for too long at one time. Perhaps it will make the journey easier."

"Thanks for the advice Lane, but don't worry about me, I'll be fine."

"How's the tea?" Lane asked.

"It's hitting the spot," she lied as she realized she hadn't taken a sip of it yet. She didn't seem to be in a mood for conversation and

Lane sensed it as he, too, had noticed the tea level in her cup had not dropped. On that note, he touched her shoulder knowing she would not take his advice. She knew he meant well, but he didn't understand. He quietly walked away and left her with her thoughts as that seemed to be where she was anyway. Strolling down to the embankment that overlooked the water's edge, Gia watched him as he lit up a cigarette. It griped her every time he lit one of those damned things up. She watched as he lifted his head to blow smoke into the air and she drifted off into her own thoughts again.

About Lane

Gia and Lane came from different worlds but had similar upbringings. They were born only five months, to the day, apart and on opposite sides of the same Province but they may as well had lived on separate planets. They were as different as day was from night, but she enjoyed his friendship, his company and his warmth. Above all, she knew without a doubt that she could trust him... well... as much as she could trust anybody.

A mutual friend introduced Gia to Lane. Gia knew only scattered bits about Lanes past life and the parts that he did share, were interesting.

Lane had built a career as an airline pilot. He told her many interesting stories about his travels and of the exotic places he had been. One of the freebies of the job was free travel for himself and his first wife. They'd wanted to get in as much travel as possible, before deciding to have children and what better way than to do it for free!

On his days off, he often made travel plans, and they would spend a few days here and there on any part of the globe. He told her they had travelled overseas and had taken in the sights of the Holy Land, parts of Germany, Switzerland, Austria, France and many other smaller countries. They could take in several countries in one day using Germany as their home base during their stay. They had a choice to either rent a vehicle or hop a train, and Gia thought that being a hobo on a train for a few days sounded exciting.

The money they had saved on flights, Lane tucked it away and used it towards other trips. They would fly, free, to Spain, go aboard a ship and sail out on a seven-day excursion. He would describe places that she had only seen in magazines. As he told the stories, he would show her pictures, home movies and slides.

He said he had always had his wife in standby mode with a suitcase at the ready. He'd check the manifest, and if he was flying to a sunny destination with a few empty seats, he'd call and have her report immediately to the airport, and she would fill one of those seats. On these occasions, the flight was usually long, and it was mandatory for him to stay over and another pilot would fly the plane out. If the plane was not due back for several days, then they would check out the Island and enjoy their days in the sun.

Gia lived vicariously through his adventures, and although it was not her who had been with him, she still enjoyed mentally travelling to these places as she watched it on film and listened to his well-told stories. It was interesting, to a degree, hearing about them, when they globetrotted around to different parts of the world. While he was off enjoying the world, and building a career, Gia had been busy making a mess of her own life.

She didn't speak a lot about her past and was always under the assumption that her life was not interesting enough for anyone to listen to her tell about it, so she did not.

Gia and Lane had known each other for many years before they were married. They each had other lives, marriages and were good friends over the years. Then, when they both found themselves alone, they began to spend time together on a friendly basis. The nearest they came to a "date" was a sandwich at his kitchen table before she headed out on the hour and a half drive home. She would think about him on the drive and in her heart, she knew he was a decent man, and she liked him a lot, but she could not push it. Not yet anyway.

She had been single longer than Lane, and she had secretly hidden her feelings for him. She was far from a kid and knew it was a combination of admiration, respect and a little bit of a crush. She just had wonderful feelings when she was near him and didn't think it would lead to more than that, so she left it alone.

Lane had gone through one of the toughest ordeals that life had to offer. The loss of a spouse is not easy, and she did not want to hinder their friendship by showing signs of interest. She had not been in a relationship for several years, and she was not eager to rush into another one. Each time she visited him she noticed that he still wore his wedding band. To her, it was an indicator that he was not ready for anything more than what they already had. Lane was friendly, kind and humorous with a big heart. He was always telling funny stories and kept Gia in stitches while she visited. She liked that about him, and it gave her something to think about on her drives home.

One day while she was in his hometown, she called him from her cell phone to see if he was going to be home. He said that he would be and invited her over and that he'd have the kettle on when she arrived. They always hugged when they saw each other, and he had great hugs, and it felt good to be in his arm even if only briefly.

He put her cup of tea on the table and joined her with his coffee, while they talked across the table. Something was different that day. She could not quite put her finger on it, but there was something different about him. 'Finger' was the operative word here. He was not wearing his wedding band! 'Finally,' she thought, 'he has taken it off.' It had taken him more than a year, but she felt it was none of her business, so she never let on that she noticed it was gone. It left a white mark on his finger since he had such a deep tan and that was noticeable enough.

Telling him it was time she got on the road, he helped her with her coat. Turning toward him, she waited for her usual peck on the lips and that wonderful hug. He looked at her differently this time, and as she looked into his eyes, she was certain he could hear her heart pound. Drawing her into his arms, he held her close to him. She was trying to enjoy it as she closed her eyes to allow herself to feel him close, but she was nervous as a long-tailed cat in a room full of rocking chairs. She hated those feelings of anxiety, Damn it!

He drew back far enough to look into her eyes and focusing on her lips he closed in for a peck only this time his lips lingered and instead of enjoying the moment she freaked out. She hadn't wanted to ruin what she felt was building into something special, so she pulled away from him and turned and practically ran out the door. Her heart was pounding in her chest, and her hands shook as she unlocked her car door. She could think of nothing else except his hug and his lips pressing briefly on hers.

It was a long drive home, but she didn't remember much about it. She had mentally kicked herself all the way home for not accepting the moment as it had been presented, to see where it would have led. All she could think about was what she should have done and all the shoulda, woulda, couldas was not going to change anything now. The moment she had been waiting for, had passed. She turned the radio on loudly to try and forget her moment of panic and finish the drive.

When she got home, she managed to calm down as she heated water for a cup of herbal tea. She had just sat down to relax when her phone rang. It was Lane, and her heart nearly jumped out of her chest.

"Are you OK?" he asked. "You ran out of here so fast I thought I had done something wrong. Was I out of line, Gia?"

"No, Lane, I'm fine. I was quite surprised but thank you for asking."

She closed her eyes as she listened to him talk. She loved the sound of his voice.

"I'm glad you stopped in today, will you be around again anytime soon?"

"I have work up there next week."

"How about lunch then?" he asked.

"Sure, I could be there around one o'clock on Thursday."

"Great, see you then."

"Bye, Lane, and thanks for calling." She was about to hang up when she heard his voice again.

"I just wanted to make sure you were home safely and now that I know you are, I'll say good night, and I'll see you soon. Night, Gia."

Hanging up the phone, she had a smile on her face and realized he made her feel like a young girl again.

Present

"Gia?" Lane called, interrupting her thoughts again as he approached her lawn chair. "Gia?" he repeated. "Where are you this time? I called to you three times with no response."

"Sorry, Lane, I didn't see or hear you walk up, I guess I was daydreaming again."

"Are you ready to go in the house, it's cooling off now."

"No Lane, not yet, I'm fine, I've waited a long time to be able to sit here and I'm not ready to give in."

"How about if I cover your lap with this?" he said, placing her favorite lap cover over her legs.

"That's great!" she said, "thank you, just what I needed."

"It's almost time to start supper; I'll call you when it's ready."

"Thanks, Lane."

Pulling the cover up closer, she smiled at Lane's protection of her. She knew her time outside was coming to a close and guessed it was nearly time to get her stuff together. She had a good start on her notes, and even though it left her sad inside, it was still a beautiful day. The fresh ocean air was exhilarating and had offset the sadness.

Before she gave up her spot on the lawn, she wanted to use her last few minutes to go back in thought to when she first dated Lane, but she was interrupted.

"Gia! Phone!" Lane called from the door; bringing her out of her thoughts.

'Damn it!' she thought, 'I can't get two thoughts together without an interruption!'

"I'll be right in!" she called back with a hint of irritation and a tad of relief to be able to get away from her past for now. Getting up, she gathered her laptop that lay closed, folded her chair and went into the house.

They ate supper with pleasant conversation, and as soon as the kitchen was cleaned up, she poured a glass of water and made herself scarce while Lane watched the news and read the evening paper. He always wanted to know what was going on in the world and Gia had no interest in the mess out there. She settled comfortably in her den where it was quiet, and her thoughts took over once again. Laying her head back against the lounge, she took herself back to when it first began for them.

The Invitation

The annual Christmas party was being discussed around the office. They were asking who would be attending and for those who were, how many tickets did they want. Gia wanted to go, and the only male person she wanted to ask was Lane, but she was not sure if he was ready for a public appearance yet. Well, the only way she would know for sure was to ask him the next time she saw him. She definitely was not going to ask him over the phone. Whichever the answer, it would be face to face, when he did.

There were still a few weeks before the cutoff date for tickets, so when she met him for lunch the next week, she would ask him then. She knew she would never go to an elaborate function, such as this, alone, so if Lane declined her invitation, then she wouldn't go either.

~

Arriving at Lane's, it was a few minutes past one o'clock. Seeing Lane standing on his deck having a smoke, sent her mind directly to mush and she could barely park her car. 'Do not pass go just go directly to mush.' Roaring in, she forgot to lower the gear and stalled in the middle of the driveway. 'What am I, twelve?' she thought. 'Why am I acting like a schoolgirl, this is Lane, for God's sake!'

Watching her for a few seconds, he yelled down for her to leave the car there, that it had likely flooded anyway. If he noticed her embarrassment, the gentleman in him allowed him not to let on. Getting out of the car, she walked toward him, and he reminded her that the gears were close together in her little car. That was his way of telling her he had not noticed that she had not geared down. 'Ya right! Like she believed that one!' Feeling certain now that he thought she was an idiot.

Lane walked toward her as she got out of her car and although she was still embarrassed, it didn't show. She had an uncanny way of not showing how she was really feeling. She was keen at not showing her true emotions when she was hurt, embarrassed or frightened and she made sure her heart was always under cover. Her mind was going in a direction where she didn't want to be, and before she knew it, Lane was giving her a welcoming hug and brought her away from the dark place in her mind.

"It's nice to see you again, Gia."

Smiling at him, she told him it was nice to be there.

"Lunch is ready, are you hungry?"

"A little bit, yes, and a cup of tea would taste great."

'It's ready, let's go inside," he said and flicked his cigarette unto the driveway.

When they sat down at the table, she said, "I have a favor to ask you."

Sitting his coffee down, he looked curiously at her and said, "Oh, and what would that be?"

"The Company is having their annual Christmas party and I was wondering if you'd consider being my escort."

To her surprise, and without even a hesitation, he said he would.

"It's been a long time since I've been to a function of any kind. Since Melanie died, there really hasn't been anything I've wanted to attend. Thank you for asking me, Gia, I'd love to be your escort."

With that out of the way, they enjoyed a great lunch, and before long, it was time for her to get back on the road.

'Well, now that he's said yes, there's no turning back,' she thought, heading down the highway.

The Escort

Watching from her window, Lane walked toward her house. This was the first visit since they both found themselves single. He had a garment bag over one shoulder and held on to the hangers with two fingers as it hung down his back and carried a duffle bag in the other hand. Her heart was racing with excitement with a little bit of fear mixed in there somewhere.

'Stop it!' she told herself, 'it's only for one night!'

Lane was going to stay overnight, but an agreement was made that he would sleep on her sofa. She had previously offered him the guest bedroom, but he said he'd prefer the sofa. Just knowing he would be in her house, while she slept, gave her a familiar feeling of panic rising up from the past. She went to the door to meet him. He had that same friendly smile that she adored and as he sat his bag down, she took his garment bag, hung it up for him and returned for her hug.

'He always smells so good,' she thought. Closing her eyes for a few seconds, she enjoyed his wonderful hugs.

"I'm glad you agreed to escort me tonight Lane, thank you for coming."

"It's not a problem Gia, I think it will be fun, is the coffee pot on?"

"As a matter of fact, it is!"

Putting her arm through his, she led him toward the kitchen. She was quite proficient at hiding fear. By the time they finished their coffee and got caught up on each other's news, it was time to get ready for the party.

~

"Wow! Aren't you just the handsome dude, Mr. Walters!" Gia said as he stepped into the hallway and walked toward her.

He was wearing black dress pants, a soft pastel green shirt and a sports jacket and she could smell his aftershave that was becoming familiar by now.

"And look at you Ms. Lake, you look lovely."

"Thank you, Lane."

It was snowing lightly by the time they left, turning it into a beautiful night. Opening the door on her side, he helped her into the car. Thanking him, she watched as he went around and got in beside her. 'Perfect!' she thought, 'always the gentleman.'

Recognizing some of her co-workers, she introduced Lane to a few of them. There were too many to worry about, so the ones who mingled with them got an introduction. When you are mingling with lawyers, police officers and the like, most of them could care less who you are, if you are not in their cliques.

Dinner was being served, and they sat at a table that was set for four and glad that no one joined them. As luck would have it, they were first to be served. The waitress suggested they go ahead and eat and not wait for the others as there were too many to be served. There were curious glances aimed at their table, and it tickled her because absolutely nobody in the room knew who Lane was, and Gia liked it that way. Secrets were her specialty.

Standing around the bar after dinner, Lane ordered a beer for him and a wine spritzer for her, while the tables were being cleared to make room to dance.

The music was not bad although it was mostly for the younger crowd, but Lane and Gia got a few dances in before they noticed was snowing heavier and decided it was time to head back to her place.

Being a good driver, Lane got them safely into her driveway. Once inside, the house was warm and inviting.

Making a cup of coffee for him and an herbal tea for herself, she asked if he wouldn't mind starting the fireplace. Excusing herself, she slipped away to get out of her party clothes and change into a pair of lounge pajamas. Padding barefoot back to the living room, she went to where Lane was sitting with his coffee.

"You look comfy," Lane said, "do you mind if I get out of these duds?"

"No, go ahead, and I'll turn on the late news."

"I'll be right back then, thanks; I'm feeling a bit overdressed now," he said nodding toward her in her pj's. They both chuckled as he sat his coffee mug down.

Making up a bed on the sofa, she kept talking to herself and forcing the panic away, telling herself again it was only for one night and he would be gone in the morning. When Lane returned, he was dressed in a pair of blue print lounge pajama and a blue long-sleeved tee shirt. They sat with their cups, carried on with casual conversations, and listened now and then to the local news. Gia was getting sleepy and said it was time for her to go to bed. She told him to watch television for as long as he wanted. He gave her a hug before she left the room.

Knowing Lane was out there in the living room, there was not much rest for Gia. Thoughts of him made her quite nervous and she couldn't settle down. She never could sleep with her bedroom door completely closed. When she heard him in the bathroom brushing his teeth and getting ready for bed, she laid there fearful that he would come into her room. 'Stop it!' she said as she talked herself out of panicking and gave a silent prayer of thanks as he passed her door and went back to the living room. From then until morning she struggled with fitful sleep.

"Good morning, beautiful," Lane said with a cheery smile as she entered the kitchen.

"Good morning," she said and returned his smile as she noticed he was already dressed and had made coffee.

"Coffee smells wonderful."

"Yes, it does," he agreed, "here's a cup for you."

"Thanks, would you like breakfast?" she asked.

"No, I never eat at this time of day; I'll wait till later."

"Are you sure, it won't be any trouble."

"Yes, I'm sure, thanks anyway. They sat drinking their morning coffee together and before long he was on his feet and getting ready to go home.

"It was a great evening last night Gia, thanks again for inviting me. It felt good to be out among the living again."

"You're welcome; it was fun and thank you for agreeing to escort me."

"Sorry to run off so early but I'm meeting my son in a few hours. We'll talk soon?"

"Sure, we will, I look forward to it."

He held her for a few seconds, smiled, tossed his garment bag over his shoulder and left.

Alone again, she could never decide whether she wanted it or if she wanted company. She loved her solitude; there was no doubt about that. She enjoyed being alone, and most of the time she was. She was not afraid of being alone, and she enjoyed her own company. She was not one who needed to be entertained, pampered or spoiled.

There was nothing she needed, materialistically. If she didn't have it by now, she didn't need it. She had long since realized that "stuff" did not make her happy, not that she ever figured out what would. She was just having a difficult time deciding if she wanted another relationship, knowing it was bound to fail. She wasn't certain she even wanted to bother. Relationships take work and with most of the ones she had it seemed as though she ended up doing all of it.

'Why was that?' she wondered. 'Why did she always allow people to walk all over her?' Was she so pathetic at relationship building that she took whatever was offered? It was not only male relationships but female friends as well. That thought took her back to her friendship with Faith Barton, but she was not ready to deal with that story yet.

Present

Lifting her head up off the lounge, Gia looked at the green-lit numbers on the clock. It was midnight and the house was quiet. Been so deeply engrossed in her thoughts, she hadn't heard Lane go to bed. The living room was in darkness except for a night light on in the kitchen. Darkness was not an option for her, and night-lights were an absolute must. Opening the fridge for more light, she lifted herself up on tip-toes and reached into the cupboard for a glass. Taking the water pitcher out, she poured herself a glass of water. Her mind was exhausted, but her body was not ready for sleep.

Over the years, she had become somewhat of a night owl. She couldn't remember just when it happened. She had lost so much sleep fighting the darkness that she needed to sleep longer in the mornings to catch up. She had never been one to get up early and never saw the point in it anyway. There were lots people who loved rising early, but she could not remember ever being a morning person.

Sitting in the living room, in almost complete darkness, she was thankful for the silence. The house was rarely this quiet now because Lane always wanted the television, radio or anything on that made a noise. Gia loved the silence. That was one more thing that she and Lane did not have in common. Of course, in the few years they had been married, she had to admit there were many other things in which they didn't share an interest.

Sitting in the dimly lit room, her mind returned to her first real date with Lane. When he had agreed to escort her to the early Christmas party, she had refused to call it a 'date.' Even though they had chatted on the phone, they had not seen each other since then.

The Date

New Year's Eve was fast approaching, and the wheels were turning in Gia's head. 'Should she invite Lane to go to the dance at the Club or should she just mind her own business and 'let sleeping dogs lie?' Needless to say, she had awakened the dog. She went to the phone and called his number, and he answered after several rings.

"Hello?"

"Hi, Lane, it's Gia."

"Well hello there, how are you?"

"I'm doing fine," she said, "I have an invitation for you, are you interested?"

"I might be," he laughed, "what's up this time?"

"A New Year's Eve dance at the Club, want to come with me?"

There was complete silence on the other end of the phone, and she thought, 'Here comes rejection.'

Cutting through the silence, "It's OK if you're busy Lane because I haven't bought tickets yet."

"No, that's not it, really, my son has asked me to sit with the grandkids, so they could go out. They don't have definite plans made yet either, so it isn't a done deal by any means. Let me give him a call and see what they are doing, and I'll call you back."

"Wonderful, I'll wait for your call, but in the meanwhile, I'll call the Club and see if there are tickets left."

"I'll get back to you as soon as I can."

"OK, Lane, talk to you soon."

In the meanwhile, she called the Club and inquired about tickets. They told her there were still several left and asked her if she wanted to put a few on hold. She said yes, and if her plans changed, she would call them. Taking her name, they reserved two tickets for her. "Now," she said aloud, "the wait begins." Slowly the nerves began to unravel, and she wondered why she couldn't mind her business.

She nearly jumped out of her skin when her phone rang. "Hello?"

"Hi, Gia, it's Lane. Plans have changed, and I don't have to sit with the kids after all. How did you make out with tickets?"

"I have two on reserve if we want them."

"I believe we do," he said.

"You'll come then?"

"Yes, I'd love to, Gia."

"Wonderful, come down about the same time as before, that will give us plenty of time to get ready."

"It's a date!" he said.

"Yes, it is. See you soon."

'A date,' she thought, 'I'm going on a date!'

It was a long stressful week for Gia as she waited for the countdown to Lane's arrival.

Leafing through a magazine, she noticed his car pull into the driveway. The magazine could have been upside down for all she knew because she couldn't remember a single article that was in it. Hearing his car door slam, she went to the door to greet him.

"Hello!"

"Hi, Gia, how are you?"

"I'm fine, thanks, and you?"

"Ready for a coffee, got any?"

"I sure do, I have one with your name written all over it."

Smiling at her, he pulled her close to him, kissed her on the cheek, and they went inside. Hanging his garment bag up, she led him into the kitchen. In just a few minutes he had a steaming hot mug of coffee in his hand. Walking out onto the back patio, he lit up a smoke.

"Have you ever thought about giving those things up, Lane?"

"Many times, but I guess I'm not ready yet. It's a dirty, smelly habit and I know I should quit and maybe I will, one of these days."

"Well then, we can only hope," she said as their eyes met.

He knew she disliked it and she knew he was addicted. She didn't think either of them would win this battle.

They arrived at the Club well after the party had started and in full swing. The music was at least stuff she and Lane could dance to this time. Lane continued to take smoke breaks by stepping outside. The Club gave smokers a choice of smoking on the sidewalk or the deck that overlooked the Bay. Needless to say, he chose the deck. Lane wore a sports jacket, so he was warm enough to step outside, but Gia was dressed in party clothes, so she waited inside for him. Whenever she looked out at him, she could feel that familiar feeling of panic trying to creep into her soul. Trying to shake it off, but she couldn't, so it lingered there, on her shoulder, like a demon.

"Earth to Gia," Lane teased. "I step away for a few minutes, and you leave the planet."

"Oh, sorry Lane, I guess I was far away."

"Care to share."

"No, not really, we aren't here for therapy sessions. Let's have some fun."

"You got it, let's go Gia, the night is still young."

As the evening wore on, the countdown to midnight crept closer. Noticing a slight change, Lane was aware of Gia heading into panic mode. He didn't want to pry so he let it go and hoped it would not spoil the rest of the evening. He remembered when she ran out of his house when he held her differently and kissed her a little longer than their usual peck, so he didn't a hammer over the head. Knowing if he wanted to keep her in his life, he had to be sensible.

The bandleader began to shout the countdown. "Ten! Nine! Eight! Seven! Six! Five! Four! Three! Two! One! Happy New Year everybody!" Dropping from the ceiling, the net opened to balloons and confetti flying around, horns blowing, people in party hats kissing everybody and wishing them well and Gia was watching it all in amazement. Turning towards him, she saw Lane a few feet away from her and as if in slow motion, he turned toward her at the same time. Their eyes met and held as her heart rate sped up. Feeling the smile leave her face, as Lane stepped closer. Reaching for her, his fingertips on each side of her face, he drew her close to him. In one swoop his lips were on hers, and it was something she had not experienced in a long time... feelings. Pulling slightly away, he looked at her and whispered over the crowd of noise, "Happy New Year, Gia." Temporarily, she was fixed in a gaze. Darting from her eyes to her lips, he kissed her again. Like a dagger to her heart, someone on stage began singing 'Unchained Melodies,' sending a shot of sadness to her soul.

For those agonizing moment, the song took her back to the one person she could not forget, and she wished with all her heart that he was standing there with her. It had been their song, the one they had danced to and he would sing along to, in her ear. She held back tears at the remembrance of him. For that brief moment, it was Beau that she longed to be kissing. Coming up for air, she put her arms around him, to hide the tears. Holding each other tightly, the song came to an end and her tender moment, of a lost love, faded. 'Beau,' she thought... 'Where are you tonight?'

Shaking hands with several people, they wished them a Happy New Year before walking back to their table.

"Want something to drink?"

"An ice water would be great," she said, and she watched him walk to the bar. A long and hidden feeling of loneliness pulled at her heart and hovered over her at the thought of Beau. 'Where did that come from?' she thought. He hadn't crept into her mind for a while, but that song plunged him back into her soul. 'Damn it!'

She felt good on the inside, and she could not help but think about how silly she had been to panic. Lane was such a patient, kind and loving man, she knew she had no reason to be afraid of him. That was her heart talking, but her head was telling her something else.

"Are you ready to get out of here and go home?" Lane asked.

Her heart began pounding fast and hard and she was certain he would hear it.

'Come on,' she thought, 'you're not eight years old any longer.'

"Yes, Lane, I think I am."

"Good, let's get out of here."

When they arrived at her house, it began to snow softly, and they decided on a quick change of clothes and then take a walk. Beautiful, could only describe the night as they watched the snow falling through the glow of the streetlights. Walking arm and arm down her street, Lane asked, "Are you OK, Gia, I mean... with what happened tonight?"

"Yes, I am, I had a great time Lane, thank you for coming down."

"It was my pleasure," he said softly, turning to face her. Looking into her eyes, he kissed her again, and she melted into him.

Ending the kiss, they walked back to the house for a hot drink. Gia didn't drink liquor, except for the champagne she'd had a few times with Beau, so she never had booze in her house, and the only alternative was a beverage. She had figured out long ago that Lane was addicted to coffee, so she went directly to the kitchen to plug in the kettle.

"Here you go, nice and hot," she said as she passed him a mug. Putting her China cup down on the coffee table, she sat next to him. Taking her hand, he told her he wished the night didn't have to end.

"It has been great hasn't it?" she said softly.

"Yes, it has," he said, leaning forward to kiss her. Sitting on the couch, they held each other, talked and kissed until the wee hours.

Finally, Gia mentioned it was time for a bit of sleep and suggested if he wanted to, he could lay with her instead of sleeping on the couch. Going into the bedroom, she crawled between the sheets and he laid down next to her, on top of the covers. Snuggling up behind her, and without a chance for her to say how nice it felt, she quickly heard faint and strange noises coming from him. Before she knew it, he was into a full-blown snoring mode which was so loud, she thought the neighbors would complain. So much for her getting a bit of sleep!

Sometime before dawn, the noise must have stopped because she was awakened to the aroma of freshly brewed coffee. Yawned and stretched, she reluctantly got up and went to the kitchen. Sleep was calling her, and she just wanted to crawl back into bed and stay there till at least noon.

"Looks like you can use one of these," Lane said passing her a mug.

"Yes, thank you so much." Even before she could stop herself, she blurted out, "Has anyone mentioned that you snore?"

Pausing only briefly, she added, "Really loud?" She wanted so badly to cut her eyes at him for depriving her of sleep, but she resisted the urge. She was much too tired to be catty.

"Yes, I have been told that many times, I'm sorry if I kept you awake."

"Don't worry about it," she said, almost through clenched teeth, but she caught herself and reminded herself again to be nice, 'don't be yourself... be nice.'

"I have to get away early; I'm expected to spend the day with my son and grandkids. My stuff is ready, and at the door, so I had better be getting on my way since it's an hour's drive."

'Thank God!' she thought, walking him to the door. Kissing goodbye for several minutes, they gave each other a big squeeze, and then he was gone. She was alone again. She didn't know if being alone was all it was cracked up to be. The house suddenly seemed very, very empty without Lane in it. Going back to her bedroom, she cuddled up with the pillow that Lane had slept on, so she could smell his aftershave, and as she drifted off to sleep, she convinced herself that being alone was good, very, very good.

~

From then on, with their long-distance relationship, they spent every possible minute together that time would allow. They spent their weekends together and did some traveling. When they realized they weren't comfortable being apart, they decided to get married. Since he was retired, and she was still actively involved in her business, it was a given that they would live at her place. He had spent a lot of time there with her, and it felt like his second home and he was quite comfortable being there with her.

It was going to be a very simple wedding. They had already decided that it would be the third week in May. There were only a few people they wanted to invite, and it consisted of his son and family and a few close friends.

Gia had a friend who was a Justice of the Peace, and she agreed to marry them. They both wanted to be married in the house they were going to live in, so there was not much left to plan. She and Lane had taken care of everything themselves. They had reservations made for the wedding dinner at the hotel they were going to stay at for their wedding night. All they had to do now was count the days.

As they waited for their big day to arrive, Gia took another step back in time to her first love.

First Love (1961)

His name was Thomas Edwards, but he was Tommy to everyone who knew him. She met him shortly after her family moved to Kanyon Cove and she was madly in love before turning sixteen. Living on the same street, she could look out her bedroom window and see his house. Quitting school at eighteen, he got a job as a striker for a local bottling company. As a ride-along on a delivery truck, helping the driver unload pop along the delivery route. Being a typical boy, he had no interest in education but instead he wanted to buy a car, hang out in the pool hall and do his own thing. Sitting in a schoolroom back then was not his idea of a good time so as soon as he was able, he quit.

He literally was, one of the cutest guys in Kanyon Cove and he had the greatest hair! Emulating Elvis, he'd comb it back on both sides and into a neat ducktail in the back. Taking special care in the front, he'd flip it up on both sides while taking the middle finger on each hand and guiding the hair down to fall over his forehead, in perfection. He was not a perfectionist by any stretch of the imagination, but when it came to his hair, it had to be perfect. Gia used to watch him with his black pocket comb in his left hand as he maneuvered and manipulated the hair until he had the perfect angles. He had that 'touch the hair and you die' look on his face. He was her guy; he was her Fonzie.

When and how they met, is their story.

New Town (1961)

Four months from her sixteenth birthday, Georgia and her family moved to Kanyon Cove. A peaceful little town nestled between two hills. At the bottom of the hills was a bridge that spanned a river that split the town in half. There was not much there except a couple of service stations, a car dealership, two restaurants, a drug store, post office, a train station and several stores that made up any small town. The town's main industries consisted of a lumber mill, a factory for boat building and on the edge of town there were two bottling companies that made soda pop. It was a typical small town and could have been called, Smallsville, Anywhere. If you blinked, you were through it, as they say.

Being in a new town had Georgia wondering if she still wanted to be known to her new friends as Gia. More often than not, when it was written as such, she generally was asked how it was pronounced, and she would politely reply, "Gee Ya." Many times, she wished her name had been spelled Jorja and nicknamed JJ, and then there would be no confusion as to its pronunciation or spelling, just J-J, too easy. But life was not easy; it never was and never would be.

Taking herself on a tour, she decided to check out the town. Crossing the bridge, she saw a small diner that looked to be as good of a place as any to start. Stepping inside, she looked around the room. Everyone stopped and stared out of curiosity, at an unknown face. Ignoring them, she lowered her eyes and they went back to their own business.

It was a simple place with worn oilcloth on the floor and a large black rubber mat just inside the door. There were several booths and tables in an 'L' shape across the front windows and along the sidewall.

Deciding on a booth, she took a seat by the window that overlooked a small harbor. The counter, with several stools, was straight ahead from the door and the kitchen was in behind with a swinging door and a serving window. A pinball machine and a jukebox were near the counter. In front of the jukebox, a young girl stood looking through the glass bubble-like front as if scanning for a song title. A coin dropped and almost immediately, 'Cupid' by Sam Cooke began to play. She didn't not know it then, but it was at that moment that she'd meet her best friend.

It was a typical place where you could sit at the counter and sip pop or have an ice cream, and no one cared if you loitered.

Gia shyly and quickly scanned the room while thinking the few customers were mostly all locals. This place could likely be a daily hangout of sorts for those lingering around drinking coffee, sipping pop and shooting the breeze with friends. Every town had a hang-out and a liar's bench.

Moving her gaze to the window, she noticed several boys sitting on the edge of a small wharf dangling homemade fishing poles into the river. She guessed they might be fishing for bass.

Interrupting her thoughts, an older waitress came to take her order. She asked for a pop just as the girl, she had seen at the jukebox, walked up to her table. Gia was not a people person and had been comfortable just sitting there alone taking in the sights. She was surprised at the girl's sudden and uninvited appearance and somewhat amazed at her boldness. The girl seemed a bit forward and not the least bit shy as she approached Gia.

"Hello, I'm Patti Stevens, mind if I sit down?" she said nodding toward the empty side of the booth and slid into place uninvited. Gia never took her eyes off Patti as she wiggled into the seat across from her. Many thoughts flew across Gia's mind before Patti was settled into her spot. 'Who is this girl? What does she want with me? What a nerve!'

"You must be from the new family who just moved in on Bridge Street near the post office."

'The bridge itself must not have been enough of a focal point; they needed a street named after it too?' Gia smirked to herself.

"Yes, I am, I'm Georgia Lake, it's nice to meet you, Patti."

"Well, it's nice to meet you too, Georgia," she giggled with a slight accent.

"Please, call me Gia," she said in an automatic response.

"OK, 'Gia' it is!"

The blonde waitress brought Gia's drink and smiled broadly as she placed it on the table and Gia thanked her. She had a pleasant and friendly smile as she turned her attention to the girl.

"Is this a friend of yours, Patti?" the waitress asked.

"Gia this is Nora, she owns the place."

"It's nice to meet you, Nora," Gia said as she handed her change to pay for her pop.

Nora gave her a palms-up gesture, handed her a straw, and said, "This one is on me, welcome to Kanyon Cove, Gia, and welcome to my place."

"Thank you," Gia said, and she was touched by the friendliness she felt here in this quaint little restaurant. Gia turned and looked out the window at the boys on the wharf and nodded toward them and asked, "bass?"

"Yes, but they rarely catch any, they are only there for something to do. Would you like to meet them? They're very cute!"

Overwhelmed already by just having to contend with her, Gia mumbled, 'maybe later' and sipped pop up her straw as she watched the young fishermen. One, in particular, had caught her eye.

Gia noticed again that Patti had a slight southern accent, but she didn't know if it was for real or put on. Patti was a pretty gal with long blonde hair, blue-green eyes that she enhanced with a bit of mascara and a touch of pale green eyeshadow. She wore a Barely Nude lipstick; just enough to know it was there. It appeared to

Gia that makeup was not necessary because she would have been just as attractive without it, but it was not her business to comment. She learned that Patti was seventeen and Gia had not quite reached her sixteenth birthday.

"Have you seen anything of the town since you moved here? Taken a tour, or met anybody?"

"No, this is my first time downtown. My sisters and I are still unpacking boxes and organizing, and I needed to get out for a while."

Gia glanced out at the wharf, and Patti noticed her stiffen slightly.

"You OK?"

Pushing her bottle to the center of the table, she slid to the edge of the seat and muttered, "I think I'd better get home."

"You just got here! Relax gurl," she drawled and tapped Gia on the hand. "What's gotten you into a dither anyway?"

Gia's eyes darted again to the wharf, and she saw one of the fishermen staring up at the window where she sat. Shifting several times in her seat, she felt uncomfortable. Getting up, Patti went around to Gia's side of the booth.

"Scooch over," she said waving her fingers and slid in next to her. Looking out the window, Patti saw the boys glance up and she waved to them.

"What are you doing?" Gia gasped. She couldn't believe Patti's nerve and fear was clearly setting in. 'Damn her anyway, what is she doing!' Now that panic had made its appearance, Gia considered Patti's behavior as unacceptable. To Patti, it was a friendly gesture, but to Gia it was sheer and absolute fear.

"Oh my Gosh! They are coming this way! Patti! What am I going to do?"

Patti touched her arm as she slid back across the booth. She asked her what was wrong as she could clearly see Gia was nearing hysterics.

"I have to go home!" The words weren't out of her mouth when the restaurant door burst open and a small commotion was happening in the entry. Typical teenage boys elbowing each other to see who could get inside first, but they were just having fun. 'Fun' was a concept in which Gia was not familiar.

"Hey, Patti! Who's your friend?"

Gia looked as if she were going to pass out and Patti glared at them and gave her head a quick nod towards the counter to non-verbally say 'not now.' As they headed for the pinball machine, one of them glanced at Gia with concern.

"I can't stay now Patti; I have to get out of here!"

"What's the matter with you Gia, what's got you so freaked out?"

"You wouldn't understand Patti; you shouldn't have done what you did. You shouldn't have brought them in here."

"They are harmless; they are my friends, Gia." she drawled.

"Your friends? You're 'friends' with boys?"

"Ah, yeah, aren't you, boys are people too?" Patti drawled, furrowing her eyebrows in question.

"Friends with boys? Are you insane? Why would I be friends with boys! Yuck!" Gia was practically hissing at Patti in a loud whisper.

Patti stared, wide-eyed, at her with her mouth opened but nothing would come out. "Ummmm, I think we should talk, Gia."

"We are talking!" Gia snapped and glanced over toward the pinball machine, she locked eyes with one very handsome fisherman for several seconds.

"Who is he?" she whispered practically in a hiss.

"Who?"

Nodding toward the pinball machine, "Him, but don't look right now he's looking this way!"

Patti made a 'tsk' sound and said, "that's my friend, Tommy Edwards, why?"

"He keeps staring at me," she said cupping the side of her face, so he wouldn't see her lips move, "what do you think he wants?"

Without Gia's notice, Patti gave her head a nod for Tommy to come over to the booth.

Standing in front of the booth, his arms crossed over his chest, his hands tucked in his armpits and his feet slightly apart in a stance that belonged only to him.

"Hello," came a voice as smooth as silk, that somehow calmed her for a few brief moments. Rolling her eyes up at him, he smiled down at her. Their eyes met and it melted her inside. She already loved his rich, dark, cola colored hair, his smile that made a dimple appear in one cheek, his perfect, even white teeth and eyes the color of smooth dark chocolate.

"Hello," she answered and gave a sharp glare at Patti and a swift, quick kick under the table. She saw something special in Tommy, but she had a lock around her heart the size of a bear trap that not even he would penetrate.

*Sucking in a deep breath, she became slightly panicked as Tommy brazenly slid in beside her and introduced himself. Wearing an old baseball cap and smelling of fish and bait, but to everyone, this was a normal sight to them. He had his elbows on the table with one arm resting on top of the other. He held a hand out to her in a greeting, and when she saw it opened to accept her hand, she flinched and nearly came out of her skin.

"Whoa!" he said and raised both hands as if she'd just pulled a gun on him. "Sorry Kitten, I didn't mean to scare you, I was just going to say it's nice to meet you."

Gia wished with all her heart that this could be a normal conversation, but she knew it would never be.

"I'm sorry, I have to go, please let me out," Gia rambled nervously.

Tommy slid out of the booth and Gia glared at Patti, non-verbally thanking her for ruining her tour. Running out the door, she heard the smoky voice of Patsy Cline appropriately singing 'I Fall to Pieces.'

Patti and Gia

Patti's brazen spirit had prompted a friendship like no other that either one had ever had. Theirs was a true friendship, and when they needed each other, they were always there, no matter what. Patti was almost a year and a half older than Gia, but they didn't care. Patti thought of Gia as the younger sister she never had. They shared most of their secrets, (except the one that Gia shared with no one) like real sisters did and loved each other as such.

They went to dances together, and they sat in their favorite booth at Nora's restaurant that overlooked the wharf and sipped cokes through straws while planning their weekends. They borrowed each other's clothes, jewelry and shoes and did each other's hair and even shared nail polish. Where you saw one, you saw the other. They could be found with their heads together giggling and planning almost every day. They spent as much time with each other as humanly possible. Patti knew most of Gia's secrets and vice versa, and they had many, too many, for teenagers to have. It would be difficult for Gia to confide her big secret to anyone. As time went on and Gia began to trust her, she felt that when the time was right, she might be able to give up this secret to her best friend. Until then it was her secret and hers alone.

~

It was at one of the dances that Gia saw Tommy Edwards again. Dressed in clean jeans, he also wore a crisp white tee shirt and a well-worn jean jacket. He had a smile that melted her heart, whenever she caught his eye. Inside her heart, she was secretly head over heels in love with him, but in her head, she feared admitting it. He was a few years older than she was and it was a bit scary, but she tried not to let it show. He was very handsome with dark brown hair and deep brown eyes that touched her soul when he looked at her.

It was a new experience for her to feel this way about someone. She had never been in a position to love or be loved up to this point. Tommy was the first male person in her sixteen years of life that she actually had those feelings for. The male population to her, spelled fear and she did not trust even one of them.

Patti, on the other hand, was very familiar with the boys and was a bit on the wild side. It bothered Gia slightly, or maybe she was a teensy bit jealous. Gia wished she could be as open with herself and her feelings as Patti was, but she knew she never would. Her father had made sure that would never happen. It did not matter to Gia though; she loved Patti for who she was and accepted her and her wild side for what it was.

Gia had been in town for only a few months, and she had already made a trip to the local doctor's office with Patti when she feared she had contracted a venereal disease. Patti was frightened out of her wits and needed Gia's support. Gia may have been the younger of the two, but she was more levelheaded than Patti would ever be, and Patti drew from that. They were both relieved when they found out she was free from diseases and Gia thought she would learn something from her experiences, but she did not. Gia had learned in grade school that having sex at a young age and having too many sexual partners could likely cause problems in adulthood. If she had learned this vital information in her health class, then what had Patti learned?

~

Several more months had passed, and Patti called her on the phone and asked her to please meet her downtown. Gia could hear the distinct sound of hysteria in her voice. Dropping the phone, she left it dangling from its cord and ran out the door. She ran all the way to where Patti had asked to meet her. When she got there, it looked as if Patti was going to faint.

Seeing Gia approaching, she ran to her and collapsed in her waiting arms.

"Patti, my God! What is wrong? Why did you want to meet here?"

Crying hysterically, she could not speak, and Gia held on to her until she contained herself. Looking around at her surroundings, she had no idea what this place was.

Lifting her head off Gia's shoulder, she looked at her with red and swollen eyes, and it nearly broke Gia's heart.

"I'm pregnant, Gia." The words stung Gia like a wasp bite.

"What!?"

"I'm pregnant, and I need you to come inside with me."

"Inside? What is this place?"

"It's an abortion clinic, of sorts, and I need you to come inside and stay with me."

"You're having an abortion? And what do you mean 'of sorts'?" Gia yelled, in a high-pitched voice.

"Please, keep your voice down and yes I am having an abortion. I have no choice, Gia. They have medical staff that come to this office every few weeks for special appointments. Not many people in town know about it because it's kept pretty hush-hush."

"You always have choices, Patti!"

"Not this time, Gia. I don't have a choice. If my parents find out that I'm pregnant then my life is over. I won't be able to go to college, I won't have a career, and my life, as I know it, will be over for me."

"Why are you only thinking about this now, Patti? If you knew all this before then why didn't you protect yourself? What is the matter with you, are you insane?"

Patti let her vent, and she listened to every word knowing she deserved it. It was exactly what her mother would have said, and she knew it, so she let her rant. Besides, she needed to hear it again anyway. Gia was so angry with her friend right then she wanted to kick her ass, but she knew it was too late for that.

"Are you finished ranting?" Patti asked. "I know all this is scary for you and what you are saying I needed to hear. But I have to go inside now, please come with me, I need you, Gia."

"Oh my God, Patti, I don't know if I can go in there!"

"Yes, you can, you have to! I can't go in there alone!"

Gia chewed, nervously, on her lip and shifted her eyes to the ominous looking building and then back at Patti.

"OK, I'll go in with you, but I don't really want to."

Patti hugged her again.

"Let's go," was all she said.

When they entered the building, both of them were shaken to the core. They looked as if they were holding each other up and, in their hearts, they knew that was exactly what they were doing.

A woman walked over to them and they both took a step back at the same time as if the woman had a boa constrictor around her neck.

"Are you Patti?" she asked looking at Gia.

"No, she's Patti," Gia said as she pointed quickly to her friend. She felt as if she were five years old standing there with her friend, trying to hold her up.

The woman turned from Gia and said to Patti, "We're ready for you dear," and held her hand out to Patti as if she were going in to have a splinter removed.

"We have to get this over with, the office is closing soon so we can move on," the nurse said.

Patti reluctantly let go of Gia and asked the nurse, "Can my friend come inside with me?"

The nurse shook her head and answered, "No, I'm afraid not but she can wait here, it will not take that long."

Patti disappeared with nurse 'Rattchett,' and as soon as Gia heard the door close, she nearly fell to her knees. Her legs would not hold her up, and she reached for a chair behind her and sat down. She leaned forward, put her elbows on her knees, dropped her face into her palms and cried. She had heard such horrifying stories about abortions and hatchet jobs and young girls having lifelong complications. She was so afraid for her friend that she closed her eyes and felt an overwhelming urge to pray as she had never prayed before and to ask God to protect her dear friend and keep her safe.

"Please dear Lord in Heaven; Patti really needs you right now. A lot more than she thinks she needs me. I pray for a hedge of protection around her Lord and ask that no harm will come to her. Stay with her Lord and see her through this terrible ordeal. Keep your hands upon her and bring her through. I ask it in your Holy Name, Amen."

She learned to pray at an early age and sometimes felt that prayer was all she had.

Gia was still in the same position when she felt someone sit down beside her. She slowly lowered her hands from her face and scarcely turned her head when she saw Patti's shoes. She quickly dropped her hands, jumped to her feet and smiled when she saw Patti sitting there. She looked a bit pasty faced, weak and ragged but she had walked out under her own steam.

"Patti," she said with sheer relief, "are you alright?"

"Yes Gia, I'm okay, thank you for staying with me," she said as she stood up and gave her a hug. Gia closed her eyes long enough to silently say, 'Thank You God' and asked if she needed to sit back down.

"Yes, let's sit for a few minutes before we get out of here."

"Are you sure you're alright, Patti?"

"I will be as soon as I get home and get some rest."

"It goes without saying that no one is ever to know about this, Gia."

"Of course, Patti, I would never betray your confidence."

"Thank you, Gia, you are such a good friend to me."

"No more than you are to me. 'Best Friends Forever,' remember?"

They smiled at each other and Patti said, "Yes, girlfriend, I remember."

Present

Gathering up her glass of water, Gia headed off to bed. Lane was sound asleep in their king size bed. She gently pulled the bedding down and slipped in on her side. Lane stirred only long enough to turn over, and he was gently snoring again. She had learned to hate his snoring. Sometimes it was so unbearable she would take a warm, soft throw and curl up on the spare bed to sleep. Even from there, she could still hear it through the wall but not as loud. Then there were times when it would lull her to sleep, and other times she would lay there seething and wanting to strangle him with her blanket just to get rid of the noise.

His snoring steadily got louder and louder, and she knew it was useless to think about settling down to sleep, so she headed for the spare room. Listening to his snoring resonating through the stillness, she got up again, grabbed her throw, stomped out of the spare room and headed for the living room couch. She had the glow from the kitchen night light, which gave her some comfort. She opened the window an inch to allow fresh air to flow inside. Pulling the mini blind up, she hoped to avoid the inevitable flapping sound caused by the breeze blowing in through the slats. She lay facing the window. Off in the distance, she could see the streetlights and traffic lights downtown. She was far enough away that she could not hear anything, but she knew there was life moving around out there. She watched in silence as she thought about how she fought sleep and hated the nights.

Nightfall made her anxious, nervous and tormented. The older she got, the more profoundly distraught she became with her nighttime anxieties. She had gone for nights on end without sleep until she relented and made an appointment to see her doctor. She needed something to help her sleep. Still, when she had taken the pills he'd prescribed, she had lain awake for hours fighting the medication. She did not want to go to sleep, and she had fought hard to stay awake.

Her childhood trauma still haunted her. She had been afraid to fall asleep for fear of being carried off again. She hated the darkness, she hated the nights, and sleep had become her enemy. Gia lifted her head off the couch and looked at the green LED numbers on the clock that showed it was after midnight. The house was deathly quiet.

The living room was in darkness as she padded to the kitchen. Opening the fridge, she reached into the cupboard for a glass, took the jug out and poured herself a glass of water. Her mind was exhausted, but her body was not ready for sleep yet.

She began to drift back to the night that had been indelibly imprinted in her mind for decades. Since she could not get to sleep anyway, she quietly opened her laptop and began to type. As the words spread out across her screen, fresh tears spilled slowly down her cheeks. She was tired and sentimental. She allowed herself to go back there even though it was well into the haunting, dark hours. Reaching for a tissue, she wiped tears away, so she could see the screen, and she began to type again. It was time to get it out and down on paper as to how she'd suffered at the hands of a monster.

The Abuse

She was only eight years old when her world turned upside down. Her carefree, youthful days were over, and after a dark and scary night of horror and torment, she was lost forever.

That dreadful night when she had gone to bed in a room, she had shared with her two older sisters but woke up in another room, lonely and afraid. A voice from the darkness whispered in her ear and brought her out of a deep and peaceful sleep.

"You're my little girl tonight," she heard the voice say.

"Wake up, Gia," he said with a gentle shake.

The voice was forcing her from her sleep.

She was hurting somewhere, why was she in pain? Becoming fully awake, she opened her eyes and it was pitch black in the room except for a bit of light to indicate a window but it was not the window from her own bedroom. Fear quickly engulfed her. Other than that bit of light, she could not see her hand in front of her. Where was she? This was not her bedroom! The window was on the wrong side of the room. Where was Meagan? It was so dark and so scary that she was even afraid to let someone know she was awake. She was absolutely sure it was not Meagan beside her so who was it? Her pajama pants were gone, and she was naked from her waist down. The pain and discomfort continued. She was fully awake now but frozen in fear. By instinct, she began to move, to try to rid herself of the discomfort. The movement caused her to give herself away.

She heard a voice in her ear again. Whispering so close to her ear that she felt the breath on her cheek and she soon realized who it was and what the pain was! She could smell something, what was that? It was the smell of cigarette breath! It was her father! And, he had his finger up inside her! The pain! What was he doing? Where was Meagan? Why did her sister not know she was missing from their bed!

She could hear his voice telling her to lie still, telling her it was alright. 'What was alright?' she thought, 'this can't be alright,' she was in pain, and her father was causing it!

So many thoughts at once and nothing made sense. She could hear his voice telling her to lie still, telling her it was OK. 'What is OK?' She was old enough to know that what he was doing was wrong! At eight years of age, she did not have any understanding of what he was doing or why he was doing it, all she cared about was that he was hurting her, and she wanted it to stop. But it didn't stop, and neither did the pain. She whimpered in protest and tried to turn aside, but he hissed at her through clenched teeth.

"It's OK Gia, keep still! Shut up before someone hears you!"

He fumbled for her arm, took her hand, forced it downward and told her to touch him. She was frozen in fear, and her arm went ramrod straight as he tried to push it down toward him. She had her hand into a tight fist, but he wrenched her fingers opened. When she touched him, she had no idea what her tiny hand was holding. It felt huge and was bigger than her hand would fit around. It frightened her even more than she already was.

"That's my good girl, that's what daddy wants from his favorite girl."

She tried to remember him ever calling her 'his favorite girl' or a favorite anything, and she could not. She couldn't remember him ever being 'friendly' to any of the children. Now suddenly, she was his favorite!? Was she doing something that someone finally appreciated? Was this the only thing that would allow her to be accepted by him?

She was certain he could hear her heart pounding. She wished with all her might that her heart had stopped beating in that moment. It was a deafening sound that filled her entire being with the boom, boom, boom heartbeat that coursed through her body and up into her ears. Gia was certain she was going to explode as she listened to the pounding sound of her own heartbeat.

She heard him whisper in a barely audible voice.

"Move your hand up and down, like this," he whispered so close to her face that she could smell stale cigarettes on his breath. He put his hand on her arm and moved it in an up and down motion that he obviously wanted from her. "That's a good girl; make daddy feel good," he whispered in her ear as he jammed his finger up inside her repeatedly.

His breathing changed from normal breaths to short quick pants as if he had been running. The next few minutes passed at a snail's pace and suddenly, what had been stiff and ridged in her hand was now a deflated sticky mess. In a flash, he had bolted out of bed. She heard his pants being zipped, his belt buckle rattle and a hurried, breathless bunch of ramblings, then he was gone into the night.

She lay alone in dead silence, frozen in fear, in a room that was as black as pitch. Tears streamed down the sides of her face and onto her pillow as she wiped the sticky mess from her hand onto the sheet. She hardly dared to breathe or say one word for fear he would return and pounce on her for disobeying him. Anybody who lived in this house knew you did not cross 'daddy.'

At the young age of eight, not knowing what he wanted from her, or even what she had done, it became locked deep inside of her. As she lay in the darkness, she began to remember what he rambled about as he left the bedroom. He had spewed threats at her and told her that if she told another living soul, she would be sorry. He also threatened that she could be separated from her family and she would never see them again. He would keep that threat because he didn't need an excuse to be abusive. She knew or thought it to be the truth, at the time. Any reason was good enough for him. She promised herself, in that moment, that she never would tell another living soul as long as he was alive. Pieces of her soul died there in the pitch-black room, and nobody cared.

When the room became light the next morning, she saw her pajama bottoms in a heap on the floor. Grabbing them, she pulled them under the covers and slipped them on before the other siblings stirred in their rooms. She could feel that she was sore down there and she went directly to the toilet. It was then that she noticed blood. This only added to the trauma she had endured in the middle of the night. She went to her mother and told her she was bleeding 'down there.' She figured this would be her one and only chance to tell her mother without actually giving up her secret and it died there in an instant. Her one and only chance was as dead as she felt at that moment. Her mother told her to go to the kitchen and tell Meagan, and she would show her how to put on a pad. She told Gia she must have started her period early.

From that very moment, she began a love-hate relationship with her mother for not clueing in to her fear and for not giving her the protection that she deserved. She had already lost it with her father, and now her mother had let her down too. Her heart sank in disbelief that her mother had no questions, that she did not see her pain. There would never be another opportunity for Gia to talk about this again. She knew the time had passed and her mother did not help her. Her heart was broken. She'd wanted her mother to make her feel safe again and tell her everything was going to be all right, but instead she blew her off and sent her to Meagan. There were no questions as to why her eight-year-old daughter was bleeding. Why would she start her period at such a young age, especially when there were absolutely no signs of maturity and why could she not see the panic on her daughter's face and the pleading in her eyes. The moment was gone.

Gia had wanted her mother to read between the lines because that was all she had to work with. She'd wanted her to read her mind, see her panic and clue in that something was not right. She could not come out and tell her mother exactly what had happened only hours before. Her mother should have known, that is what mothers do, they know! Are they not supposed to have a motherly instinct about these things?

They were always told that mothers had eyes in the backs of their head. They knew all, saw all, and heard all, and children were not able to get anything past them. It seemed that was not the case in Gia's situation.

~

Gia became deathly afraid to be left alone with her father after that night. She had always been afraid of him, but this was a different kind of fear and for a different reason. This was paralyzing. Her entire family grew up with a fear of him. He was mean, selfish, hateful and not very likeable. That night cemented it for her, and she began a lifelong road of hatred towards him.

Life became confusing for Gia now. She hated her father, and she wanted to hate her mother, too, but she was all she had. She clung to her mother's leg, hid behind her apron and panicked whenever she heard his footsteps. She wanted to be wherever her mother was. If she left the house, Gia wanted to go with her, so as not to be left there with him. She figured by hiding behind her mother; then he wouldn't know she was there. In her terrified state of mind, she hoped that if she couldn't see him then hopefully, he couldn't see her either. That did not work. Every time he saw her wrapped around her mother, he would tell her to get the hell outside with the rest of the kids. Many times, while hiding behind her mother, to get out of sight, she'd open her mouth to speak, and nothing came out. In her little eight-year-old brain, she knew if she spoke aloud then he'd hear her and when that happened, he'd chase her out of the house and away from her mother.

Gia began to stutter after that, and it added to the already long list of resentments. When she figured out that her father resented her clinging to her mother, she began to cling to her older sister. Gia had been completely traumatized, and so she clung to her sister as if she were her lifeline. Where Meagan was, you were likely to find Gia. Meagan became more than a lifeline to Gia and most of the time she used her as a shield to try to keep out the bad stuff. It didn't matter what her thoughts were or how she felt; it just seemed that her life had been filled with bad stuff no matter what protection she used. There was no armor strong enough, to protect a child from someone she already mistrusted. She had lost the ability to smile and nor did she have the desire to.

Even though there was never another incident of that nature with her father, Gia did not know there was never going to be 'a next time' so the fear stayed with her as she waited for it to happen again. From then on, when she went to bed at night, she made sure she wrapped herself tightly around Meagan. Holding on for dear life, so if she were to be carried off again, he would have to awaken Meagan in order to loosen Gia's grip.

~

Sleep was almost non-existent for her except for a few hours here and there, and any slight movement would wake her. While lying in bed, praying for morning, Gia overheard harsh words between her parents. She had never heard them fight and scream at each other before. It was late into the night, and they probably thought it was safe to raise their voices.

"If you quit your job, we're done!" she heard her mother scream. "I've had it with you quitting your jobs and taking off for no reason! You have responsibilities, a family and you need this job!"

"I have to go, Anna, I want to go! I'll be back at the end of October."

"No, you won't!" she yelled, "if you leave, don't come back!"

"What are you telling me? If I leave for this other job, I can't come back home?"

"This 'job' is only for a few months," she yelled, "and the one you are leaving is full time! There is always someone looking for work, everyone except you, that is! By the time you get back, the position will likely be filled, and then what? You lay around until something else falls into your lap? I don't think so, Brad! You go, if you want to, but do not come back here when the job is over! I'm done with this and with you!"

Lying in the darkness, she listened to every word. Being a light sleeper, she was awakened by the slightest sound. This was foreign to her though. She never knew of them fighting.

~

He left just before she turned nine. She could still remember that day as if she were still living it. The feelings were just as vivid as they were when she watched him walk down the driveway. She had not taken her eyes off him until he was out of sight and out of her life. She remembered the layers of fear peeling off her like onion skins as she watched every step he took until he disappeared from her sight. At that very moment, she felt that if she had not been so terrified of God, she would have dropped to her knees, right there in the driveway. She wanted to thank God for taking him away and to ask Him to please keep him away. It could have been known as one of the happiest moments in her life although there were very few moments to compare.

~

Meagan had barely turned seventeen when she got married, and Gia figured she had wanted a way out too. Meagan was not there for Gia now, and the trauma never seemed to stop. At thirteen, she had begun to 'blossom' into a woman, and the drama only got worse. Anna's boyfriends would hang around long after she'd gone to work. One night one of them even tried to get into her bed. She was afraid of every one of them, yet her mother would leave the house knowing she still had two teenage girls home alone, a temptation for any man. She did not have the decency and respect for her daughters to ask her friends to leave before she left for work.

She soon began to live in a world where she would not let others inside. Her thoughts began to move along in a fantasy world. She didn't want to be herself any longer; she wanted to be anyone except who she really was. She became very secretive, and she never cared to share her thoughts with anyone. She hated it when she was questioned about what she was doing. She had felt alone in the world since she was eight years old and even before that when she was lied to and had promises broken in her young life.

She hated being asked how she was or how she was feeling. Nobody cared how she was so why did they have to ask. They asked the question but did not wait for her to answer. She was a mess inside, but no one noticed, and she said nothing. She could not confide in another living soul. So what could she say, and who really cared anyway? She was thirteen and almost grown up, and she kept telling herself that she could take care of herself since no one else ever had.

Present

Closing the laptop, Gia felt worn to the core. Setting it aside, she wiped at the tears that had rolled down her cheeks from having to recreate that horrible time. Knowing it was close to daylight, she closed her eyes and felt the nighttime slip away as she drifted off.

~

"Hey, you, did I keep you awake with my snoring again last night?"

"No actually, I didn't quite get to sleep in there, but it was getting pretty bad, so I came out here."

"I'm sorry, Baby," he said as he kissed her good morning.

Gia stretched and yawned, got up, went in to brush her teeth then came back for coffee.

"Did you get any sleep at all, you look beat."

"Yes," she said, "I got some."

"How's the book coming? I heard you on the keyboard quite late."

"OK, it's coming along," she answered, and left it at that. She didn't want to rehash what she'd already written.

"It's another beautiful day, are you going to sit out again?"

"I think I might do that, Lane. What about you?"

"I'm going to finish cleaning up the flower beds and get them ready for new plants."

She heard him go outside and he went about gathering up his gardening tools. He had taken her chair outside for when she was ready to go out. A bit of time had passed when he came back inside for a bottle of water. He saw that she was still in her pj's.

"Gia, it's a beautiful day and you aren't dressed yet. You're going to miss the best part of the day. Aren't you coming out?"

"I'll be out in a little while; it's barely past ten o'clock," she said trying to keep her voice from rising and her temper intact. For those who could sleep a full night didn't understand that while they were asleep, she was still struggling. She had never been a morning person and ten o'clock in the morning was not missing half the day, for her it was just beginning. She dragged the bottom of her cup along the countertop until she ran out of space, then carried it into her bedroom.

She had decided to walk on the beach and would surely need a shower when she came in out of the sun. She quickly washed her face, applied her cream, and she was ready. Runners would be the appropriate footwear to go along with her raggedy edged jeans. She got a warm sweater out of the closet, grabbed her hat and headed outside and down the path. Lane had already taken her chair out for her and placed it where she had been yesterday.

"Thank you, Lane," she called, and as he lifted his head, she nodded toward the chair. Smiling at her in acknowledgement, he went back to his gardening.

It was a beautiful morning and the quiet ripple of the tide relaxed her while the sun brought out good feelings. Standing near the edge of the cliff, she cupped her eyes and looked out over the water. It seemed like only a short time, but when she noticed the angle of the sun, she knew she had been there, lost in thought, for quite some time. Lane came up behind her and put his arms around her waist. It startled her, but his hands relaxed her, too. She laid her head back against his shoulder and closed her eyes.

"You look exhausted, Gia."

"You know, I think I am, mentally. This book is taking me to places I don't really want to go, and I can't seem to stay away from them. It is very exhausting."

"Would you like a cool drink or something?"

"Yes, I would, Lane, thank you."

"OK, Babe, wait here, and I'll bring you a bottle of water."

He kissed her on the back of the neck, and she smiled and touched the side of his face without turning around. He was a great guy, and she was glad to be with him. Brief thoughts of their wedding night floated to the surface, bringing an ugly moment, but she had to let it go in order to be civil.

Walking down the steps to the beach, she made her way to the water's edge and stood looking out over the peaceful bay. There was not a ripple on the water, not a boat in sight and not even a seagull.

Sitting down on a piece of driftwood, she tried not to let her mind go to places where she would be unsettled. Looking back toward the house, she saw Lane coming toward her, so she gazed out at nothing in particular, and before she knew it, he was at her side.

"Sorry I took so long with your water, Gia," he said offering her a cool bottle, "I got held up with a phone call," he said, and sat down beside her. "Why the sad look?"

"Just reliving all this stuff again," she shrugged and reiterated, "it's taking me to places in my mind that I'd rather not go. It's just difficult going back there."

"You've been doing that a lot lately, haven't you?"

"Well, yes, I must. I thought I had worked through all of this stuff. Why did I start this damned book anyway? Will I really be able to set it all aside again, once it is done? A strange thing has happened to my mind over the last little while, especially since I began to write. Maybe I have always been a scatter-brain, but I was too busy to notice. The problem is that whenever I let my mind turn to the past, it immediately goes to the unpleasant parts... not necessarily to the bad things that were done to me or what happened accidentally, but things that I did that I regret... things I said or did, or failed to do, that hurt the people closest to me. Things I did so that I seriously embarrassed myself, decisions I made that were just plain stupid, inconsiderate, selfish and hurtful to other people, people who trusted me. I know there must have been some good things that happened that on a given number of days, I did the right things. I can't get any pleasure out of looking back at them though, because the bad days, keep jumping front and center in my memory and make me feel so regretful that I could cry. So, what I must do is try not to look back so much and keep my mind focused on the present and the future. I cannot allow myself to look in the rear-view mirror of my life. Although I know there were some nice things there, there are also many sad memories mixed up with good ones. It seems I am lingering mostly on the bad ones right now. I really feel this so-called 'journey' I am on will help eliminate some of the sadness I feel about the past and help me to deal with it." She shrugged her shoulders and said, "But then, they are all the little moments that determine our lives."

"I'm sorry that you feel you must go back there Gia, but perhaps once you've made the 'journey,'" he said lifting his fingers to form quotes, "and your book is written, then hopefully your pain will be over. If you must go through it, you may come out on the other side a little lighter, and perhaps it will bring back a smile or two."

"Maybe Lane, but you know when I look back to when I was young it scares me to think that I have gone through more than half of my life already and know that not much of it was spent being happy. That's the part that makes me the saddest."

"It will, Gia until you let it go and maybe this journey, you're taking, will help you to do that."

Listening to Lane, she held her water bottle between her palms and gazed out over the water. Lost in her thoughts again, his voice drifted out across the water.

Sensing she was no longer listening, nor had she opened her water bottle, he stood up and touched her on the shoulder. Absent-mindedly she touched his hand as he walked away. She'd changed her mind about taking a stroll down the beach to stretch her legs and get fresh air in her lungs, so she climbed back up the steps to higher ground.

Gia needed a break from all the walks down memory lane and the stress from having to relive it all over again. Instead, she sat on her canvas chair and enjoyed the break rather than opening her laptop.

Miles of beach, water and solitude spread out before her when she spied a young couple ankle deep in the water. 'Where did they come from?' she thought. The temperature of the water changed only a few degrees from summer to winter, and even at ankle deep, it was freezing cold. One had to be tough to take a swim in these waters. In their town, they boast of having the highest tides in the world and more than likely, the coldest.

Once again, a feeling of loneliness for Beau crept in as she remembered a romantic time on another beach, in another life, somewhere in Maine. Closing her eyes, she allowed the feelings to creep in again as she travelled to their one-time love nest on that beach from so long ago. She and Beau had been strolling hand in hand along the beautiful water's edge before they headed home from their trip. On the way back along the boardwalk, they found a little hideaway consisting of crabgrass, driftwood and mounds of clean warm and dry beige sand. Ducking in, he checked out the log, helped her to sit down and joined her. Putting his arms around her, she snuggled closer. The sun was hot and delicious, and they were feeling the effects of it. He kissed her face, her hair and her lips and when he felt her response, he picked her up in his arms and laid her down on the warm, soft sand.

It was just before noon hour and the beach was not yet alive with visitors. For all they cared, the beach could have been crawling with people, and it would still have been only the two of them. She loved him so much that only he existed in her world anyway. Time had stood still as they made love among the sand dunes. Afterwards, they lay perfectly still, relaxed and smiling at each other. Their arms and legs were wrapped, in a trap-like position, so that neither one could escape, nor did they want to.

The time came for them to leave and they laughed hysterically realizing they had sand in places where sand should never be. They straightened themselves up as much as possible, they shook the sand off themselves and headed back to their hotel for a shower before the long drive back across the border and home.

These were the places her heart went, and she had no control over it.

Present

Slowly, she walked back to the house still carrying her precious memory of Beau in her heart. She felt like writing a bit when she got inside. So, she opened her laptop and began to think back on her years with Tommy.

Early years

Anna was not thrilled with her friendship with Tommy. She thought he was too old for her, but Gia didn't care, and she saw him every chance. She'd made sure to finish her homework as soon as she got home from school, so she could be with him in the evenings for a few hours.

When she'd finished school, Patti invited her to the city as a roommate. After heading off to the big city, Tommy soon followed, and he found a job too. They saw each other as often as time would allow but not on a daily basis. Gia worked her shifts and headed back to the apartment. She and Tommy survived on phone calls and a few dates a week, which satisfied them both for the time being. Gia loved being away from home. This was her first job and although she didn't see Tommy as often as she'd hoped, she loved the city and the freedom from her mother. Life was perfect being with Patti again.

Patti had left Kanyon Cove a few years before Gia, to attend university. They didn't see much of each other with their schedules, but it felt safe for Gia knowing Patti was around.

This was the best move Gia felt she'd ever made since, at times, the tension between her and her mother had become unbearable. She could not find it in her heart to totally forgive her for a lot of things that had happened to her. Her father was to blame for the abuse, but she'd expected her mother to protect her from him and the others, but she did not. At this point in her life, her mother did not know about the abuse. Gia still held on to her secret and she knew she would as long as her father roamed this earth. Her mother could not understand why she wanted to leave home at such a young age and Gia didn't have the heart to tell her it was partly to get away from her.

Gia had been in the city just over a year when she got a call from her mother telling her that her father had passed away. Relief had spread through her body as if a hundred-pound weight had been lifted from her shoulders. Funeral arrangements were underway, but Gia hardly heard any of it. When her mother started to tell her where and when, Gia cut her off.

"I don't care when or where the funeral is Mom, I have absolutely no interest in details. Thank you for calling."

"What! You're not going to the funeral?"

"No, I am not."

"Why not, he was your father!"

"I don't care who he was, I don't owe him anything!" she yelled into the phone.

The First Honeymoon

Several years into their courtship, Gia and Tommy were married. It was a very small and intimate wedding with her best friend, Patti, by her side and Tommy's cousin stood beside him. Gia's mother was there, but no other guests were invited. Her mother took several pictures during and after the ceremony. Anna had arranged reservations for them to have their wedding supper at the finest restaurant in town. It was a happy time for them, and they were both glad there was not a big to-do. This day was all about them just as it was supposed to be. They thanked everyone who helped make their day special and they were off to the airport after a brief time at the restaurant.

They were packed and ready to go even before the ceremony. All they wanted was to be alone somewhere on a beach. The money they saved on the small ceremony went toward their two-week honeymoon. As they sat on the plane waiting for take-off, Gia could feel knots forming in the pit of her stomach. The four-hour flight was going to be stressful for her, to say the least.

Looking out the plane window, they saw the sea-green water and the sandy white beaches, and their excitement grew. Barely able to wait for the plane to land, they wanted to get started on their honeymoon. Gia forgot about the knots in her stomach for a while and concentrated on their excitement. She wanted Tommy to see that she was as happy as he was, and she was determined to do that.

Their suite was elegant, and the manager of the resort was true to his word. Management had left a huge wicker basket of tropical fruit, fresh flowers and a bottle of champagne in an ice bucket for them to enjoy at their leisure. The view from their balcony was magnificent and second to none. They could see forever, across the crystal-clear water. They were high enough up so that nothing obstructed their view. They saw surfers, colorful sailboats, hand gliders, islanders selling their wares along the beach. Thatched roofed sun shelters and chaise loungers were scattered all along the beach. Beach towels, with the hotel logo on them, were strewn across the sandy beach while vacationers enjoyed themselves in the water. Sunbathers laid on the hot sand, children were building sand castles and lovers strolled hand in hand.

As they watched from their balcony, Tommy put his arm around Gia, and he instantly felt her body stiffen slightly from his touch.

"Are you OK, Baby?"

"Yes, I'm fine," she lied.

"Are you sure? You seem tense."

Gia stood beside him with her eyes closed and inhaled deeply. She wanted so badly to run as far away as she possibly could, but there was no place to run. She felt the same way as when she was eight years old and trapped in bed with her father. Panic set in, and her heart began to pound in her ears.

"You have got to relax, Kitten," Tommy said as he pulled her closer to him. "How about if we go down and check out the beach," he said trying to ease her nervousness.

"I'd like that, let's get changed," she said, and Tommy sensed relief in her voice.

~

"Last one in is a rotten egg!" Tommy yelled and dove into the water and out of sight. Gia was still trying to adapt to the water and managed to get herself in, up to her waist. She was high up on her tippy toes as she tried to find where Tommy was. Suddenly, he surfaced in front of her causing her to squeal in delight. He placed his hands on each of her hips and lifted her high up into the air and dropped her face first into the water. Diving in behind her, they surfaced together in laughter.

"It is absolutely beautiful here, Tommy."

"From where I'm standing, I must agree," he said as he gazed into her hazel eyes. They were standing in the water neck deep, and her long red hair was floating on top of the water behind her. He was deeply in love with her, and she took his breath away while his body wanted her so badly it ached. Wrapping her in his arms again, he held her close, hoping it would make her feel safe and loved. He felt her heart pounding against his chest, and he knew she was afraid of something, so he was careful not to press himself closer. He wished she would share her fears with him and help him to understand what it was that terrified her. He had never pressured her about it, but he had known for some time that she had encountered something traumatic. She was determined to hide her feelings. He was only guessing, of course, and he had nothing to go by except for when he felt her tense up whenever he tried to get close to her.

"Are you ready to go back to our room?" he asked her softly. He could tell by the look in her eyes that she was not, but he left it up to her.

"It's still early, Tommy," she said.

Agreeing to stay, it gave her more time to adjust to life as his wife, and what came with it. He didn't know how long it would take, but he was willing to wait.

They romped, played and splashed in the water and spent a bit of time lying on the beach under a thatched sun shelter. Gia was fair skinned and stayed out of the sun as much as possible. Her time in the water was exposure enough. Tommy drifted off to sleep as the tropical breeze swept over his body and as Gia watched him sleep, she wondered how she was going to cope. 'How was she going to allow Tommy to touch her in that way?' She wished, for a brief moment, that she had not gotten married.

Tommy and Gia hurried back to their room to get ready for dinner. They had reservations, and there was just enough time to shower the salt off them, get dressed and rush off to the restaurant. Gia's skin was a little pink from being in the sun too long and she had not taken the time to reapply her sunscreen. Now, she could feel the burn especially on her shoulders. Tommy thought it made her look healthy and glowing, but Gia knew where sun damage could lead.

Seated at a table on the patio, the sea breeze was blowing slightly so that they were comfortable. Tommy noticed that Gia was relaxed more than she had been earlier, and he wondered how long it would last. He leaned across the table, took her hand and told her how lovely she looked.

Gia had difficulty accepting compliments and never really knew how to respond when she got one. Perhaps it was because she never considered herself as anything other than plain and when she was told she was pretty, beautiful or any other term, she thought it was just a lie. Her mother was always quick to point out that if you gawk at yourself in the mirror for too long, you were considered conceited. Many times, as a child, she would stand with her back to the mirror to brush her hair, so her mother wouldn't catch her looking at herself. She didn't want to hear her mother tell her that she was nobody and no one cared what she looked like anyway. She could still hear her voice, "You can stand there as long as you want but you are going to look the same when you walk away." How could anyone think she was pretty if she did not? It must be just another lie to get something out of her.

Tommy interrupted her thoughts and asked her if she had heard what he said. She said she had and thanked him as best she could for the compliment. Looking at him intently, she asked, "Are you serious?" She could hear her mother mocking her, as she asked the question.

"What about, Kitten?"

She loved it when he called her 'Kitten,' it reminded her of their first meeting at Nora's Place. He had called her 'Kitten' even before he knew her name.

"Do you really think I'm pretty?"

"What kind of a question is that Sweetheart, you are a beautiful woman. Do you not think of yourself as beautiful?"

Tears sprung to her eyelids and he quickly moved to the seat closest to her.

"Baby are you OK? What's wrong?"

She reached for her handbag, took out a tissue and dabbed at the corners of her eyes.

"What's wrong, Honey?" he asked again.

"Why don't I feel pretty Tommy, why does it feel like it's a lie?"

"What do you mean?"

"My mother always indicated that I was egotistical whenever I looked in the mirror and told me the results wouldn't change when I walked away. I've heard it all of my life, so I figured everyone must have seen, in me, what she saw."

Tommy could see the sadness in her eyes. "I'm sorry you had to go through that, Kitten. I never knew about that part of your life, you never confided much in me."

Holding her hand, he felt he shouldn't say anything, but he couldn't help himself, so he moved in for the kill while he had the chance.

"Gia, I know there is something else that's been burdening you. We have been together for a long time, and whenever I try getting close to you, you freeze up on me. Loving you the way I do, I felt certain that somewhere, down the road, you'd trust me enough to talk to me. To explain what the problem is, so that I'd understand and possibly help you through it."

Visibly shaken, she asked, "Can we skip dinner and go back to our room?" Leaving their table, they went to the elevator and headed up to their floor. Breaking down, Gia walked into Tommy's arms as soon as the elevator doors closed. Holding her tenderly, she sobbed into his shirt as they waited for the doors to open again. Luckily, no one else got on with them, and the elevator went directly to the top floor. Gia clung to Tommy as he unlocked their door. As it swung open, he scooped her up in his arms, kicked the door closed with his foot, and carried her into their room. Holding her close, he rocked her back and forth, as he stood there while she cried in his arms. The day had just gotten the best of her, and she was ready to collapse. Her nerves were completely frazzled thinking about her wedding night. Silently wishing again that she had not gotten married, so she wouldn't have to face this night. Lifting her head up off his shoulder, he lowered her slowly to the floor.

"You OK, Baby?"

"No Tommy, I'm not, can we go out on the balcony and talk?"

"Of course, is there anything I can get for you before we go out, something to drink, perhaps?"

"I'll have a glass of ice water please."

Walking out onto the balcony, she blew her nose and waited for Tommy to follow her. Carrying two glasses of ice water, he set them down on the table. Walking over to the railing, he wrapped his arms around her. Her reflexes kicked in and her hands automatically went up to touch his arms as they stood there in silence looking out over the bay. 'Old habits die hard.' The wind blew her hair back off her face, and he felt it whip lightly across his cheek. Taking a deep breath, she turned to look at Tommy. Reaching up, she touched his face and asked him to sit with her. Gia looked as if she didn't know where to begin or even if she wanted to, but she knew she had to be honest with Tommy if they were going to be together.

"Tommy," she swallowed and began, "this is very difficult for me to talk about. No one knows about this yet, I haven't even told Patti and you know she is my dearest friend in the world, and I know that eventually, I will have to tell my mother. Slowly, she began telling him about her father molesting her when she was eight years old, the trauma it had caused, and how it had triggered suspicion inside her mind, causing her to think that everyone lies to her.

"How can I trust other people when I couldn't trust my own father?" she asked. She tried, with difficulty, to explain that she had always felt that she was unlovable and the only time she felt safe was when she was alone. Hearing herself speak the words, for the first time, sounded as if she was living in someone else's story.

Tommy sat and listened to everything she'd told him, and his heart was heavy as he listened to the woman he adored, share the pain that she's kept locked up for so long. Everything that had happened or did not happen between them, became crystal clear, and he reached for her hand to comfort her but did not interrupt. Before they realized it, they'd been on the balcony for more than two hours. Tommy could only imagine how difficult this evening must have been her. He also knew it was up to him to try and make her feel safe. Sensing her reluctance to go inside, knowing what was expected of her, he tried easing her mind.

"Gia, what your father did, was sick and demented and it was not your fault," he said sympathetically. He noticed that she was vibrating badly. "Honey, you are shivering, let's go inside."

"I can't, Tommy," she blurted.

"Yes, you can, you need to get some rest Kitten; you're exhausted," he said tenderly. Seeing the terror in her eyes, his heart went out to her. Tears streamed silently down her cheeks and as he reached out for her, she nearly jumped out of her skin.

"Gia, it's me, Tommy, you don't ever have to be afraid of me. I'm not going to hurt you and I'm definitely not going to force you into anything that you don't want to do."

"You're not?" she asked with pleading eyes.

"No, Sweetheart I'm not," he said with a gentle smile, while bending his knees to look into her eyes. He could feel her relax a bit as soon as she heard his words. He put his arm around her shoulder and led her back inside.

"Go and get yourself ready for bed, you're about to fall off your feet."

Glancing at him, she was leery of what she was hearing. Looking at her he winked, smiled and nodded toward the bathroom. Seeing sheer relief on her face, he knew he was doing the right thing. She was exhausted, and the pressure of this night had gotten the better of her.

She knew she could not have kept her secret from Tommy any longer. She went into the bathroom and closed the door.

~

As the days and weeks went by, the patience he had shown her was incredible. Feeling his love and patience, caused her to love him even more. Over time, he showed her that making love, with someone you love, is a special bond between two people. He assured her that it meant more when there is love involved, and he showed her just how special it could be. Taking small steps, he didn't want to intimidate or overwhelm her at the prospect of making love, and he tried to reassure her that it was a natural thing to do. When she relaxed enough to be with him intimately, it made her fall more deeply in love with him. They had a great marriage and a bond that could not be broken by anyone or anything.

~

Shortly after getting home from their honeymoon, they made the decision to move from the city and go back to Kanyon Cove. Tommy was self-employed and installed furnaces, so, no matter where they lived, there was always going to be furnace work, and he could always get new clients. Gia worked in real estate, and the same was true for her location. She could sell properties from any town or city and she wanted to do it in Kanyon Cove.

At their first opportunity, they began their search and planned a trip home to search locations. Gia made phone calls, printed off interesting property sheets, and had gotten a few leads to make their trip worthwhile. On their first drive home, they found the 'perfect' location. A waterfront property had just been listed and they were the first to view it. It boasted of two bedrooms, two bathrooms, a private patio and beautiful sunsets. There was space for both of them to set up home offices. What else could they ask for in purchasing their first home? The paperwork was finished quickly, and before they knew it, they were packing up their city lives and moving home.

Life Happens

Being married for several years, they both had successful businesses, and were blissfully happy, until the day an unexpected knock came at the door.

"Mrs. Edwards?"

"Yes, I'm Georgia Edwards."

"You need to come with us Ma'am; your husband has been in an accident and has been taken to the hospital. If it's OK with you, we'll drive you."

Shock overcame her, and she did not stop to ask questions. She guessed that an officer must have grabbed a sweater, that hung by the door, and her handbag, from the table in the entry. He must have had the sense to lock her door because she sure as hell was in no shape to remember to do it. She just walked blindly, as they led her by the elbow, to the police car and helped her into the back seat. Once inside, one of the officers asked if there was anyone they could call. Giving him their neighbor's phone number, she asked him to tell them about the accident.

"What happened to Tommy?" she asked as reality set in, and her tears were free to flow.

"He was t-boned at an intersection by a drunk driver."

"How bad is it?"

"I'm afraid it's pretty bad Ma'am. We're almost there so hang on until you can talk to the doctors." The siren screamed as they raced through traffic to get to the hospital entrance.

Freaking out in the back seat of the police cruiser, she felt like a caged animal. It was her first time in a police car and the siren was almost unbearable.

"Please hurry!" she said as panic started to take over.

"We are Mrs. Edwards; we're going as fast as we can."

Seeing the hospital in the distance, her heart pounded wildly, and she was sure she was going to pass out. She knew the police officer was talking to her, but she couldn't hear what he was saying. At the hospital they pulled up right behind the ambulance that had brought Tommy in. It was still in front of the emergency entrance with the back doors open.

She heard someone yell, "She's going into shock, get over here!"

The same police officer was screaming at a doctor who was just inside the entrance. She remembered seeing lights flying by her, then darkness and then lights again. She could not figure out what the lights were, 'why are they over top of me and why am I moving?'

Then, she realized she was on a gurney flying down the corridor to emergency.

"Tommy! Where is he? I have to see him!"

"You will, Mrs. Edwards just as soon as we check you out to be certain you're stable. Hang in there with us for a few more minutes and we'll take you to the floor where Tommy is."

She was so tired.

"Stay awake, Mrs. Edwards, we need for you to stay awake, OK? Can you do that for me?"

Her only thought was how tired she was and how badly she wanted to go to sleep. Someone placed a cold cloth on her forehead and brought her around enough so that she could understand where she was. Then she remembered that Tommy was here, too, and she had to see him!

"Please take me to see Tommy; I have to see him now."

"Let me help you sit up Mrs. Edwards, and we'll see if you're OK to leave. You gave us a bit of a scare you know. You had a slight drop in blood pressure and passed out for a few minutes. It looks as if you haven't had much to eat today, young lady."

Sitting up slowly, she sat still on the gurney and was lightheaded for only a few seconds, and then the dizziness passed. Swinging her legs carefully over the side, she slid down off the bed until she felt her feet touch the floor. She was a little weak but OK to leave, but not before drinking a glass of orange juice. She asked someone where Tommy's room was, and they took her to the waiting area to wait for a doctor.

"He's still in surgery, Mrs. Edwards."

"Already! How is he?" she whispered.

Inhaling deeply, he pressed his lips together before speaking. "I'm afraid it doesn't look good," he said honestly, "but we can always pray for a miracle. He was pretty banged up Mrs. Edwards, and he will be in surgery for some time. I suggest you try and get something to eat or at least a cup of coffee while you wait. You need to keep your strength up for when he comes out." Then, in a voice that was barely audible, he said, "If he comes out, Mrs. Edwards."

Grabbing her before she lost her balance, he led her to a leather couch and sat her down.

"Oh my God, it's really bad, isn't it?" she cried.

"Yes, it is, we have to be truthful with you right now. Tommy is in critical condition and if he comes out of surgery, he will be in intensive care for some time."

Gia felt her strength slip away as she digested his words. 'How was she going to go on without Tommy? He was her life; he was her everything. He must make it through this. If anyone can, Tommy can.'

Gia was still in the waiting room in shock and terrified while trying to keep it together. She wished someone, anyone, would give her an update on Tommy's condition. She paced the floors until her legs ached and she tried to sit down only to jump up again at every movement in the hallways. She was tired physically but mentally she was so strung out she knew she would not close her eyes until she heard something.

'Patti,' she thought, 'I have to call Patti.'

People began to gather in the waiting room, faces that were blurred and meaningless to her. She wanted them to go away. She looked mindlessly from one face to another, but they were all strangers. Each face could have been that of a neighbor, but she didn't recognize anybody. She could hear phones ringing, questions being asked with vague responses, and she could relate to not getting answers. She heard magazine pages being flipped, someone was working on a crossword puzzle, which was her and Tommy's favorite thing to do every morning. Looking around, she saw someone pull a novel out of her handbag, which likely meant she was here for a while, too.

More people gathered, new faces appeared, and Gia became increasingly uncomfortable in this crowd. Just as she was getting ready to bolt, Tommy's doctor appeared in the doorway. Making her way through the mass of people, she kept her eyes on the doctor. Questions began to form in her mind, 'How is Tommy doing? How long has she been here? What time is it? These were the first questions she wanted answers to as she approached him nervously. The look in his eyes spoke volumes, and her heart sank.

"Mrs. Edwards," the doctor said touching her shoulder, "your husband is out of surgery. He's managed to hang on through the long hours in there, and it's a miracle that he did. He is in ICU and will be there indefinitely. You should come with me now because there are no guarantees that he will make it much longer."

Gia gasped and nearly collapsed but managed to grab the arm of a nearby chair.

"Please take me to him," she cried and followed him down the hall. Feeling numb, she didn't know how her legs got her down the hall to the elevator and up to the ICU. Following blindly behind the doctor, she felt like a child being led to a dark and scary place. She knew she could not go back there right now. Tommy needed her to be strong for him like he had been for her.

Entering the ICU, she held her breath, looked around at several patients in the room and had to ask where Tommy was. The doctor pointed to his bed, and she clamped her hand over her mouth to stifle a scream.

"What?" she hissed softly.

Touching her arm, he nodded his head. Walking slowly toward his bed, she could not believe it was her Tommy lying there hooked up to several tubes that came from every possible vein and orifice. He was horribly bruised and swollen so that she could not find anything recognizable about him. She was staring down tubes, machines, hospital blues and a cacophony of bells, buzzers and beeps. He had a tube down his throat helping him breathe, an intravenous drip of meds on a pole, bags of blood, and a catheter hung over the side of the bed. Several machines were beeping, and a monitor was lit up showing his heart rate and pulse. The beeping was endless, and Gia was devastated as she concentrated on the machines that kept Tommy alive and breathing. Reaching for a tissue on the table next to his bed, she quietly blew her nose and then took another one to wipe her eyes. She disposed of them and grabbed a couple more knowing she'd need them.

Rolling a stool up close to his bed, she sat down. Looking around, she strained to make sense of it all and tried to think of what she could possibly do for him, but she knew there was nothing anyone, except God, could do. She knew He had a plan for Tommy, and she prayed it was to keep him alive for her. Staring at his motionless form, she tried her best to see something familiar, so she would know this person actually was Tommy. Dropping her eyes down to his hand, she saw it.

"Tommy!" she whispered as fresh tears escaped. She saw the wedding band that she had slipped onto his finger several years before. His hand was badly swollen, and the ring was barely visible. She was surprised they hadn't cut it off for circulation purposes. There are reasons for all things, and this was her way of recognizing him, actually, the only way. She didn't know if she should touch him. Her hand hovered over him afraid to hurt him if she rested hers on his.

There was a nurse close by at all times, and she kept an eye on Gia as well as Tommy. Seeing that Gia was in an agitated state, she walked over to her and whispered, "It's OK to touch him," she whispered, patted her arm and walked away, chart in hand.

Gently, she slipped her hand under his, and it felt oddly cool. She remembered his hands were always toasty warm. She was still having difficulty believing this person was her Tommy, but she knew it was, from the wedding band that looked exactly like hers.

"I love you, Tommy," she whispered as tears slid down her cheeks. "Try and hang on Baby, I need you."

She kept hearing the doctor's words over and over in her head as he told her he may not make it. The possibility of Tommy dying was beyond her comprehension. There was no way he would die and leave her.

"Squeeze my hand Tommy, if you can hear my voice, if you know I'm here with you. Please squeeze my hand, Baby."

The nurse came over and touched her shoulder, and Gia jumped to her feet as the stool spun on its wheels.

"I'm sorry, I didn't hear you," Gia said.

"I'm sorry, too, Mrs. Edwards," she said reaching to quiet the stool. "I shouldn't have come up behind you like that." Smiling at

Gia sympathetically, she said "I just wanted to tell you that, in all probability, it is likely too soon to expect a response from your husband. He hasn't been out of surgery very long, and it will be quite a while before the effects of the anesthetic drug wears off. But that's a good thing, Mrs. Edwards; it gives his body the time it needs to heal internally. I know this is a scary place for you to have to be, especially alone, but I can assure you that your husband will not regain consciousness any time soon. I'd advise you to go home for a while and get some rest or be with your family. Someone from here will call you if there is any change. Go home and get some rest."

"Do you mean he doesn't know I'm here?"

"No, in all probability, he likely doesn't, not yet anyway, which is why you should get as much rest as you can for when you need to be here."

She was reluctant to leave but knew the nurse was right, and she did need to go home and get some rest. She sat again for a few quiet moments searching again for some recognition of Tommy, but there was none, just the wedding band. She silently thanked God for giving them the insight to buy twin bands. She gently tried to twist his band around his finger, but it was swelled so badly it wouldn't budge. She leaned over and lightly kissed his wedding band as a single tear dropped on his hand.

~

The water felt refreshing as Gia stood under the shower spray. Leaning her head against the shower stall, she felt the hot water run down her back. Sadness lay heavy in her heart while her tears mixed with the spray. She thought of Tommy lying in the hospital, banged up beyond recognition. She envisioned his handsome face, his lean athletic body and his smile that always melted her heart.

Tommy was very athletic and loved to play hockey in the winter, baseball in the summer and the occasional game of golf. Both were captains of their bowling teams and bowled every Sunday night from fall on into the spring. It was the one activity they could do together, that they both enjoyed. Tommy wanted to teach her how to play golf, but she knew it was his time with his friends and she didn't want to intrude on that time.

The water had cooled off, and Gia felt a chill run through her as she stepped out of the shower. She wrapped her hair in one towel and her body in another as she made her way to the bedroom. She sat down on the cedar chest at the foot of her bed and stared blankly into nothingness.

Waking up the next morning, she was still wrapped in towels but with no remembrance of leaving the cedar chest. It was very early morning, and not quite daylight yet, so she lay in bed and tried to let yesterday's events sink in. She no more than allowed her mind to open when her phone rang. The ringtone in the still of the early morning sent a shock through her body like a gunshot. Grabbing her cordless phone from the nightstand, she hit the 'talk' button.

"Hello?"

"Mrs. Edwards, it's the hospital calling..."

"How is Tommy?" Gia interrupted before the nurse could finish.

"There was no change through the night, but he is showing signs of conscientiousness, so perhaps it's best if you get down here."

Gia clicked the off button and flew off the bed in a panic. She dressed as quickly as she could, tied her hair up in a ponytail and sped off to the hospital as fast as she dared. Driving into the first available parking spot, she ran to the entrance. Once inside the doors she saw the elevators and pressed the floor to the ICU. There was a new shift nurse at the desk as she got off the elevator, so Gia went to her and introduced herself.

"Oh, yes, Mrs. Edwards, please come with me."

Feelings of anxiety and distress, she was close to passing out. Seeing spots before her eyes, weakness and nauseous crept in, and all she wanted to do was to sit before she fell. She could not remember eating anything after she drank the orange juice the day before and she was beginning to have the same feeling as then. Finally, she was at Tommy's bedside. There was very little change in the swelling, and she noticed there was more bruising than yesterday. She rolled the little stool up to his bedside and slid her hand under his. She looked down at his ring again and then up to his face.

"Tommy, sweetheart, it's Gia. Can you hear me, Honey?"

She searched his face for any sign that he was in there somewhere and suddenly she felt a little tug on her fingers.

"Tommy!" she whispered, "can you hear me?"

She waited for only a few seconds and he tugged at her hand again. The swelling was so bad he could not squeeze, but she knew he was trying to communicate with her. Her heart leaped with joy knowing Tommy was conscience. A nurse came over to her, touched her shoulder and nodded her head for Gia to step aside with her. She gently released his hand and stood up to move to the side.

"He has been in and out of conscientiousness for the past hour or so," she said in a whisper. "He may not be able to speak to you yet but give him some time, and I'm certain he will. He's still not 'out of the woods' yet, Mrs. Edwards, he is still very critical, and he needs to rest so his body can heal. Sit with him and let him know you are here and that'll give him comfort in knowing he isn't alone."

Gia nodded as she listened and glanced from the nurse to Tommy to make sure if he moved, it would not go unnoticed.

"Thank you, may I go back now."

"Yes, of course you can, is there anything I can get for you?"

"I would love a cup of coffee and piece of toast if it's possible."

"I'll see what I can do for you, now you go to your man," she said with a drawl as she winked at Gia.

"I'm here Tommy," she said as she rolled the stool back up to his bed. She slipped her hand back under his and he tugged in response that he knew she was there. Gia laid her head down on the bed and closed her eyes to thank God for bringing Tommy this far.

"Here's your breakfast, Mrs. Edwards."

Gia raised her head and looked at the nurse who in return said, "It surely does not hurt to pray, child."

Gia thanked her for the food and coffee, and she sat watching Tommy's face as she ate every bite. There was a fruit cup, toast and cereal. She ate slowly since she could not remember her last meal; she wanted it to stay down. She noticed Tommy's hand move slightly and she reached for it to reassurc him she was still there.

"I'm here Baby, get some rest."

Many hours had passed, and there were no other signs from Tommy, so she decided to go home. Gia was reassured that he was resting comfortably and that they would notify her if there were changes. She went home to spend another lonely night alone. She was up early the next morning and went back to the ICU to wait.

~

Opening his swollen eyes, Tommy tried to make sense of where he was. He had been taken off the ventilator and was now breathing on his own but with an oxygen tube up his nose. A flicker of his eyelids caused her to spring to her feet. "Tommy! You're awake!" She had waited for so long to see another glimmer of conscientiousness from his swollen body. Tommy searched for her through his badly swollen eyes that opened only in slits.

"Baby?" he whispered faintly, barely forming the word.

"Yes honey, I'm right here," she said as she held his battered hand and leaned as close as she could to his lips. "You should try and rest."

Tommy sensed that his situation was not good, and he wanted to say as much as he could while he was able.

"Baby," he whispered in short gasps, "try to move forward, don't live in the past. Forgiveness is a wonderful thing. Find the strength to let go." He gasped and paused between rushed words, seemingly knowing he was running out of time. He was barely audible and slowly losing breath, but he continued. "Don't give him any more power, let it go, Babe." His breathing became shallow as he struggled once more for words. "I love you, Kitten, I always will, be strong for me, Babe."

Gia knew he was talking about her father, how his abuse had followed her every day. She knew Tommy wanted her to be free from the torment he had caused her.

"I love you, too, Tommy," she croaked through her tears.

He looked straight into her eyes and tried to wink at her through his swollen eye as she heard the buzzing sound escape from the monitor.

Her face went from a hopeful smile, at hearing his voice, to utter disbelief. Her spine went from semi-relaxed to poker straight as she raised her head to look at the instrument panel above his head. She watched in horror as he flatlined before her eyes. Her body went into total shock as a doctor, and several nurses rushed in and surrounded his bed. Someone rolled her stool out of the way but not out of direct view of Tommy. It seemed, for a few minutes, that her body was suspended in the air as she watched the doctor take his pulse; a nurse was checking monitors while another checked IV's. A team with a crash cart came clamoring through the door as Gia watched in a hypnotic state.

Shortly afterwards she heard those awful words that she'd only heard on television, "The time of death, ten thirty a.m."

The doctor stepped in front of Gia and reminded her that Tommy was too weak for them to attempt to paddle him back to life. She could barely hear him speak from the confusion in the room. She listened to the loud, steady buzz of his life support system and suddenly it was as if she'd gone deaf. There were no sounds in the room as someone unplugged the machines leaving the room deathly quiet. In those few minutes, she watched as if in slow motion, the cluster of people that had surrounded Tommy's bed. Someone had a hand on her shoulder, and she vaguely heard the words, "I'm sorry, we have lost him."

Total shock engulfed her as she tried to take in the doctor's words. She never took her eyes off Tommy's face, and only seconds ago, he was speaking to her.

"No, no, no!" she said as she moved her eyes and stared at the person in front of her. Being in total disbelief mode, she could not even cry for her Tommy.

"I'm sorry, Mrs. Edwards," she heard again. Sadness filled her body and she began to tremble as she looked down at his hand and saw the swollen skin around his wedding band. Glancing momentarily at her own matching band, she rose to her feet as if she were filled with helium.

"Mrs. Edwards? Georgia? Can I call someone to come for you?"

Searching the room in confusion, she tried to find the voice that was speaking to her but to no avail. Then she realized the person with the voice was behind her, holding her up.

"No, no one, just give me a few minutes, please."

"Sure," the voice said, "sit here."

"Thank you," she responded reaching for the stool. Dumbstruck, she could not yet bring herself to cry, but her insides were screaming.

'Where is Patti?' she thought. 'Why isn't she here?' Then she remembered, somehow, that Patti was out of town, 'Damn it!'

She had listened carefully to every word that Tommy had said to her. Although she was numb with grief, she knew exactly what he had meant and what his words were telling her.

From the time they met until he had taken his last breath, they had known each other for a dozen years, and now it was over in a heartbeat.

Leaving the Hospital

Stumbling blindly from the ICU, Gia made her way to the elevator. With shaking fingers, she pressed the button to the main floor. Turning around slowly, she pressed her palms and her cheek against the coolness of the wall and closed her eyes. She felt the jolt when the elevator came to a stop. The doors opened, and she pushed herself away from the wall and stumbled out into the lobby. Her vision, blurred by tears, caused her to trip into the arms of a stranger.

"You OK?" he asked.

She stared at him blindly as he held her at arm's length searching her face.

"Are you OK?" he asked again, to which he got no response. "Can I call someone for you?" He could see that she was in a traumatic state and walked her over to the information desk. "Excuse me, could you help this lady, she seems to be in shock," he said to the attendant behind the window.

"Bring her around here, sir," she said as she twirled her finger in the direction of the door around the corner. "Thank you," was all she said as she focused her attention on Gia. She only needed to ask one question before she was in total understanding of why this woman was in shock. "What's your name, dear?" she asked offering Gia a tissue.

"Gia Edwards, Georgia Edwards," she elaborated.

"Edwards?" she repeated, Mrs. Thomas Edwards?"

"He's er... was my husband."

"I'm so sorry for your loss, Mrs. Edwards, is there someone I can call for you?"

"No, my friend is out of town, and there is no one else. Could you call a cab for me, please?" Her car was in the parking lot, but she knew she was in no shape to drive. She didn't want to leave Tommy there alone, but she had no choice.

Fresh tears rolled down her cheeks as she waited for the taxi. The cab pulled up, and the driver got out and opened the door for her. She practically crawled into the back seat. She gave the driver her address and then continued to cry knowing she was going home alone, only this time for good.

Her home looked unwelcoming when she stepped out of the cab. She felt apprehensive as she stood on the sidewalk. It was a long walk from the sidewalk to her house, and her steps slowed as she approached the front door. She wondered how she was ever going to go inside and expect life to go on. She fumbled as she tried to find the key slot in the doorknob.

Turning the key, she heard the dreadful 'click' and pushed the door open. She gave herself a few seconds to breathe before entering. Stepping inside she turned her body as she closed the door. She was not quite ready to accept the room. She touched her forehead against the coolness of the steel door. For a few moments, she just leaned against it, unable to face the emptiness. Reaching across, she twisted the deadlock. The hollow 'clunk' of the bolt sounded like that of a prison cell being locked. She turned again to press her back against the door then slowly let her body slide to the floor, like a ragdoll. She felt undeniably defeated.

She'd lost track of time, and as she got to her feet, her instinct for hiding from the world began to process. She made her way around the living room closing the mini blinds and pulling the drapes. Then, she stumbled from room to room closing all the blinds, drapes and turning off all the night-lights. There were no lights, no sounds and no sense of joy at being home. She carefully made her way back to the couch.

This was the first time, in her recollection, that she wanted to be consumed by complete and utter darkness. She didn't want to be anywhere else. The room was as black and as cold as her thoughts and feelings were. She seated herself in the middle of the couch, drew her knees up to her chin and felt unable to move another muscle. She was dumbfounded as she sat in the darkness. There was stark, deafening silence with only the roar of white noise in her head. Tommy was gone; she had watched him die. She sat there alone with a heavy heart. It had been only a few days ago that Tommy had been in this room with her. To say 'what a difference a day makes' would have been an absolute understatement.

It had seemed like hours before she made her way to the bedroom. Stripping off her clothes, she got into the shower. This time she had had the good sense to pull on a shower cap, so she didn't have to deal with wet hair. The first splash of water was a shock to her body and caused her to inhale deeply, but she didn't care. Even the water felt heavy and uncomfortable. It was not at all soothing. As it pelted against her skin, she began to cry. Her tears mixing with the water had no beginning and no end. Stepping out of the shower, she rummaged the medicine cabinet. She needed something to help her sleep.

~

Vaguely, she heard a constant thumping at her door. Then she heard someone calling her name. She didn't care who it was; she just knew who it wasn't.

"Gia! Open the damned door! Gia! It's Patti! Let me in!"

Groggy from the sleeping pills, she could not grasp the concept of Patti being at her door. 'She's out of town,' she thought, her mind was just playing tricks on her. Wrapping her housecoat around her body, she made her way down the darkened hall.

"Gia?" she heard again, "open the door, it's Patti!"

Relief overcame her as she unlocked the door and wrapped her arms around Patti's neck. Patti's heart broke in two when she saw Gia. Her long hair was matted, her eyes were swollen almost shut, and she barely recognized her best friend.

"Gia, Honey, I'm so sorry!" she said as she held her. They were both sobbing lightly at first, but as soon as Patti showed signs of sympathy, it became a full-fledged howl from Gia. She finally had someone to hold her! Her friend was here!

"I heard about the accident, on the car radio, on my way home. Gia, I had no idea how serious it was. I wish I had been here for you. I came directly home. Gia, why are you here in the dark? You hate the dark.

"I... can't... face... the... day," she sobbed, her body going into spasm as she tried to speak. "Patti, Tommy is gone!" she howled.

"I know, Sweetie, I'm so sorry," she said as she held Gia close. She rocked her back and forth and patted her back for a few minutes. "Sweetie, you have to pull yourself together, we have things to do."

"Wh..what things?" she sobbed.

We must go to visit the pastor, make arrangements for Tommy's funeral, and then we're going to talk to the women's group at the church to plan his reception. So, go in there and get presentable and do something with that hair, it looks like a rat's nest!" she said pointing towards the bedroom. Patti gave her instructions as she went about opening drapes and mini blinds to bring light back into the house. "Gia, go!" she said pointing towards the hall.

"What? No!"

"Yes, Gia, go and get dressed!"

Once Patti had gotten Gia up and running, the funeral arrangements went smoothly. Their first stop was the florist shop to choose the appropriate arrangements. They made their way to the church to speak to Pastor Andrews. He had taken notes on their requests and had agreed to pass the information on to the woman's group.

They took a lunch break, and although Gia was happy to sit down, she was not hungry. She ordered a cup of coffee and sipped it as she watched as Patti ate.

"One of these days all that fat is going to kill you," she said as Patti dipped her fry into a separate bowl of gravy.

"Yada, yada," she replied while giving her hand a flip and taking a big bite out of her burger.

"How do you eat that crap?"

"A burger wouldn't hurt you," she said pointing to Gia's tiny frame.

"Gross!" she winced and looked around at the other patrons. She watched them eat. "How do people eat this stuff?" she said again, puckering her face as if she smelled something bad.

"It's a burger joint for God's sake! What did you expect?"

"Tsk!' Gia clucked.

"Shut up!" Patti said, glaring at her, "so I can eat guilt free."

Gia really hated 'stupid.'

Back at Gia's house, Patti posed the question.

"What are you going to do now, Gia?"

"Oh Patti, please, don't ask me questions that I can't answer right now. Allow me, to at least, get through the funeral tomorrow before I have to plan the rest of my life!" Feeling agitation setting in, she began to silently and slowly count to ten. She could not afford to alienate Patti; she was all she had.

~

Gia barely remembered the service or the reception. She did, however, remember Tommy's name being mentioned throughout the service, but her heart ached so badly she cried through it all.

She remembered being led to the basement after the service. There were wall-to-wall people. Some were sitting, but most were standing around holding plates of food and a cup of something. She didn't want to be there and asked Patti to please, take her home. She told her that she had a headache and wanted to go home and go to bed. Patti knew she had spent far too much time in bed, so she tried to keep her there a little longer.

"Would a cup of coffee and some aspirin help?" Patti asked and was in no mood for an argument.

"Sure, a couple of aspirin and water please." As she waited for Patti to return, she scanned the room. There were so many faces that she didn't recognize. 'Who are these people?' she thought.

"Here you go," Patti said handing her a glass of water and the pills.

"Thanks, Patti, but I'd really like to go soon."

"Sure, as soon as the crowd begins to thin out."

Gia tried not to roll her eyes, but Patti caught her.

"Be nice, Gia!" she hissed.

~

She saw Tommy come in. He looked around the room, and when his eyes met hers, he winked, smiled and began to walk toward her. Gia stared, wide-eyed, at him. Joy enveloped her at the sight of him. In her subconscious mind, she knew he was dead, but in her heart, she just wanted to hold him. When he got to her, he reached out to touch her but before they connected, skin to skin, she woke up. The usual confusion of dreams and the push-pull of emotions caused her to panic when he reached for her. She sat bolt upright in her bed realizing she'd had a nightmare.

She buried her face in her hands. She shook her head back and forth and tried to recall the funeral from the day before. It had been brutal as a few moments, here and there, surfaced. She remembered bits and pieces of the service and how it stung each time Tommy's name was spoken. Afterwards, she recalled the buzz of constant chatter, the scrapping of chairs and the milling around of dozens of nondescript faces. People were coming up to give her their condolences and hugging her. Her head was pounding, and she wanted to go home.

She could no longer contend with all the confusion around her. Was it any wonder Tommy wanted to reach out to her in her sleep?

"Tommy," she said aloud, "what do I do now?"

She slowly dropped her hands from her face almost expecting the past few days to be an actual nightmare, but everything was still the same. The house was dark and cold; there were no movements, no aromas of coffee coming from the kitchen and no whistling sounds as Tommy brewed up a pot. She was so alone... so... so... alone.

Falling back onto her pillow, she became absorbed in self-pity and began to cry again. She was sorry now that she hadn't allowed herself to stay in her nightmare, so Tommy could hold her and tell her it would be all right.

Her doorknocker brought her out of her pity party with a start. She sat up again, not wanting to answer it. She listened hoping whoever was there, would go away. Before the thought could properly form, Patti was standing in her bedroom door.

"I thought you'd still be in bed, Gia, its three o'clock in the afternoon!

"How did you get in?"

"I have a key!"

"But I let you in the other day," she frowned.

"Yes, because you had the deadbolt locked. Have you even eaten?"

"No, I haven't eaten, and I'm not hungry."

"Well hungry or not, you're getting out of that bed!"

"I don't want to!" Gia whined as she heard water running.

"Get up and take a shower right now!" Patti ordered as she pulled the bedding off the bed.

Gia clucked but obeyed.

While she showered, Patti changed the sheets and pillowcases and made up the bed. She was in the kitchen making her something to eat when Gia appeared.

"This is awful, Patti."

"Yes, it is, and it is going to be awful for a long time. That doesn't mean that you don't have a life to live. By that, I mean there will be no lying around feeling sorry for yourself. You have a business to run, a house to keep and lots of things to do to keep you busy."

"Not yet Patti, please," she whined.

"Stop whining Gia; this is your life now and if you don't start to live it, you will drown in self-pity. Depression is not a place where you want to go. You are strong, you are beautiful, and your life is not over. Tommy's life is over, Gia. It was his time to go, his number was up, and he was called home. That does not mean you have to stop living yours. Tommy would not want that for you. I'm sorry that I've been so harsh with you these last few days Gia, but I had to be because I would not have forgiven myself if you were to go beyond the point of no return. You have to stay strong, and you must fight every day to stay strong and not get depressed and live on pills. It would kill me to see you go there."

"I know you're right, Patti, but it hurts so much."

"I know it does and it will get better in time," she said as she wiped tears off Gia's cheeks and gave her a big hug. "One day at a time, my friend."

~

One day at a time, one week at a time, one year and then two years. Time heals all wounds. Gia had decided to take her maiden name back. She didn't do it to disrespect Tommy's name; it was her way of moving on.

Tommy's death had taken another piece of her soul that she would never get back. Her father had taken the first chunk years ago. Her soul was being chipped away, and it was beyond her control.

Gia got her business up and running again, and her life was back on track. She learned to accept the fact that Tommy had lived out his numbered days like we all will. She gave thanks for the time she was allotted with him, and now it was over, and she was moving on.

One day her nephew, Ty, came to ask for a favor.

The 'Friendship' 1976

Several years after Tommy's death, Gia was doing her best to function on her own. This was a new concept for her, and she had to learn to live with it. She tried losing herself in her business. During the day, she was busy, but the nights were still long and lonely.

Patti had been a blessing, but she knew that she had her own life in the city and Gia had to learn to live on her own. Spending time alone was almost unbearable, at times, but she was thankful for her nephew, Ty. Spending time with him was a blessing. She continued to go to his little league baseball games to cheer him on, and she also drove him to Scout meetings. She did what she could for him, and it helped them both at easing the pain of losing Tommy. His parents had busy lives, so Ty spent a lot of time with Gia.

His Scout Troop was having their annual father and son banquet, and this year it was being held at the local Knights of Columbus hall. Ty asked if she'd go with him since his dad was away and his mom had to work. She accepted and felt honored that he would even consider her as his escort.

~

Arriving at the banquet hall a bit early gave them time to walk around and look at all the badges, flags and trophies that were on display and would later be presented to the troop members. The tables were set up nicely, and each one had a woodsy centerpiece appropriate to the occasion. They were all made similarly, but not exact, with pinecones, bark and boughs.

Making their way back to their table, Ty chatted nonstop, and Gia took the opportunity to glance around the room at other groups. Most attending the function were young fathers and their sons. She continued nonchalantly to search the room, and she came across another female sitting alone at a table. When their eyes met, the other woman lifted her hand in a sort of a wave, and Gia lifted hers up enough to reciprocate and be sociable. She then turned her attention back to Ty and his chatter. A friend of Ty's walked up to their table and Ty greeted him and introduced him to her.

"Aunt Gia, this is my friend Chance," he said with a big grin, "we are in the same troop."

"Hello," Chance said nervously and pointing behind him. "Um, my mom wants to know if you will come and sit at our table."

Gia looked around, to where he was pointing, and it was the same woman who had waved at her. She had her arm waving in the air beckoning Gia to join her at her table.

'Oh Geez!' Gia mumbled to herself. Instant red flag! There was no reason why this person could not have gotten up from her table, walked across the room, and ask to join them. Instead, and as if by obedient instinct, Gia got to her feet and headed over, Ty in toe.

"Hi, I'm Faith Barton, thanks for joining us. We may as well sit together and chat while the boys do whatever they are here to do," she said flipping her hair back off her shoulder.

"Hello, I'm Georgia Lake, but call me Gia; it's nice to meet you."

During the conversation, Gia found out that Faith was a single mom and was also her son's escort to the event. That night a friendship, of sorts, formed between them. When Gia pulled up a chair and sat down, Faith's mouth never stopped. Gia learned more about her than she would ever have time to process, in such a short span of time. Gia sat and listened halfheartedly, smiled and nodded in all the right places. Every now and then Faith took time to inhale. 'This was going to be another 'it's all about me' person,' Gia thought.

With legs like a giraffe, she noticed that Faith was tall, slim and attractive. She had bleached blonde hair, big blue eyes and a deep raspy voice. Gia guessed the raspy sounding voice was caused from years of smoking. From what she was saying, she was a big-time party girl and was always ready for a good time.

Faith was quick to reveal her adventurous side, in detail, even though they were virtual strangers. Gia listened as Faith prattled on about her escapades and she envied Faith's spirit and her 'tell-all' sense of total abandonment and 'take me as I am,' attitude.

It seemed that Faith and Patti had similar backgrounds when it came to men. Faith had the same free spirit as Patti because when she met someone that she was attracted to, she had no problem sleeping with him. She didn't care if she ever saw them again; she just lived in the moment. Gia so wished she had some of the carefree attitude that her newfound 'friend' had. She allowed a moment to wonder what it would be like to give herself freely to a man she didn't know very well or not at all. Before she finished the thought, she felt an ugly shiver go through her body and knew she could never do it.

Wrapping up the event, the girls noticed they had chatted through the entire evening.

Faith invited Gia to visit and they exchanged phone numbers, and Faith insisted on Gia visiting her soon.

After a few days had passed, Gia called her. Faith asked if she was coming to visit and she accepted the invitation. When Gia pulled her car in the driveway, Faith waved from her second story balcony.

"Hi, there!" she called, "I'm so glad you came! Come on up and sit in the sun with me."

Faith had been dressed in long sleeves and a long skirt the first time Gia met her. Now that she saw her in shorts and a halter top it was evident that Faith was a sun worshiper. The deep lines on her tanned face, the skin on her hands and arms looked like crepe paper not to mention the rest of her skin was heading south. She noticed several dark brown sunspots on her skin as well. There was a cigarette in the ashtray with smoke rolling from it. Gia silently thanked God for the outside air. She knew that Faith was six years older than she was, but she already had signs of ageing prematurely, and it looked as if she didn't care. At thirty-six years old, she could have easily passed for forty-five, due in part to her, 'I don't care' attitude. She lived for today and to hell with tomorrow. Nicely tanned, she boasted that she spent every possible sunny day in her lounge chair soaking up the rays. She admitted that she rarely wore sunscreen but instead used lots of baby oil to draw the sun in and had implied that she would worry about the wrinkles later.

"Aren't you afraid of sun damage?"

"Pfft," she answered with a flip of her hand and a furrowed brow, "that's why they make moisturizer."

Gia pulled a lounge chair over to a partially shaded area of the patio and sat down.

"What can I get for you, Gia? Would you like a glass of iced tea?"

"Yes, I would Faith, that sounds lovely."

Faith appeared with a huge pitcher and two glasses on a tray. Sitting it on the patio table, she poured a glass for Gia and one for herself.

Scanning her surroundings, she could hear pieces of ice tinkling into their glasses as Faith poured the iced tea.

"Here you go, I hope you like it tart; I have lots of lemon in it."

"As a matter of fact, I do like it tart, thank you."

Taking the glass, with a napkin under it, Gia took a sip.

"This is really good, Faith."

"Thanks, it's my mother's recipe."

"You'll have to share!"

Faith took a long drag off her cigarette, inhaled deeply and tilted her head to the side to blow it out of her lungs.

'That is so disgusting,' Gia thought, as she watched the smoke roll out of Faith's mouth and nose.

Out of nowhere Faith said, "Would you like to go out with me tonight? There's a party going on at a friend's place, and I'd like you to come."

Gia didn't know any of Faith's friends and her instincts were telling her to say 'no,' but she agreed to go.

"Great! Could you pick me up about nine?"

'Wait, what!' Gia thought, 'she invites me to a party and expects me to drive her there. Is this normal?' She noticed that Faith didn't have a car in her driveway.

The party was a bust, for Gia anyway, the instant she walked through the door. There were people standing around in a smoke-filled room with music so loud she could feel it pound in her chest and she wondered why the neighbors hadn't complained.

Faith saw someone she knew and left Gia standing in a room full of total strangers. Gia's first and only thought was, 'What the hell am I doing here!' She was disgusted with herself for even agreeing to come. She was also disappointed in Faith for abandoning her before she got her feet inside the door. No one spoke to her, and no one noticed that she was in the room. 'This was a feeling she could totally relate to.' Gia did not smoke or drink and was totally out of her element. 'Alone in a crowd,' has never rung truer.'

Faith was across the room where all the men were, and she saw her throw her head back in laughter while blowing smoke. She noticed that Faith only wanted to be where the men were. It was not long into the party when she noticed Faith talking with a man and then disappearing into a room with him.

Stepping outside, she welcomed a breath of fresh smoke-free air. Her eyes stung, her lungs hurt, and she wondered if perhaps there was more than just cigarettes being smoked in there. Although she drove Faith here, she certainly didn't feel a responsibility to stay and take her home. She was still pissed that she'd left her to her own devices without even one introduction. She made her way across the crowded parking lot to her car. Climbing in behind the wheel and gave a 'see ya' wave into the dark and drove off.

Bright and early the next morning her phone rang, and right on cue it was Faith.

"Hello?"

"Gia! Good morning! What happened last night? Why did you leave the party? I looked for you everywhere and couldn't find you."

Annoyance reared its head instantly, and Gia knew she was ready to blow.

"Faith, I don't want to sound rude here but what the hell were you thinking? You took me to a total stranger's house, you never introduced me to a single person and then you disappear into a back room with a man. What did you want me to do, wait outside for you to come out like a damned taxi with the meter running? Yes, I left, what else did you expect me to do?"

"I'm sorry, Gia, I thought you knew some of the people there."

"What? Faith think about what you just said. You and I barely know each other, what makes you think I'd know any of your friends?"

"Well, I just want you to know that I had to get a taxi home last night and I don't think it was fair of you just to leave me there."

"Hello! Do you even hear yourself? It is way too early in the morning for me to wake up to this crap!"

Hanging up, she was as mad as a hornet. 'Why don't I ever look at call display before answering the damned phone?' She was still in shock from the audacity of that woman! She was pumping adrenalin now and knew she would not get back to sleep, so she threw the comforter off her body and headed for the bathroom to brush her teeth. Donning her housecoat, she left the ties hanging at the sides and walked to the kitchen.

Gia finished her first cup of coffee and muffin. She was nicely snuggled into her favorite chair, working on her second cup and reading the daily paper, when the phone rang again. Picking up the cordless, she forgot to look at call display and heard Faith's voice again.

"Hi Babes, are you busy?"

'Damn it!' she thought as she rolled her eyes up to the ceiling.

"No, why?"

"Would you like to go out with me today?"

"Where would you like to go this time, Faith?"

"I have a hair appointment and then I'd like to do a bit of shopping, wanna come along?"

"So, if I come along, who is driving?"

"Well you are, of course, silly, I don't have a car," she said with that raspy laugh.

"So, this is a taxi call, then?"

"Don't look at it that way, Babes; I would like to spend time with you. We haven't seen each other since the party."

"That was only last night, and you can always visit me. Faith, we are only a few blocks from each other, walking distance, actually. Come on down before your appointment, visit with me and then I'll drive you over."

"Oh, Babes, I can't today, I have so much to do before my appointment, can't you just pick me up here?"

Gia could see a pattern starting already but in case she was wrong, she agreed to pick her up, but it wasn't sitting well in her craw.

"Oh, thank you, Babes, my appointment is at two, see you then!"

'Babes,' she'd learned, was a pet name that she used on everybody, so it was not meant as anything special towards Gia.

It was exactly as she had predicted. Faith was wrapped up in chitchat with her hair stylist and friends who were all there for a hair-do and left Gia to one side without even an introduction.

She sat in the waiting area observing the chatter and the laughter, and it seemed she did not exist to anyone in the salon. 'God! This is getting so old,' she grumbled to herself, 'can we all just say 'loser'!!'

The magazines on the table were as old as Methuselah's goat, and she wouldn't have touched any of them with a ten-foot pole. She could only imagine how many other people had licked their fingers to turn the pages. She shivered at the thought. It didn't matter where she was; she never bothered to read or flip through magazines. She'd sooner sit with her hands under her armpits to avoid touching anything.

Finally, when Faith was finished, Gia tramped along beside of her while she shopped. When she was done, Gia asked if she would like to come home with her for a cup of coffee.

"Not today, Gia, I have to get home, the kids will be home soon, perhaps another time?"

"Sure Faith, another time, then."

"Talk to you soon Babes, it was a nice day, bye!"

Sitting behind the wheel, she was flabbergasted when she didn't even get as much as a 'thank you' from Faith.

~

Gia got the feeling their friendship was one-sided from the start. It was Gia who did most of the calling and visiting. Whenever Faith did call, she needed a ride somewhere or a pal to go to a club or a dance.

Over the years Gia had always been "Johnny on the spot" because she thought that was what friends should do for each other and the word 'no' had never been part of her vocabulary. She sent birthday and Christmas cards to Faith every year, but it was a rare occasion when she'd get one in return. There were occasions when they did have a good time together. There were lots of laughs and talks about some of the adventures they'd gone on and the stunts they'd pulled and never got caught. The double dates they went on, the losers they had dated. They often compared stories and giggled like two teenagers. They lied for each other and, in all probability, lied to each other. So, it occurred to her that 'if they will lie for you, they will lie to you.'

Faith could talk her into just about anything, and Gia would do it just to prove she was Faith's friend. She could not understand why she felt the need to prove herself to anyone. It was a part of Gia's makeup. Her way of getting people to like her and most of the time all it did was enable people to use her.

~

A few years into the friendship, she got yet another call from Faith, and again she needed a ride. It did not end there as Gia was about to find out.

"Let's go to the casino?" Faith asked.

Since Gia had never been to a casino, she thought it would be fun.

"Sure, that sounds like it might be fun."

"Great! Pick me up around nine."

Gia rolled into the driveway, on time, honked the horn to let Faith know she was there. She waited. Several minutes passed, and she honked again, and still, she did not appear. She got out of the car and stomped to the door. Chance answered her knock.

"Hi, is your mom home?"

"No, a friend showed up and drove her downtown, but she said if you wanted to go down that you were welcome."

"Thanks. Who is here with you tonight, by the way?"

"Nobody, mom leaves us here alone all the time."

Hearing his words, it stunned her. It was not that long ago when she told her she could not visit because the kids would soon be home from school. That was in the middle of the day, and this was nighttime! She could feel her back teeth begin to grind... liar! 'If they will lie for you, they will lie to you,' echoed in her head.

Getting back in the car, she decided to drive to the casino out of curiosity. Walking in, she stood and looked around, and sure enough, there was Faith laughing, joking and blowing smoke with a circle of men.

Faith had told Gia once that if her men friends were married, she didn't care, that she would 'do them' anyway. If their wives wouldn't take care of their men, then she would. Her ego would not let her believe that all they wanted from her were sexual favors. When they got what they wanted from her, they still went home to those wives. The same wives, that Faith saw as uncaring hags that didn't have a clue how to care for their men.

Walking up to Faith, she tapped her on the shoulder. Faith's face dropped in disbelief when she turned around.

"Hi, I-er-um really didn't think you'd come," Faith stammered.

Gia raised an eyebrow, cocked her head and said, "Really? Why not? You invited me."

Faith heard a hint of annoyance in Gia's voice but ignored it and turned back to her friends hoping Gia would go away.

"Hey, Faith, who's your friend?" one fellow asked.

The green-eyed monster appeared, and Faith did not want to introduce her to anyone in her circle. She looked at Gia as if she had forgotten her name. Gia cocked her head again, smiled and looked her straight in the eyes as if to say, 'Well, go ahead, introduce me.' She loved watching Faith squirm.

"Um, ah this is Gia." As soon as her name escaped her lips, she turned her back on Gia and started talking to the men.

"Faith you're not playing nice here, let's invite Gia into the conversation," one man piped up.

If looks could kill, then Faith would have laid Gia out on the floor with one look. Faith hated the fact that Gia still had long natural red hair while Faith had to dye hers. Gia looked at least ten years younger than she really was, and Faith looked more than ten years older than she actually was, wore too much makeup and smelled of cigarette smoke.

The same man elbowed his way past Faith, and he looked straight at Gia.

"Hi, I'm Scott, Scott Taylor; can I buy you a drink?" he asked while nodding his head towards the bar.

"No thanks, I'm driving."

Gia was a nervous wreck just being in this room and here was this man trying to get into her space. She was acting brave to prove a point to Faith but inside she was a mess. Faith was plainly in a fit of jealousy since all the attention was not on her now. Gia did not want Scott's attention, but she secretly enjoyed annoying Faith.

Scott was on a mission and was not about to let Gia go without at least a contact number. Seeing that Faith was trying to shuffle her off, he knew she wanted Gia away from the group.

"Excuse me; I'd like to talk to Gia for a second if you don't mind." He never took his eyes off her and Faith was livid. Scott was tall and very good looking, and he knew it. Once he got his eye on Gia, he was like a dog with a bone. "Can I have your phone number, Gia?"

"What? Are you serious right now? I don't even know who you are, why would I give you my phone number?"

"Be-cause-you-want-to?" He drawled with a raised eyebrow and cocky grin.

Leaning in close enough to show him she was not to be messed with, she said, "I really don't think so, so get over yourself, and get out of my face." With clenched teeth, she backed away. Scott smiled at Gia and put his hand on her arm to stop her from walking away. She looked back at him and instantly her eyes went down to his hand, when she glared up at him, he removed it as if it were on a hot stove.

"Thank you," Gia said, and she walked away. Scott was watching her as she turned, and her long hair swung around, seemingly in slow motion, and he was mesmerized with her.

He walked over to Faith and spun her around, so she could look at him and asked her for Gia's address and phone number. His request only made Faith fume a little more, and she snorted that she didn't know. In the meanwhile, her men friends began to wander off to avoid being a part of the scene that was about to take place.

"What do you mean you don't know? She's your friend, for God's sake!"

"I haven't known her that long and I've never been to her house," she sneered.

"Have you ever called her then?"

"Um, er, well yes I have a few times, but I can't remember her number."

"You're lying!" he said with his face curled up in a sneer, "I know you, and you are so green right now Faith and let me tell you what, it really doesn't become you. Are you that insecure that you can't give me Gia's phone number without all this jealousy and drama?" he said waving his hand in the air. Faith thought he looked a little like a drama queen himself at that moment.

She was speechless. None of her male friends had ever spoken to her that way and she had to pull in her horns. Seeing the look on his face, she relented and gave him Gia's number.

Scott left Faith standing there totally alone and wandered around the casino to find Gia but to no avail. While he had been standing there arguing with Faith, Gia had gone into the lounge and ordered a tall glass of ice water, with a wedge of lemon, then found a table and sat down. No one seemed to notice her when she went in, and that was how she wanted it. She had felt invisible her entire life anyway, and this was no exception. Same shit, different day. The room was dimly lit but light enough that she could just barely see unfamiliar faces in which she had no interest.

Scott had walked around the casino a few times thinking he might have missed her and was certain she must have gone home. He strolled into the lounge, eased his way up to the bar and ordered a drink. It never occurred to him she would be in the bar since he had already offered to buy her a drink that she had declined.

In the mirror behind the bar, he caught a glimpse of her, and his heart leaped a little with excitement. Taken totally by surprise, since he'd never let a woman get to him before. He had never found anyone he wanted to spend any amount of time with and certainly would not commit to any one woman. Most of his lady friends lasted for a few dates and then he was on to another one.

No one held his interest, nor did he want them too. He was out for a good time, and he planned to have one.

The bartender served him a drink and taking it; he moseyed over to Gia's table. "Excuse me, is this seat taken?" he said with a grin.

Just as she was about to open her mouth, Faith sashayed in and sat down before Gia or Scott knew what had happened.

"Gia, can I talk to you?" Glaring up at Scott with squinted eyes, and said, "alone."

Gia looked up at Scott, who was as stunned as she was, and said, "Later, Scott?"

Her words gave him a glimmer of hope that she would at least talk to him again. Smiling, he nodded and walked back to the bar. Sitting on a barstool, he watched the two women from time to time in the mirror. He realized how much he enjoyed looking at Gia and wondered why he had not seen her around before. Glancing up again he noticed that Faith was leaning in close to Gia and was curious as to what was going on. He hoped Faith was not painting a dim picture of him.

"Gia, did you bring money with you?" Faith hissed.

"Yes, why?"

"Would you lend me a few bucks?"

"Faith? Are you telling me that you came to a casino broke?"

"The guys usually give me gambling money, why do you think I'm being nice to them? Men are men, you can tell them anything, and they'll believe it. Come on Gia lend me a few bucks; I'll pay you back."

A red flag went sky high once again, but Gia ignored it and agreed to lend her some money.

"How much do you need, Faith?"

"How much did you bring?"

"That's not the point!" Gia said through clenched teeth, "how much do you want?" She was trying desperately not to raise her voice and cause another scene.

"My God, Gia! Do you have to be so difficult?"

At this point, Gia was ready to kick the chair out from under her.

"If you want money, then tell me how much you want, or get away from my table! I'm not about the drain my wallet for you Faith."

Scott could see the tension building at Gia's table and thought he should go over to see if he could help but decided against it. Meanwhile, he kept a close eye on them through the mirror.

"A hundred bucks!" Faith snorted.

Gia opened her wallet, gave her fifty dollars and told her to get away from her table.

"I can't gamble with fifty bucks!" she said almost in a screech.

"You should have thought about that before you left home!"

"I wouldn't have to ask you for money if you hadn't shown up! I would have had all I needed from the guys."

"You invited me, you idiot!" she said, slamming her palms down on the table. "Why do think I'm here? I would never have come to this place otherwise!" she said waving her hand to indicate the room she was in to get her point across.

From where Scott sat, he knew she was pissed off. He smiled to himself and thought, 'this gal can take care of herself,' and was secretly glad he had not interrupted them. 'This one's got spirit' he thought, and he liked that about her. Seeing fire in her eyes, he lowered his head and smiled broadly, knowing how annoying Faith could be. He and the others usually just gave her money to gamble to get her away from them for a few minutes. It was a joke between the men because they knew they would get their money's worth later.

Looking up from his drink, he saw that Faith was gone, but Gia was still there.

"It was looking pretty tense here for a while," he said with a grin.

Gia just rolled her eyes and waved toward the chair for him to sit down.

"Thanks," he said as he heard her take a deep inhale. "You look frustrated."

"What is up with her anyway? Is she always this dense? Who comes to a casino without money?"

"She does," he added, nodding his head towards the door that Faith had just left through. "Because," he continued, "we usually feed her gambling money, it keeps her away from us for a while. She thinks we are all dumb idiots, but we know her game and we always have."

Gia could not help but laugh, and so did he. He noticed how pretty she was when she smiled.

"I hope you don't mind Gia, but I forced your phone number out of Faith. Believe me, she didn't want to give it up," he added, hoping she would not be angry.

"She had the nerve to ask me why I was here when she was the one who invited me!" Gia said waving her arms toward the casino.

"I'm glad she did."

Looking back at him, she didn't say a word. Caught in a stare, they just eyed at each other for several second until Gia dropped her gaze.

"I have to go Scott but call me if you want to."

"Oh, I want to," he said as he nodded his head. She stood and looked into his eyes for a moment longer, picked up her handbag and walked away from him.

Following behind her, he said, "Let me walk you to your car."

"Thank you; I'd like that."

"No problem, it's my pleasure."

"The fresh air feels good," Gia whispered into the night as they walked across the parking lot.

"You are a breath of fresh air, Gia."

Right on cue, she felt like a kid again. She didn't know how to accept a compliment from people.

It looked as if she was blushing and he smiled to himself. She was indeed a breath of fresh air. 'Who blushes today?' he thought.

"Can I call you tomorrow?"

"I'll be away tomorrow, Scott, how about the weekend?"

"Great, the weekend it is then," he said as they stopped next to her car.

"Good night, Scott."

He just smiled and nodded the same to her and watched as she drove away. He didn't bother to go back inside; instead, he walked to his own car and drove home.

~

Gia and Scott had been seeing each other for several months, and although she would not fully give her heart or herself to him, there was something about him that she liked and something that she just couldn't did not trust. He was fun to be around, very generous with gifts and flowers but not true to his word. Gia was beginning to get suspicious of his behavior.

Several times after they'd made plans, Scott hadn't shown up, or he would arrive hours late. Usually, after these episodes, she noticed a pattern forming with flowers arriving the next morning. At first, she thought they were to say 'I'm sorry' but a phone call to explain would have sufficed. She was not one to ask questions but did cause her to observe and take mental notes of dates and times. She quickly came to realize her suspicions were true. A journal or a diary wasn't necessary she was quite proficient at remembering details. Given the fact that she was quite adept at game playing, she knew exactly what was happening. It was justifiable to her when she did it but to have it done to her was another story. She decided to play his game but only for a short time.

She remembered a story he'd related once at the beginning of their friendship. Scott was the youngest of three. His older siblings and parents had spoiled him beyond reason. They made him feel as if he could do no wrong and when he did, they'd justify it without consequences. It was as if he had no conscience when it came to hurting people or letting them down. It didn't matter to him one way or the other. As he grew up, he was convinced that he could do no wrong and he thought he was privileged. His attitude was; 'how I act is my responsibility and how you handle it is your problem.' He was insufferable most of the time.

Games were his forte as she remembered a story he had once told her. In the fall of the year, when leaves began to pile up on his neighbor's lawns, he would see bags and bags of leaves by the roadside waiting for pick up. Night after night, he would drive off to the shoulder of the road, deliberately hitting the bags of leaves to blow them apart. The next day he would see the neighbors raking them up again. He would just grin and wave as he was passing. This continued for several years. Each time the leaves were raked up again and were placed in new bags. One night, on his way home, he saw the fresh bags of leaves by the side of the road, and again he veered off to the side to blow them apart. Only this time he was the one who got a surprise. Someone had replaced the leaves with a bag of bricks. When he drove over them, thinking it was leaves, the only thing that was blown apart was his right front tire. Payback is a bitch.

Scott did not have the good sense to come up with a reasonable explanation for his behavior, and it was beginning to happen too often for her liking. In this day and age, there were phones on every corner and in every establishment. There was absolutely no reason to stand someone up.

Gia put it on the back burner long enough to see how it would play out. She was not going to let this go until she saw it through, so she waited. She knew he would call; it was just a matter of time.

He called a few days later and asked if she wanted to go out and see the movie, they had both talked about seeing. Agreeing to go, he asked her to be ready by eighty thirty, and they would catch the nine o'clock show. By ten thirty, Gia was in her housecoat sipping on a glass of water trying to concentrate on the book she was reading while fuming on the inside. 'If he were to show up now,' she thought, 'he would be dead meat!'

The doorbell rang the next morning. Opening it to a delivery person sent her blood to a boiling point. Smiling at her when she opened the door, it was as if he knew something that she didn't. Passing her a long, narrow box, it was obvious they were long-stemmed roses. As soon as she touched the box, she felt a jolt of hatred run through her body. She thanked him and closed the door, not even offering the guy a tip. She was certain he had already been well paid, for his trip.

'There was always something about flowers,' she thought. It seemed every time she got them it changed everything from then on. It was like they were a bad omen to her.

When this particular box arrived though, she was certain she knew what they stood for and why they were sent. It was tied with a beautiful bright red ribbon that was nicely done in a fancy bow with a small white envelope tucked securely underneath. Anyone in their right mind would have been ecstatic and honored to receive such a thoughtful gift, but not her. Under different circumstances, maybe, she could have mustered up a little happiness but not this time.

Taking the box into her bedroom, she laid it on her bed. Looking at it for several minutes, she began pacing, panther-like, around the room. Slipping the envelope out from under the bow, she pulled robotically on the ribbon's end. Watching as the beautiful bow unraveled itself into just an ordinary piece of ribbon. Taking the top off the box, she slowly folded back the layers of white tissue paper, exposing the flowers. Pulling the card out of its envelope, she read, 'All my love, Scott.' They were the most beautiful, perfect bouquet of red roses and baby's breath she had ever seen. Yet, there was something inside of her that would not accept or appreciate their beauty. Instead, she tossed the card, and the envelope, in on top of the roses and folded the tissue back over them. Laying the ribbon on top of the tissue paper, she put the lid back on and slid the box under her bed.

Knowing why the roses arrived at her door, made her even angrier. "Does that jerk think for one minute that these few red roses would make up for what he's doing?" she said aloud. Clearly, every time he stood her up, flowers of some sort arrived the next day. Speaking volumes that they were 'flowers of the guiltiest kind.' He obviously only sent them when he was guilty of something. 'Creep,' she muttered giving the box a kick with the toe of her slipper. Hearing it slide a little further under the bed caused her to smirk just a little.

She was used to having jerks in her life and there were always going to be jerks. She had no 'true or deep' feeling for this particular jerk but, it made her blood boil to think that he had such an enormous ego. So much so, that he obviously thought her to be an imbecile. It didn't take a rocket scientist to figure this guy out. He was a jerk! He loved playing the game. He had to see how far he could go; it was the thrill of the hunt. Gia was the master of the hunt and knew exactly what he was doing.

It had been several weeks, and Gia had not accepted any of Scott's calls. If he could not call to cancel a date, he certainly was not going to call to make one, only to stand her up again.

~

Patti, her long-time childhood friend, was in town and had stopped in for a visit on an evening that Gia was alone, as usual. Since there was no mention of Scott, Patti took it for granted it had ended between them. She knew about the 'new guy' and had met him on several occasions but what she wasn't aware of was that Gia was biding her time. She also knew that Scott was a snake because she had seen him, out and about, several times just in the few days she was in town and he was never alone. So, while she was there face to face with Gia she decided to jump in with both feet.

"I'm sorry about the breakup, Gia"

"What break up is that?"

"You and Scott...?" she said with a questioning tone.

"What makes you think we've broken up?" Gia patted the spot next to her on the sofa. "Sit down here and tell me all about it!"

"I saw him the other night at the casino with someone else and on several other occasions recently. So, I just took it for granted it was over between you two."

"This is a very interesting piece of information, Patti." Gia said with raised eyebrows and a triumphant smile. "Tell me more, girlfriend!"

"Well, it's just that I saw him once and he was with a gal I hadn't seen before and other times just locals hanging off him."

"You're certain it was Scott?"

"Oh, I am sure," she said nodding her head, "I would not have said anything to you unless I was."

Gypsy Heart   127

"Well thank you for the heads-up, Patti, I appreciate the honesty."

"You know I am always honest with you, Gia, but I don't want to cause trouble for you two either."

"What makes you think you're causing trouble; it looks like the troublemaker is Scott. Did he see you on any of these occasions by the way?" Gia could feel her heart seizing up but, true to her nature, it never showed.

"No, I'm sure he didn't."

"Good then, because I'll have a little fun with this bit of information."

"Oh Gia, you scare me when you have that look on your face."

Gia laughed with Patti and told her not to worry, she'd be okay.

"Oh, I don't doubt that Gia, I would never want to be on your bad side."

"Well let's hope you never are." They laughed like teenagers and slapped their hands in a 'high five.'

"One good thing is, thank God you never slept with him."

"When would I ever have had an opportunity? Besides, with all his shenanigans he'd be too tired anyway! It's just as well; I'm not in the mood for syphilis."

They enjoyed the rest of Patti's visit as Gia took the opportunity to fill her in on Scott's behavior over the last few months and that she had just confirmed her suspicions. Scott definitely is the snake that she thought he was, and she was spot on regarding her trust issues with him. Giving him the benefit of the doubt for far too long, she took some of the blame for hanging on way too long. She always had to prove her point no matter how long it took!

Several days later, Patti went back to the city and Gia was enjoying yet another evening at home. Settling in with a book, the phone rang, and it was Scott. It had been weeks since she had taken one of his calls. This particular call was the one she had been waiting for. From the sound of his voice, you would have thought she was everything to him.

"Hi there beautiful, how are you tonight? It's been a while since we talked"

"I'm fine thank you, how are you?"

"I'm doing alright; I miss you, and I was wondering if we could get together later."

'Here it comes' she thought. "Get together later? For what?"

"We haven't seen each other in weeks, Gia and I haven't been able to reach you on the phone, and I miss you."

"That's because I've been avoiding you, Scott."

"Avoiding me? Why?"

"How dumb do you think I am? And... what makes you think I would ever believe that you miss me?"

"Of course, I miss you, what are you saying?"

"What I am saying is... that you are a liar, Scott, and no, I do not want to get together with you later or ever for that matter."

"Why, what's wrong, Gia?" Scott asked, obviously pretending he had no idea what she was talking about.

"You want to know what's wrong, Scott? Where would you like for me to begin? Oh, wait... how about all the nights you stood me up, by conveniently forgetting about the plans we had made. Or... what about all those flowers that arrived after all your no-shows? Or... how about the women you were with on all those nights that you were supposed to be with me. Is that a good place to start Scott?"

"What are you talking about Gia?"

"What were the flowers for, on the mornings after you stood me up? Where were you on those nights that you couldn't call me? Why was it that every time you were a 'no show,' the next morning, I would have a delivery guy at my door? What's up with that?" She continued with the flurry of questions, so he could not interject. "Am I the one you thought about calling after everyone else had gone home?"

Dead silence fell on the other end of the phone and Gia could picture him trying to come up with something lame to feed her. Since she had never questioned him before, he was at a loss for words, and she knew it.

"I can explain that Baby if you'll let me come over."

"If you come over here Scott Taylor, you may not leave in one piece, so you'd better stay far, far away from me. Do I make myself clear?"

As she clicked the 'end' button on her cordless phone, she heard, "I'm sor…" just before the call ended. 'Sorry my ass,' she grumbled, 'sorry that you got caught, is more like it!' Damned cordless phones! She would have loved to be able to slam the phone down in his ear, to show how angry she really was, instead of a little 'click.' 'What a time not to have a good old-fashioned telephone with a receiver,' she thought.

~

The roses had been under her bed for at least two weeks after she gave them that final kick. She got down on her knees and lifted the bed skirt to see where the box was located. Reaching for it, she pulled it out, and laid the box on the bed and took the top off. Laying the ribbon aside, she folded the tissue back, and smiled to herself… 'perfect!' They were as black and dead as her heart felt toward him. Putting it all back together, she tied the red ribbon around the box and made a bow as best she could, then called a courier service. When the delivery person rang her doorbell, she gave him Scott's address, paid him and closed the door. She made a mental note to call Patti with details.

Faith called not long after Gia closed the chapter with Scott. She had obviously gotten the scoop from the men at the casino and Gia thought it was a call to gloat, but it was not.

"I'm sorry about what happened with you and Scott. Sometimes these things have to be found out on their own. While I'm at it, I want to apologize for my behavior as well. The way I was acting, you would have thought it was jealousy talking and I wouldn't have blamed you for thinking that way. I knew Scott was the 'playboy slash bad boy' type but he really seemed to genuinely care about you, Babes."

"I'm sure he did Faith, but he cared about many others as well and to me that makes too many in a relationship."

"I thought he would have been different with you, though."

"It doesn't matter now Faith, once a snake, always a snake and it's over. He can do as he wishes and with whomever he wants to do it with."

"Would you like to come over?" Faith asked.

"No, not really, I don't feel much like getting dressed and going out, maybe another time. Thank you for calling."

"OK, Babes, another time."

As she hung up the phone, she thought that Faith could be such a sweetheart at times. She still had her hand resting on the phone when she realized that her relationship with Faith was over as well. As one sided as it was, she'd had good times with her, and many bad times but still she knew in her heart that it was finished.

~

It had taken her a few years to realize that Faith had never been a real friend. Especially not like she and Patti were. She would never have another friend like Patti. Friends are there for you no matter what. Friends dropped in on each other uninvited and always with an open invitation. A true friend will hang out with you when you need them, and they will leave you alone when you need to be left alone. She thanked God every day that Patti had the good sense not to leave her alone after Tommy died. It comes with instinct if you really care, and she never once got that from Faith. She never received a call from her just to say, "Hi, how ya doing?" or "How was your day?" The only calls she'd even gotten from her were when she wanted or needed something and to express her feelings about Scott. She knew that Faith had a better friend in her than she ever had in Faith.

She felt blessed to have Patti in her life. Maybe someday perhaps the two of them would retire on a beautiful tropical island and grow old together.

Patti Stevens

Gia's thoughts went back again to a few years after Patti had the abortion. Patti had moved to the city and shortly after Gia and Tommy had followed. Circumstances had brought Patti back to Kanyon Cove. Her mother became sick, and her dad needed Patti at home. Her stay there was going to be a long one, so Gia took over the apartment they were sharing. Both Gia and Tommy were home for a two-week summer vacation.

A new guy moved to Kanyon and Patti was smitten with him. His name was Tony Walker. He and his mother had moved to the area when they'd purchased a local beach property after his father died.

Patti, Gia and Tommy were at a beach party when Patti saw him walking down the beach toward the crowd. She introduced herself to him and invited him to join them. Patti learned that Tony was an American and that his father left his mother quite well off. She soon realized that she wanted Tony, his name, and all that came with his name, no matter what. She began ingratiating herself into Tony's life at every chance.

Gia and Tommy went back to the city after their vacation days were over and life returned to normal. They had just returned from their honeymoon when Gia got a call from Patti. As soon as she picked up the phone, she knew something was not quite right.

"What's wrong, Patti," she asked when she heard her friend's voice tremble.

"I think I'm pregnant," she sobbed into the phone.

Gia slumped her shoulders and closed her eyes as the air escaped from her nostrils. Flashbacks hit her in the gut. "What?" she said through clenched teeth.

"You heard correctly Gia, and I'm afraid to tell Tony. I believe he is only with me out of obligation anyway because I chased him until he couldn't run anymore and now this."

"Are you insane? Have you learned nothing after that ghastly trip to the clinic?" She was hissing into the phone and then began to frantically rub her forehead, which is what she sometimes did when she was looking for solutions.

"Why haven't you told him? He may be able to help you."

"I want to do a home pregnancy test first."

"And if it's positive?" Gia realized she was raising her voice when Tommy looked up at her and cocked his head in question. Smiling at him, she waved her hand as if nothing was wrong. "Did you do this deliberately to get Tony to marry you?" she hissed into the phone with her hand cupped around the mouthpiece. She could tell by the sound of silence that she had nailed it. Gia just closed her eyes and shook her head. She had gotten her answer.

Tony felt obligated to marry Patti after learning the news. Once they had gotten through the wedding and life settled down for everyone, she had a miscarriage. They both knew that Patti married for all the wrong reasons. She knew there was money in Tony's family, and she thought she had enough love for Tony to hold out for it.

~

The years that followed had taken its toll on Patti and Tony's marriage. Gia believed that Tony felt trapped while Patti pretended that she was happy. Happiness to Patti was dollar signs and the good reputation that came with the Walker name. She'd pulled it off quite well, as Gia learned.

~

After Patti had gotten her through the tragedy of losing Tommy, and she began to move forward with her life, Patti had fallen back into her old habits.

One night, Gia's phone rang. Picking it up, she heard Patti's voice on the other end.

"Hey, girlfriend, what are you up to tonight?" Patti asked.

Gia hit pause on the remote control and said, "I'm watching a movie, why?" She knew something was up from Patti's tone. She heard excitement in her voice that had not been there for a long time.

"Would you cover for me if Tony calls?"

"Where are you, Patti?"

"I'm at the Royal Inn."

"You're at a hotel right here in Kanyon? Are you insane?"

"I know you disapprove Gia, but right now I need you to cover for me in case Tony calls."

There was a long silence, and Patti asked if she was still there.

"Yes, I am, and you know I don't like this, Patti."

"Yes, I know you don't, but will you anyway?"

Gia knew the minute she'd asked, that she would do it, but it didn't make her feel any better knowing she would have to lie if Tony called her. The pleading sound in Patti's voice turned her to mush, and she knew she would do anything for her friend, right or wrong.

"Yes, you know I will, Patti."

"Thank you, girlfriend, I'll call you tomorrow."

"You'd better!"

Gia's heart sank at the thoughts of Patti being out in the open with another man and right here in town! What was she thinking? She knew what small towns were like. She knew she had to let it go and pray that Tony would not call her. No such luck. Five minutes hadn't passed before he was on the phone asking if she had seen Patti.

"I was just talking to her Tony; she's meeting with a client in about ten minutes. She said she tried to call you. Where are you?"

"I've just stopped for a drink, at the bar, at the Royal Inn."

When the words hit her brain, the pulse in her neck began to thump.

"Are you drinking alone?"

"As a matter of fact, I am."

"Why don't you come over here for a few minutes and talk to me instead of staying there alone?" Gia said through the pounding in her own ears. She had to get him away from the hotel and protect her friend.

"Thank you, Gia, I think I will come over. I'll be there in a few minutes."

Laying the phone down beside her on the sofa, she leaned her head back and covered her face with both hands. "Why me?" she asked aloud, as she closed her eyes to gather her thoughts.

She did not want Tony in her house, but she had no choice but to invite him over to get him out of the hotel bar. All Patti needed was to come face to face with Tony in the lobby!

While she waited for Tony to arrive, she remembered one of the reasons why she and Patti were kindred spirits. She understood the gypsy heart pattern, in Patti, much like her own. For as long as she could remember, Patti had never been faithful to anyone that she dated and oh, how Gia knew that feeling. Gia was not even faithful to herself and her own gypsy heart kept her that way.

Gia managed to keep Tony occupied for a few hours against her better judgment. When he said he had to leave, it was a relief to her but hoped it was enough time for Patti.

Patti called her the next morning to thank her for covering her ass. She told Gia that she knew she was not comfortable lying to Tony. Gia reminded her that she was not a teenager any longer and asked her why she was acting like one. She knew Patti well enough to know that nothing she said would ever make a difference in her decisions and that everything she'd said had fallen on deaf ears.

... And then there was Beau, (1989)

Jean Beaupre had arrived on assignment alone, as most of his assignments were. He was a Louisiana boy, here with the National Guard out of Georgia, USA, and setting up near Gia's hometown. He had arrived first to do the background work for the surveillance before the rest of the team arrived. Family members were to follow once he had settled into his new surroundings and would be a cover for his real work.

~

Gia had met Beau at the local club shortly after he'd arrived in town. He was there with his group, and she was there to help her friend, Chloe, make contact with him. For Gia to go to a club alone was a feat all on its own. She was not the type to haunt clubs, pubs and bars for any reason. She truly felt it was kismet to have been at the club alone and to have met Beau. Even more of a coincidence was that Chloe was late.

~

Chloe Haynes, a nurse, working at the local headquarters, had met Beau upon his arrival. She had seen him several times on lunch breaks and chatted with him. She knew Beau would be at 'Club Mix' on Friday night and made plans with Gia to go with her, hoping to 'accidentally' run into him. Something of importance came up, and she asked Gia to go on ahead and keep an eye out for him. Chloe described Beau to her and asked her to call if or when he arrived. Gia arrived alone, against her better judgment, but since Chloe was her friend, she'd do it for her. Immediately seeing friends, she joined them at their table. She sat facing the entrance in order to keep a watchful eye as people arrived. Shortly after the music began, Gia noticed a group of unfamiliar faces searching for a table. Figuring out that one of them must be Beau, she went directly to the payphone and called Chloe. She had tried her best to describe the man she thought Chloe was looking for and they both agreed it must be him.

"Chloe, if you've decided that it's him then my work here is done."

"Can you just watch him for a bit," Chloe asked, "I will be there within a half hour. Continue to keep him in your sights in case he decides to leave."

'What am I... your spy now!' she thought, "Then what?" she exclaimed.

"Just keep him in your sights and if you notice he wants to leave then try to delay his exit."

"Are you crazy, Chloe? This is your caper, and you should be here! By the way, why aren't you here if this is so important to you? I feel as though I am a secret agent in a 'Get Smart' episode," she hissed, as she watched him closely. "What am I supposed to do if he wants to leave?"

She had no idea what she would do to keep him there. She was certain that if he were to decide to leave, she would not step in and try to stop him. She was certain of that since it was not in her make up to approach a total stranger, especially a man!!!

"You'll think of something; I'll be there as soon as I can... byeeee!"

Gia looked at the phone receiver and rolled her eyes. She banged it against the front of the phone a couple of times before she hung it up. She cut her eyes at the phone again and made her way back into the room.

Noticing he never danced with anybody, but he seemed friendly and sociable. Suddenly she saw him standing alone leaning on one of the rails that led to the dance floor. 'Was this an indicator that he was inching his way to the front door?' she thought.

Sauntering over, she stood on the other side and leaned back against the opposite rail. Even though she was facing him, she was in her own world and felt quite safe standing there. Knowing he did not know her from Adam, she had as much right to stand there as he did. She felt very brave but still peered over at the door for Chloe, who still hadn't arrived. 'As soon as she arrives' she thought, 'this snoop job is over, and I'll be out of here!'

Gia glanced at Beau from time to time while he watched people on the dance floor. She tried to figure out what the attraction was that Chloe had towards him and the more glances she sneaked, the more obvious it became. She guessed him to be a few inches over six feet tall as she took in his long, lean frame. He wore jeans with a soft, white, V-neck sweater with the sleeves pushed midway up his forearms. He had one foot crossed over the other with his arms folded across his chest. His stance was one that will be forever etched in her mind.

She turned her gaze away just as he looked at her and she guessed he might have caught her staring at him. She had great peripheral vision, and suddenly, she knew he had noticed her. Nervousness creep in as she wondered, 'Should I casually walk away, should I stay? Where the hell is Chloe!?' Trying to keep one eye on the people who were dancing and the other eye out for Chloe, she turned her eyes toward the door again, but met his stare instead. When their eyes met, she couldn't move her body, she was trapped inside his blue eyes. It was as if they were the only two people in the room and time had halted. He smiled with a slight nod of his head, and pressing her lips together shyly, she smiled back. 'He has a crooked smile and his eyes sparkle,' she thought, and she was sure her heart had skipped a beat or two.

Unchained Melodies began to play, and he unfolded his arms, stood up and stretched his hand out toward her and said, "Would you like to dance?"

He had a deep, resonate voice that could only belong to him. While they held their gaze, she reached out her hand and placed it in his. When it reached his palm, he pressed his thumb firmly on top locking her hand to his, and she thought her heart would stop. Leading her onto the dance floor, he placed his hand gently on her back, folded her other hand toward his chest and pulled her close to him. She was home. Closing her eyes, she thought she had never felt as if she belonged anywhere until he folded her up in his arms as they danced. Softly, he sang along to the words of the song, in her ear. Feeling her heart beat against his chest, she was certain he could too. Leaning in a bit closer, he non-verbally told her she was safe with him. When the song ended, they lingered on the floor for a few extra seconds, while she soaked in these new feelings. When they realized the Righteous Brothers song had ended, they separated and looked at each other just as Bob Seger blasted out Old Time Rock and Roll.

As a slow and daring grin crossed his face, he nodded his head toward the floor with a 'wanna try' look and she nodded as if to say, 'I will if you will.' Gia got the impression that maybe he thought she couldn't keep up. Giving her an approving smile, with one raised eyebrow, he picked her up and swung her hip to hip, through his legs and caught her hand in time to the music. They were having the time of their lives. The other dance patrons gave up the dance floor while they put on a show for them. People had formed a circle to watch them jive! They were clapping to the music and encouraging them to continue. The crowd roared, clapped and seemed to be having as much fun as Beau and Gia were. This was one night that she would not soon forget. This was the first time in her life that she had let go and truly enjoyed herself.

She was certain she had met her white knight. There he was, tall, handsome, great personality, fantastic dancer but, first and foremost, a perfect gentleman. This night had to be a dream, and if it was, she did not want to wake up. The rest of the evening was theirs and theirs alone. They danced, they talked, they laughed and for once Gia was happy inside and out, and it showed.

As she and Beau were laughing and enjoying themselves, she looked up and saw Chloe standing off to one side of the club glaring at them. Gia waved her over, but she turned on her heel and walked out the door. Their friendship had turned to hen shit in one night.

When things wound down at 'Club Mix,' Beau walked her outside and invited her to sit in his car. Theirs were the only two cars left in the parking lot. They sat in the empty parking lot, in his station wagon, and talked and kissed for hours. Asking her for her phone number, he gave his number to her. He asked if she would accompany him, the next day, to find stereo equipment for the common room. Since the agents had no entertainment in their quarters, he was chosen to shop. This was when CD's were coming into fashion. Accepting his invitation, she said she would love to go and with that, he walked her to her car, kissed her good night and she drove home.

She was unlocking her front door when the phone startled her. "Who could be calling at this hour of the night?" she said aloud. Not having call display in those days, she was reluctant to answer it.

"Hello?"

"Hi, it's Beau."

"Hi!" she said, sounding surprised.

"I'm just checking to be certain you gave me the right number."

Gia smiled into the phone and she knew without a doubt that she loved him already. "Did you really think I would do that to you?" she said jokingly.

"It must be the insecurity in me but like I said, I'm just checking. See you tomorrow, around eleven?"

"Sure."

"Good night, Gia."

"Good night, Beau."

~

He showed up promptly at eleven and they drove an hour and a half to a place where there were much bigger malls then they had in their small town. Once inside the mall, they strolled hand in hand browsing in and out of shops. Suddenly he released her hand and walked away from her. She saw him off to one side talking to a lady who had her back to Gia. She was selling flowers just outside of her shop, and with curiosity, she watched as Beau handed her some money. Turning back toward her, she stared at his tall, lanky frame. Passing her a single long-stemmed red rose, he said, "A perfect rose for a perfect lady." He was the perfect guy. If she had to describe her feelings at that moment, she was certain she could not. She was still in 'awe' that he would even ask her out on a date.

~

They had spent the entire day together and not once mentioning stereo equipment. They went grocery shopping, and he invited her to his suite for supper. The agents, in his group, each had a two-room suite plus a bathroom. They shared a kitchen, as well as the common room down the hall. Beau cooked a great meal and they sat cross-legged on pillows at the coffee table that he had set up with a tablecloth and matching cloth napkins. He made her a wine spritzer, and they ate together and talked about how they enjoyed the day. She still felt strange and very intimidated in his presence since they had only met the night before, yet she knew she could trust him. She helped him clear the table, and they carried the dishes across the hall to the kitchen. When everything was washed up, they went back to his suite.

Music played softly in the background as they danced to Otis Redding's 'These Arms of Mine' and Percy Sledge's 'When a Man Loves a Woman.' He was wonderfully romantic, and Gia had never known romance. He was an excellent dancer as she had found out on their first dance. She could feel the attraction growing between them. Suddenly, as their lips met, Beau swept her up in his arms, laid her down on his bed, and they gave in to their passion. She had not intended to stay overnight, but she felt so wonderfully comfortable in his arms. She understood, without words, that he didn't want her to leave. He wrapped her in his arms, and they fell asleep.

~

Waking the next morning, Beau was standing by the bed with one foot propped up on the heat radiator, with his arms folded over his knee, smiling down at her.

"Good morning, it's about time," he joked. "It's back to the village with ya wench," he chuckled as if he were in a stage play.

It was then that he had told her he was off on vacation days and was heading to Vermont on his motorcycle. He said he would be gone for a couple of weeks and that he would call her when he returned. For obvious reasons, she did not believe his story. She trusted no one. Figuring that she had just had her first one-night stand, and this was the big kiss off.

Offering her a helmet, she climbed on the back of his bike. They stopped for breakfast and then he dropped her off at her house. Giving him back his helmet, he tucked it into a compartment and kissed her goodbye. She stood on her step to watch him roar off into the distance.

She had taken it for granted that he was not interested in her. She had actually forgotten that he said he would call. She went about her days with the happiest feeling inside that she had never felt before. She wouldn't allow to let him ruin it by making promises he had no intentions on keeping. 'If nothing else' she happily thought, 'she'd have a wonderful memory to carry her through.'

~

A couple of weeks later Patti dropped in for a long overdue visit. Gia was excited as she gave Patti a condensed version of her night at 'Club Mix,' meeting Beau and their romantic evening together. Patti, of course, was full of questions but before she had a chance to answer, Gia's phone rang.

"Hello?"

"Hi Gia, it's Beau."

"Beau?" Wide eyed and in disbelief at hearing his voice again, a wide smile brightened her face.

"Yes, I told you I would call when I got back. I returned last night; I'm at the office. You sound surprised or am I catching you at a bad time?"

"Actually, I am surprised; I had convinced myself that you weren't going to call me."

He could not help but laugh at her candor. She loved his laugh already.

"Can I see you tonight?"

"Sure!" She could hardly contain her excitement.

"Great, I'll see you around seven."

Excitedly, she told Patti about Beau; her heart was soaring.

Her bell rang promptly at seven. Opening it, she flung herself into his arm. She was overwhelmingly happy to see him again. He folded her up into a big hug indicating he was happy to see her, too.

"Wow! I should go away more often," he said.

They ate at a small seasonal restaurant that was at full swing for early June. It was quite crowded, but the waiter found them a table by a window. Beau ordered a beer and Gia had a glass of ice water. For an appetizer, he ordered a plate of steamed mussels. Gia had never been at this particular restaurant before, and it seemed as though everything he did for her, and with her, were 'firsts' for her. She never dreamed she'd ever eat a mussel, but he fixed one the way he liked it and asked her to at least try it. They cleaned off the plate and ordered dinner. While they were waiting for their dinner to arrive, the waiters and waitresses were bustling around taking other orders. Every time they took an order, they would say 'soup or juice?' at each table. Finally, Beau looked at her, crinkled his eyes and said, "What the hell is 'super juice?'"

He was such a character, and he made her laugh no matter where they went. There was nothing high classed or pretentious about him in spite of his position. He loved life, had a good time and he fit in no matter where he was. His attitude was 'if you can't beat em, join em.'

Gia was always afraid of doing something stupid in front of him, but his behavior was very relaxing. He never made her feel as though he was something more than she was and when they were together, he was always on her level no matter what. He truly made her feel like an equal.

From the night they met, he had spent every possible minute he could with her. He filled her heart. It seemed she had not been able to open up that part of herself or to actually care this deeply for someone, until Beau. He indeed filled her. The sound of his voice on the phone made her heart sing. His presence gave her peace; thoughts of him caused her to smile, and no one made her as comfortable inside her own skin as he did. He was her everything. Then, he mentioned the planned family visit and her heart sank. Jealousy streaked through her soul and it lay heavy on her mind. 'Would his family decide to stay? What would she do if Beau chose them over her?' She developed a plan in her mind that she wasn't completely comfortable with, but she had to see it through.

She'd asked Patti to drive her to the next town to 'spy' on Beau. She knew he would not recognize her friend's car. Just as they rounded the corner, his house came into view; they slowed the car and pulled onto the shoulder. Seeing the back end of an unfamiliar car in his driveway, she was certain it was a rental. 'She' had arrived. Gia closed her eyes for a moment and took several deep breathes trying to slow her heart rate down as it pounded heavily inside her chest. She felt sick and dizzy. She wanted to leave; she wanted to stay; she wanted to cry then she wanted to kick her own ass for even thinking about doing this. This was not going to be good.

A tall, lanky teenager, who resembled her dad, was pulling a fist full of string, with helium balloons attached, from the trunk of the car. Scanning the area quickly, she wanted to see as much as she could take in, in the few brief moments that she had. She caught the ass end of a woman entering the side door. She felt her heart drop with a thud, then 'swish, swish' as blood rushed past her ears to the point of nausea. There it is. This is what she had come to 'spy' on when she should have minded her own damned business, then she would not have felt quite this much pain. She sat watching his wife and daughter as they arrived for a visit to see his 'new' house and most especially, to visit Nova Scotia. They were in there, where she should have been. She had seen enough. Although it had been an amicable separation, and Gia was proud of him for that, but she was jealous of the family visit.

Patti looked over at Gia, touched her arm and said, "Are you OK?"

"No, but let's get the hell out of here!" she said, snapping herself around in the seat. Gia was beside herself, not only for what she had just witnessed but also for the fact that she was spying on Beau in the first place. But she had been the one with him when he went house hunting; she was who he'd called with excitement when his offer was accepted, and the deal had gone through. She was who he'd cooked for and invited to share the first meal he'd prepared in his new place. AND, it was with her that he wanted to share the bottle of sparkling champagne to celebrate his new 'digs.' She was the one who he eventually made love with on the carpet in the living room when the meal was over, and the champagne bottle lay empty on the floor.

She had known that Beau was married; he had never kept that information from her. But, seeing his wife at his home, made it all too real.

What Gia wasn't aware of yet, was that on the first family visit, his wife chose not to follow him. The town was relatively small, and the nearest city was hours away, definitely not her 'cup of tea.' Furthermore, it was not the South! They decided to go their separate ways although nothing was set to paper. His assignment was for two to five years, more likely three, and since she lived in a city, she was not about to give up her lifestyle to live in a Dog Patch northern setting.

She and Beau hadn't committed to a live-in relationship because of his limited time there. She did not want to be uprooted for the sake of a few years, but they spent a lot of time together. They traveled a bit, and he took her to parties at their quarters and made her feel special. For one of the functions, he informed her it was a formal dinner, and she wore a beautiful blue gown with a spaghetti string strap on one shoulder and strapless on the other. She was very proud to walk into such an affair with him. He was very handsomely dressed in a tuxedo and stood out in a crowd with his six-foot-two frame.

Heads turned when they walked into the dining room, and he pressed his hand lightly at the center of her back as he led her to their table. She was petrified when she saw the table settings. There were, at least, eight or ten pieces of silverware and he must have seen the look on her face because he leaned over and whispered, "Start on the outside and work your way in." However, before she touched anything, she waited for him to choose his piece first. He had told her, beforehand, that the napkin is always placed so that you can pick it up by the inside edge. It will open without shaking it. She had never been invited to such an extravagant affair, had never seen so many pieces of silverware or as many pieces of crystal glasses at one setting. She felt honored to sit down with so many important people. In her own mind, she felt extremely special, in comparison to her own jumbled world.

Once the dinner was over, she could breathe a little easier as she tried to relax in this atmosphere that she had never been in before. Gradually, as the evening wore on and people began to leave, they found themselves outside by the pool. They were the only two remaining guests as they sat on the edge of the diving board. He slipped his jacket around her shoulders as they talked and eventually, they watched the sunrise the next morning.

He was respected in his position, and it was a respect that he accepted with grace. He was not an overbearing blowhard who mistreated his authority like so many others do when their position goes to their head.

She loved him, and she liked the prestige that came with him. She did not let his prestige render her blind to his flaws. He had flaws, and she saw them, but she accepted them as one does when you are in love. He allowed her to be herself and loved her, warts and all, so she accepted him, flaws and all.

She hadn't met anyone who had a bad thing to say about him. He was kind to everyone and always said that everyone deserved second chances. He knew when to use his authority and most importantly, he knew how to use it. He had a great personality and he enjoyed his life. He also loved a good party and usually was the life of it.

~

Three years had passed in what seemed like the blink of an eye. He had bought a small house and settled in nicely and they spent a lot of time there. Yet, time waited for no man.

Beau was given notice of another assignment coming up, and that his time in Kanyon was coming to an end. Although they were not in the mood to celebrate his leaving, they wanted to celebrate their time together. Bringing out a bottle of champagne, they toasted each other. Although she was extremely proud of him and his accomplishments, she was trying very hard to make this all about him and not about the gnawing she felt in the pit of her stomach. She was broken up inside trying to deal with his joy and her sadness at the same time.

He was told where his next assignment would be and how long he had before checking in and he didn't have long to get his plans in order and leave. Before his deadline, he invited her to go on a trip with him. They'd had only a few weeks left together, and he planned a road trip to the Island. They'd driven to the ferry that had them on a forty-five-minute sail. For the next week, they drove up one coast and down the other while camping or staying in quaint Bed and Breakfasts.

Along the road, there were signs posted, with 'Cackleberry' written on them. They both decided it must be a new hybrid fruit.

Out of curiosity, Beau stopped the car at one of the signs. A lady was standing in her yard, and he politely asked her what 'Cackleberry' meant. Telling her they'd seen it on several occasions on the drive. She smiled graciously and told them it was farms, where farmers raised hens and grew berries. So, by combining the names from hens cackling and growing berries, they came up with the name 'Cackleberry.'

On one of their outings, to the Island's famous beach, they walked for what seemed like miles along the beautiful pink sand. Beau had picked up a piece of driftwood that resembled a shepherd's crook to use as a walking stick. Suddenly he stopped, poked the end of his stick in the sand and wrote I 'heart' U. Gia had her camera and she, with Beau's assistance, climbed up on his shoulders to get the entire writings in her lens. She knew he loved her and now she would have it indelibly imprinted on paper forever. Not that she would ever forget about their trip or lose the image in her mind's eye, but she still wanted the picture.

Upon their return, they learned that his house had been sold. His life there would soon be packed up and put into a moving van. She thought about him day and night, he was everything to her, and she wanted for nothing else in her life except to be with him. He completed her; he made her whole. Without him the only thing that came naturally to her was to breathe in and breathe out, everything else was a chore.

While they were together, he was the best thing that had ever happened to her. He was the only one who allowed her to be herself and accepted her warts and all.

At night, to be close to her, he would gather her in his arms, lay her on top of him, pull a sheet over them and they'd fall asleep. Waking up in the morning, she would be in the same position, and their bodies would be literally stuck to each other after being pressed together all night. They had to be touching in one way or another. If lying with their backs to each other then, the soles of their feet were touching, or they would sleep with their fingers intertwined. There was always a connection.

~

When the time came for him to leave town, she was unable to follow him. She spent many sleepless nights without him beside her. He was literally 'the one who got away.' She knew, in her heart of hearts, that he could not ask her to follow him. His assignments were mostly with the National Guard, and it was rare that anyone knew where the agents would be posted. They had packed up his life, cleaned his house before the closing date and watched as the packers loaded the moving van, compliments of his agency.

She knew her heart would never heal, and it would never safely belong to anyone else, ever again. She also knew she would never allow anyone to get that deep inside her heart. He told her that just because he was not with her, it didn't mean he did not love her and that he could love her from anywhere. At the time, it did not help her situation, but it was nice to hear.

His temporary love made her a prisoner in her own skin, and he was buried deeply inside her soul. She knew she would never get him out. She vividly remembered the morning he left. He had spent his last night at her house. She hardly slept a wink all night and prayed that morning wouldn't come too quickly. He'd gotten up early for the trip to his new destination. They had loaded the last of his personal belongings into his recently new El Camino. He kissed her goodbye in her driveway and with one last bear hug, he looked at her and said, "Have a nice life, kid." Her heart was literally breaking into pieces as he got into his car, drove out of her driveway, and supposedly out of her life.

She actually felt the total opposite from when she watched her father walk down the driveway and out of her life for good. The feelings then were of sheer relief, and this time it was pure heartbreak, emptiness, agony and a 'sinking into the darkness, feeling. Frozen on the spot, she watched as he drove to the stop sign at the end of her street, the left signal flashed, and he drove off. Tears were welling up and her body began to shake uncontrollably. He looked back to where he'd left her, stuck his entire arm out of the car window and waved it in the air. The sleeve of his shirt billowed in the breeze until he disappeared past the ball field and out of her sight. The cloud she had ridden on for three years had suddenly vaporized and sent her toppling back to earth where she had to face her life without him. Slowly, she lowered her arm, swallowed past the lump that had formed in her throat, turned and stumbled blindly into the house.

Through tear-filled eyes, she made her way to the sofa and sank down as if defeated. She looked out the window in the direction in which his car had just gone. She felt like a lost dog, waiting for his master to return. She waited, hoping he would change his mind and come back for her. Every scenario that played out in her head would never become reality. There was no such thing as White Knights in shining armor riding in on white steeds. Even though Beau was a gentleman, he was not Richard Gere rescuing Debra Winger in An Officer and a Gentleman, nor was she Julia Roberts in Pretty Woman. Regardless, she wanted Beau to love her that much, and he did not. Her time with him was like a dream, and that dream was over. She knew that life with him had ended and the nightmare of life without him was just beginning. Knowing he was never coming back for her; she fell face down into a cushion and cried and cried until she was exhausted. Her stomach muscles ached; her eyes were red and sore, as was her nose from wiping and blowing. She was left with a huge hole in her chest where her heart had been. She missed him, she ached for him, and she cried some more. "Beau," she moaned through her tears. She felt as if he had just died. The selfish part of her could have accepted his death but just knowing he was moving on without her, nearly killed her. She was absolutely lost, and she knew she would be for a long, long time. After several hours of crying and feeling sorry for herself, exhaustion overcame her, and she dozed off on the couch as huge sobs rippled from her body.

It was dark when she woke up and realized she was not having a nightmare and fresh tears began again. She had not even had her first cup of tea or a bite to eat since the night before. It was well past suppertime, so she got up off the sofa to plug in the kettle.

Wallowing in self-pity was getting her nowhere. Wanting badly to see her friend, she reached for the phone and called Patti. While she waited for her, she turned the radio on to escape the quiet, so she could hear something other than her own sobs.

As soon as she turned it on, she heard the DJ announce a new Reba tune called, 'My Broken Heart,' and all it managed to do was bring more tears when she thought there could be no more. Listening to the song, reminded her of Beau, and how appropriate the song was. 'Someone had written the song just to make her sadder than she already was,' she thought, as she tuned in to the words that were streaming from the radio. It was almost identical to her situation. There was nothing more heartbreaking than country music when sadness was all around. She listened to the words with fresh tears. What was she thinking, listening to this kind of music on a day like this! Shortly after Reba had done a hatchet job on her heart, another tune came on by Pam Tillis, called Don't Tell Me What to Do. She could still hear Beau's words, 'Have a nice life, kid.' 'How dare he tell her to have a nice life! How could she ever have any kind of a life without him?' She could barely breathe without him, let alone live and be happy! She had had enough of country music for one day, and she flipped the radio off.

Picturing in her mind, he'd soon be reaching the end of the first leg of his journey, on route to his new destination. Then he would find new friends and acquaintances and fall into lust again. The thoughts of him moving on without her caused unbelievable pain in her heart. She imagined all kinds of horrible things involving other women, and it was driving her crazy. Thinking in these terms only made her feel sorrier for herself than she already did.

Gia had never established the attitude of 'live for today and to hell with tomorrow' or 'love em and leave em' or even 'I'm here for a good time not a long time.' Some people even lived by the old saying, 'if you can't be with the one you love, then, love the one you're with.' She loved Beau with everything she had to give, and inevitably failed. It didn't matter how much she gave in time or of herself or how much love she gave, it wasn't enough, and he still walked away.

~

Patti arrived, suitcase in hand, to Gia's relief, and she was so thankful to have someone with her to talk to. They would likely spend the next few days talking non-stop about Beau and Patti was prepared to sit and mostly listen while she got the hurt out. Patti knew that Gia would, and had done, the same for her, and she was there for her this time.

Gia's phone rang a few days after he'd left and when she answered it, she heard Beau's voice on the other end. Patti quietly walked away to give her some privacy.

"How's it going kiddo?" he asked.

"About how I expected it would, Beau," she said as fresh tears slide down her cheeks. "How are you doing?" she asked.

"It was a long drive. I'm at the first stop and must wait for further instructions. I am not given a lot of info at one time; it goes with the job."

Gia concentrated on the voice she had grown to love and not necessarily on what he was saying. Her mind went back to times when his voice would calm her or lull her to sleep. That was how peaceful she had felt with him. She missed him so badly she wanted to crawl through the phone and into his arms. Her heart was torn between wanting to rip his face off for leaving her, the ache she felt from missing him and the joy at hearing his voice. She was always torn in so many directions with her feelings. She began to wonder if she would ever find a happy medium.

She had convinced herself that once he was gone, he would expect her to move on. She had assumed he would or why else would he have said 'have a nice life.' To her, it meant 'get out there and enjoy your life.' So, she had to wonder what this call really meant. Did he miss her; was he calling out of compassion, love, pity or maybe guilt? Was he not ready or willing to let go of her? Why make a call just to ask how she was doing? It should have been more than obvious how his move would affect her life; it was not a difficult concept. They had spent three years together, and she loved him with everything she had so she wondered again, what this call was really about.

"I should go, Gia, I wanted to call to see how you are. Is it OK if I call you again when I am settled? I'm not certain if I can disclose where I am going, but we can stay in contact somehow."

"I'd love that," she said, "Thanks for calling Beau; it's nice to hear your voice again. I miss you. Have a safe trip."

"Thanks, I'll call soon." And he was gone again.

Hobo Soul

When we hear the word 'hobo,' a certain image comes immediately to mind. We picture a train jumping, box-car living, raggedy-ass tramp. But there is a definite difference between a tramp and a hobo. A 'tramp' works only when forced to, and 'hobos' are workers who love to wander. A hobo loves the journey far above the actual destination.

Gia could easily describe Beau as having a 'hobo soul.' He became restless if in one place for too long. The excitement mode would kick in when he knew there was another destination with his name on it. The difference between the 'hobo' and the 'hobo soul' is that Beau travelled first class, ate the finest foods, slept in posh hotels and got paid well for allowing himself to be exposed to dangerous situations.

So, for a time, the tears were over, and they were replaced with wonderful memories that she and Beau shared.

After Beau left, she would lie in her bed night after night and think about her life with him, and every precious memory with him spilled forth at random. She'd always kept a notebook on her night stand, and she decided to write out her life with him. There were so many good memories and so few bad ones. She knew she'd never again love anyone as she had loved him, nor did she want to. He was it; the one, the only and he had walked away.

'Artificial intelligence is no match for natural stupidity.' When that thought came to mind, she was not sure if it was meant for him or for her, but the more she thought about it she was certain it was meant for her. She was the stupid one. She had scolded herself more than once for getting involved with him in the first place since she knew it was short term from the beginning. Then, on the other hand, if she had not met Beau, she may never have known what real love was, and that gave her some peace. She just had not expected the time to pass so quickly.

Memories, in no particular order, crowded her mind as she allowed herself, pencil in hand; to recall times and places that belonged to only them. Having nothing but time on her hands, she allowed her mind to travel back over some of the precious times and adventures they had shared. Flipping the pages in her notebook, she penciled each story giving each one a title. Each title had a special meaning.

Her memories

Christmas at the Cabin

Beau had bought a cabin by a lake during his stay in Kanyon. They spent many happy days and warm summer nights there. They thought it might be fun to go there on Christmas day. When they finished with Christmas dinner and had cleaned everything up, they headed out for a few days. Since the cabin was in the woods, the roads were blocked with snow. They could only get in so far, and then they had walked the rest of the way.

Gia asked Beau to get a tree, and she'd trim it. He went out into the woods and came back with a Charlie Brown tree, which was something only he would choose. It was raggedy and scrawny, but it was theirs. Gia had spent time making star and snowflake shaped ornaments, wrapped them all in aluminum foil, strung them with thread and hung them on the tree. She also strung red berries, that she'd found behind the cabin, at the edge of the woods, and added them to the tree and voila! They had a Christmas tree. Beau was impressed that it looked so cute with what little she had. They spent a few days doing things they enjoyed like walking in the woods. Their evenings were spent snuggling by the fireplace and watching the sun go down over the water. Soon it was time to go back.

It had warmed up considerably, and the warmth of the sun had melted some of the snow causing the road to become slushy for the walk back to the car. It was nice going in and walking through the soft snow, but the slush was another matter. She had not worn proper footwear and in no time, her boots were filled with water. She knew there was no sense in complaining since nothing could be done until they got to the car anyway. Before they reached the car, Beau could hear swishing sounds as they walked. He turned, looked at her and asked, "Are your feet wet?"

"Soaked," was all she said.

He looked at her with amazement and said, "Well you are quite the little trooper aren't you! Why didn't you say something?"

"Whining isn't going to fix it, so why say anything?"

The look on his face showed how much he admired her for not complaining about how cold her feet were. When they finally reached the car, he opened the passenger side door for her and helped her to sit down. He pulled off her boots, emptied the water out, and peeled off her socks and wrung them out. Opening the back gate of the car, he found a rough looking blanket and wrapped it around her feet. He started up the car and turned the fans on high, so she could warm up. Taking her feet, he laid them on his lap and taking one at a time, he rubbed them while the car warmed up. It was a perfect Christmas.

When he got notice, that his assignment was over, he had given her permission to use the cabin whenever she wanted and to check out the property from time to time until he decided what he was going to do with it. Until then, it was hers to do with as she pleased and insisted that she enjoy it.

The Birch Bark Letter

She had agreed to check on the cottage now and then so with a mixture of heavy heart and gladness she set out to do just that. Although it was heart-wrenching for Gia to go there without him, she knew she must. It was a promise she'd made to him before he left, and it was a place for her to go and sit by the water, soothe her soul and mourn him. She never said she was not a glutton for punishment. She felt close to Beau here, but she missed him terribly as well. It was an hour's drive, and then several back roads led into the lake and the closer she got, the lonelier she felt. Turning into the stumpy driveway, she stopped next to the verandah. Looking out at the lake, she remembered the canoe ride they had taken. Getting out of the car, she sauntered down to the dock.

An old Adirondack chair sat in the middle of the dock, and she wondered how it had gotten there. She thought about the night they'd made love, on the spot where she stood. Tears began slipping down her cheeks, as she stood there alone, lonely and her heart aching for him. Closing her eyes, she could almost feel him walking up behind her and wrapping her in his arms. She could smell him. Even though he never wore scented products, he had a scent all his own. She placed her arms across her chest as if to touch his arms. She wanted so badly to turn around and wrap her arms around his neck, but she knew if she moved, she would break the spell. As tears streamed down her cheeks, she let the feelings sweep over her.

'Why did she do this to herself? Why did she allow him to have so much control over her emotions?' She already knew the answers to her own questions. She loved him, and she knew she always would. The fantasy world she lived in, with him as her white knight, that never returned, was all she was ever going to have. Being in this 'world,' she was happiest. This is where Beau was, and this is where she wanted to be. Her ridiculous thoughts had broken the spell, and the moment with Beau had passed. She touched the arm of the chair and wondered again how it got there. Stepping inside the familiar cottage, she knew instantly that someone had been there. She walked around the room as if in search of a burglar but soon decided she was alone. Things were missing, personal things of Beau's. Her heart galloped at thoughts of Beau being there. She checked everything possible, and his personal belongings were gone. She was puzzled because she had just been there a few weeks earlier.

"Beau?" she heard herself say aloud, "were you here?"

She noticed a rolled-up piece of birch bark on the table, and she curiously reached for it. Holding it up with her left hand, she slowly unrolled the scroll-like note and began to read:

'My Dearest Gia,' quickly she drew her fingers off the roll, and it snapped shut on her thumb. Tears immediately welled up in her eyes as she read his words. His handwriting all too familiar to her even though she had not seen it in a while. His husky voice echoed in her mind as she wiped her tears and started again.

My Dearest Gia:

It is beautiful here at the lake. I am sitting alone on the dock, and my thoughts are of you. I always considered this cottage as 'ours' since you are the one who searched it out and found it for me to purchase. It does not feel like 'ours' if you are not here to enjoy it with me. I know it is my fault that we are not together. I take responsibility since I am the one who made the decision to leave when my assignment was over.

I am not about to interrupt your life, so I purposely did not tell you I was coming here. It is not my right to fall in and out of your life knowing I am not here to stay.

I have found a buyer for the cottage since I no longer need it. I am being sent abroad for several years, and from there I do not know where I will be. Selling the cottage will tie up loose ends here.

I suspect you will be around, to collect your personal stuff and to check on things here, so I know you will find this note eventually.

My best regards for a wonderful life and just know that you are in my heart no matter where I am in this world.

Beau xo

Looking up at ceiling, she took a deep breath and wiped away the stream of tears. It was unbelievable how much her heart ached for him. She missed him terribly. Plopping down on a chair in front of the fireplace, she dropped her face in her palms and cried, as the scroll hit the floor. She wondered if a person's heart could possibly break in half.

"Damn you, Beau!" she sobbed, "damn you for leaving me!"

Straightening her shoulders, she pressed her back into the chair and relaxed as if she were a rag doll. The scroll was lying on the floor where she'd dropped it, and as she reached for it, she saw a gift sitting on the mantle above the fireplace. Her heart stopped. She didn't know if her legs would hold her up or not and she was almost afraid to trust them. She touched the gift as if it were a piece of gold and saw her name on the tag in Beau's handwriting. Opening the box, she gasped a little. Her fingertips touched her lips as she smiled. She lifted out a precious ornament that she had admired many times at his house. It was a 'stick horse,' that sat on a pedestal and when you touched it, it rocked. It had meant a lot to him back then and had been a gift to him. She never thought he would ever part with it, but there it was, sitting in the palm of her hand. She knew, for certain, she would keep it forever.

The Race Horse

He was long and lean, and many times she referred to him as her racehorse because he kept himself in great shape. He ran, he played several sports, including golf, hockey, and football and when Gia was with him, they took long walks. On a rare occasion, they had slight disagreements, as all couples do. One time they were lying in bed, words were being exchanged, and they could not come to an agreement. Beau slid over, laid his head on her shoulder, rolled his eyes up to her and said, "Talk to me like I'm a racehorse." They both began to laugh, and the disagreement was soon forgotten. Agree to disagree was his motto.

Surprise Party

It was Gia's 43rd birthday. She had received an assortment of birthday cards and best wishes that she had always gotten. On this particular birthday, she was at work when she saw a florist come into the building. There were hundreds of people who worked there and in passing, she thought how lucky someone was to be receiving such a beautiful bouquet. Someone called her name, and she thought it must be a colleague with a question for her. Raising her head to see who it was, she looked directly into the bouquet of flowers.

"Gia Lake?" he asked.

"Yes."

"For you ma'am," he said and passed her the vase.

Slowly, she reached for the delivery. Thanking him, he nodded and left her with the flowers. Sitting the vase down on a bare spot on her desk, she looked for the card. Turning the envelope around, she lifted the flap and read, 'Happy Birthday, from the Cove Dweller.' It took a few seconds for it to register and when it did, a smile spread across her face.

Shortly after he'd moved to the area, he had bought a small two-bedroom cottage in Hartley's Cove, hence the 'cove dweller.' She was surprised and overjoyed that he would think of her and had actually remembered her birthday. They had only been dating for three months. Thinking about how sweet it was, she took her camera out of her handbag and took a picture of the bouquet... as if she would ever forget about this moment.

That same evening, he surprised her with a birthday dinner at a local resort. It was a warm August evening as they strolled through the grounds after they'd finished eating. The beautiful sunset was a perfect ending to a perfect day! As the sun sank low on the horizon, he folded her up in his arms and whispered 'happy birthday' into her hair. She closed her eyes, wrapped her arms around his back and whispered, "Thanks, Beau."

Saving a Life

Beau had a plan to renovate his house in Hartley's Cove. Shortly after purchasing it, he set out to remove the old electric range, replace it with a countertop stove and wall oven. His plan was to install the wall oven under his kitchen counter. It was an open concept kitchen, so there were no 'walls' in which to mount an oven. She heard him go into the larder and turn off a switch, so he could make connections. Something moved her to go to the kitchen, and she followed her premonition. She walked up behind him as he positioned himself under the counter ready to grab the wires to connect the oven. "Are you sure you're safe under there?" she asked.

"Yes, I just turned off the fuse box," he told her.

She was very uneasy as she stood there, and her gut was telling her otherwise. "Wait!" she said as she moved around to the other side of the counter. "I just want to check something out." Flipping the light switch to the 'on' position, the kitchen lit up!! Beau banged his forehead as he came scurrying out from under the counter with a look of shock on his face. He grabbed her and wrapped her in his arms. "Thank God you did that; I could have fried under there! I was sure I turned the fuse box off." He had not pulled the main circuit breaker to the 'off' position that cut the power to the entire house. "You just saved my life Gia; how did you know to do that?"

"It just didn't feel right, Beau. This is an older house, and some have both a fuse box and a circuit panel. I know you are doing the best you can here, but you are an amateur when it comes to home renovations. This is your first home and your first attempt at this stuff. I just went with my instincts, and something told me to double check, and I'm glad I did."

He had reminded her on several occasions that she had indeed saved his life.

Sweetness

She was at Beau's place waiting for him to come home. He'd had a meeting after work, and she knew he wouldn't be long. Time passed. The longer she waited for him, the worse she felt. Since she didn't know how long his meeting would last, she decided to go home. Home is where she usually wanted to be when she felt ill. She left a note on his counter telling him of her situation and drove herself home. Going directly upstairs, she stripped her clothes off and climbed into bed. She must have just missed Beau by a few minutes because shortly after she settled herself down under the covers, her doorbell rang. She got out of bed and slipped into her pajamas as she peered out her bedroom window and saw Beau's car parked in the driveway behind hers. She went downstairs and opened the door for him. He simply held out his hand and said, "Come with me."

"I'm not dressed."

"You don't need clothes, you can 'not feel well' at my place just as well as you can here. You don't have to be alone so come on, grab a sweater; you're coming home with me."

Taking her by the hand, he walked her to his car, opened the passenger side door, helped her in and drove home. When they had finished the ten-minute drive, he tucked her into his waterbed and laid down next to her with a book while she fell asleep. He was sweet, kind and he spoiled her and made her feel loved.

The Camping Trip

Her doorbell rang one day. Beau was standing on her step when she opened the door. "Put a few things in a bag and come for a bike ride with me," he said. "A toothbrush is about all you'll need and a warm sweater; I have the rest."

She knew better than to ask questions when he was on a mission. They went out to his motorcycle, and he passed her one of his leather jackets and said, "Put this on and here's a helmet." They were each dressed in leather boots, jacket and a helmet. She climbed on the back, and they drove off. As they glided down the road, she wrapped her arms around his waist, laid her cheek on his back and smiled to herself. They ended up on the far side of the province at a beautiful beach where he pitched a tent, made a fire and had supper heating in no time. He was quite adept at this camping thing.

He had told her many stories of the biking adventures he had taken for weeks at a time. Therefore, he knew what he was doing, and he knew how to get around with the bare essentials. He would bathe in rivers and streams; sleep out on the sand under the stars or snuggle up in a tent. He told her that he usually stopped in the late afternoon to give himself time to set up his tent, eat and still have time to read before darkness set in. She jokingly referred to him as her nomad.

This was an overnight trip, but the places he found to take her were amazingly beautiful. On their way back, the next day they got caught in the rain. He casually pulled the bike over to the side of the road, opened up a hatch on the side of the bike and pulled out yellow rain gear. She thought they must have looked like two big ducks riding down the road, but it was great fun.

Secretary's Day

Gia was sitting outside on her patio getting a few minutes of sun when she recognized Beau's car. She felt her heartbeat quicken as it did whenever she saw him. She saw the signal light as he made the right hand turn and pulled up across the street, from her place. It was in the middle of the afternoon, and he was still in his work gear. Her heart filled at the sight of his handsomeness. She stood up as he got out and opened the back door of his car. When he stood up, he slid something behind his back, and she smiled at his romantic side. As he began to cross the street, she moved across the lawn to meet him. He leaned in for a quick peck and then brought a beautiful bouquet of tiger lilies from behind his back. He must have seen the look of surprise on her face as he handed her the flowers.

"What's the occasion?"

"It's secretary's day, at work, so I brought you a bouquet also."

"Thank you, Beau, they are lovely!"

"And so are you," he said with a smile and kissed her again.

She loved him more every time she saw him.

He told her he couldn't stay and that he was just a 'delivery boy' and had to get back to work. "Can I pick you up later for dinner, at my place?"

"Sure, I'll look forward to it."

Watching him leave, she tenderly touched the flowers. He was her everything.

Her pencil was busy as floods of memories poured into her mind. She continued with her short stories.

Buskers

Next, she remembered the time he took her on a three-hour drive to the city where 'Buskers' were performing on the waterfront. It was the first time she had ever seen them. It was a beautiful hot, sunny summer day as they strolled along the waterfront in the city. Each 'Busker' did his act for the public. It was something she would never see again without the memory of Beau.

They stopped more than halfway home to find a place for a quick take out and then he drove to a provincial park. They had a picnic under a shady tree before continuing home. After they had finished their sandwiches and drinks, he propped himself up against a tall tree and she sat next to him. He put his arm around her and turned her around, so she was facing him. She laid her cheek on his chest, and he stroked her hair as they chatted. Life was so easy and simple with Beau.

Missed Trip

Another time she remembered arriving at his place only to find a note for her. He wrote, 'Na, Na, Na, Na, Nah. I have been called away to the city for meetings tomorrow - if you had been here you could have come along.'

It made her smile just knowing that he wanted her with him. Even though she had missed out on a trip, she was content knowing she'd be missed.

A Day Trip

One Sunday morning he woke her up early and asked if she wanted to go for a ride. He hadn't said where they were going; they just ate breakfast and left. They caught a forces plane and flew across the water, so that he could visit his mom and dad for twenty minutes! He'd rented a car and drove all over his hometown showing her the places that were important to him as a child, and it pleased her that he wanted her to know about his young life. When he finished the tour, they boarded the plane and headed home. Who else but Beau would think of travelling such a distance just to visit his aging parents? She didn't need all the memories to remind her of how wonderful he was; she already knew that part of him. It just made her lonelier for him and the man she knew he was, and she missed him. These precious memories made her smile through the sadness.

Christmas

For Christmas one year, Beau gave her a Lamb Chop hand puppet. She thought it was a rather strange gift, but he was always full of surprises. When she put the puppet on her hand, she felt something hit her fingertips. A surprised look washed over her face as she realized something was in the puppet's head. Beau watched her with his boyish grin as she struggled to pull it out with two fingers. It was a small velvet jewelry box, and she turned the opening toward her and slowly lifted the top. She had admired a 'Stairway to Heaven' ring in a jewelry store window on one of their walks. She was excited as he took the box from her, removed the ring from the center slot and slipped it on her finger.

"Merry Christmas, Gia," he said as he pulled her to him. She smiled up at him through happy tears.

Carnival

He had taken her to the carnival, and as they strolled around the grounds, they had stopped at a booth with a row of rifles attached on mounts. He paid for a round of time and began to shoot. He asked her if she would like to try and her immediate response was to say no. She had never held a rifle before so instinctively she figured she couldn't do it. The game was set up so that objects would pop up for a few seconds here and there and he wanted to see how many of the targets he could hit before they disappeared in the allotted time. Gia smiled as he kept missing most of the them, but he was laughing at himself, too.

She envied people who couldn't do well but still were able to laugh at themselves and have fun doing it. Suddenly, she had an overwhelming burst of excitement inside her as she put her hands on one of the rifles. She thought, 'I can do this!' One popped up near her, and she pulled the trigger, bang, down it went, and her excitement grew. Another one popped up, and again she aimed and pulled the trigger before he had a chance to pull his and again the target went down. She went from target to target as fast as she could feeling very competitive as she downed every last one. Beau looked at her with crinkled up eyebrows and playfully said, "What?" as he pulled her into a bear hug. "You just put me to shame woman, and I'm trained!"

"I know, right!" she said feeling very proud of herself for even daring to try to do something new.

Football

What Gia knew about football would fit on the head of a pin, but Beau was a big fan of the game, and Gia endured a full Grey Cup game just to be with him. The only thing that stood out about the entire day was a great play made by quarterback John Elway and how Beau roared when he scored.

Their entire day was spent in bed in front of the television. They ate when they were hungry and got out of bed only to rustle up something to eat, which was usually Gia's job since the game was so important. Her other job assignment was bartender and what she knew about liquor would also fit on the head of a pin. He reminded her of how he liked his drinks, and he showed her how to pour a perfect glass of beer with no head.

She recalled how Beau got when liquor had taken over. His true feelings came out, and he would put his heart on the line and tell Gia exactly how he felt about her. 'Drunken words are sober thoughts.' She knew how he felt and had from the beginning, but it was always nice to hear it spoken to her in actual words. It was just her own insecurities that she had to deal with. Beau was not one to verbalize his feelings and reminded her now and then that there was a difference between knowing how someone feels about you and hearing about it. He told her that people should know how someone feels about them by the way they treat them, not by what they say. She knew how Beau felt about her.

She'd stopped writing at this point and remembered that he had also admitted to not loving her enough, which was when he left town without her. This information had not consoled her when he told her that he had loved her too much to ask her to risk her safety to follow him around to dangerous places. He never knew where he was going to be and most of the time, he, himself, needed bodyguards. He had loved her enough to protect her but not enough to let go of the life he had chosen. This job was his life.

Personal Ads

When the three years with Beau ended, Gia tried to re-adjust to life without him. She didn't know where he was and there was next to no contact for security reasons.

She had a knack for doing things without thinking them through, and this was no exception. As she sat looking over the weekend newspaper, she came across the personal ads. 'Mind your business,' she warned herself, 'just turn the page and move on to the antique cars section or yards sale items, anything, just turn the page.' However, the last voice she ever listened to, was her own.

'I'll show you!' she mumbled to herself. Beau was gone, and she was going to show him that she could move on without him. 'Bigger and better things ahead, you'll see!' There were numerous ads to choose from of various age groups, color and race. Some even into kinky stuff that she had only read about!

Gia didn't want to be alone in this venture, so she talked a friend into posting an ad too. They tried not to sound desperate but, who in their right mind posted ads? Surely, nothing good can come from looking for love in a newspaper. However, she posted it anyway even though she knew it was a bad idea from the start. But was she doing it for herself, or to prove to Beau that she didn't need him? 'He'd moved away, he'd moved on,' she grumbled, 'and she was alone.' Hindsight is great, and when she seriously thought about what she was doing, she wondered how she was going to meet a perfect stranger when most men frightened her! There were no single, available men in her hometown. Sure, there were men who were cheaters and those who were looking for a good time and a one-night stand, but she was not into that. She was not looking for someone who entered a club wearing jogging pants, a dirty t-shirt and a gold band on his ring finger. All she could do was roll her eyes when she thought about it.

Single white female... and so it began. Letters started coming in from an unknown post office box in the city. It was exciting getting letters from perfect strangers. They all wanted to meet her, but she didn't want to meet anyone, her heart still belonged to Beau, but he was gone. Responses came from a retired teacher, a firefighter, and a laborer who worked at a quarry, just to name a few. In her notebook, she began to write about the experiences as she remembered them.

The Teacher

Zack Glendon. He sent her beautifully penned letters. He said he liked her ad and was interested in meeting her. She smiled as she read his words. He wrote that he was a retired physics teacher and recently widowed. He had beautiful penmanship, and she guessed it came with the job. He signed his letter with his name and address, which indicated he was not a game player. He sounded kind and caring. He was a little older than she was, but she didn't give it a second thought. She was apprehensive about meeting someone new, but it was exciting, and she loved the attention. It gave her something to think about besides Beau and the heartache she felt.

It frightened her a bit when he asked for her phone number, and she wondered if she should get involved this soon. She answered his letter, and she asked him to send a photo. She decided to add her phone number along with a picture of herself and mailed it. Then she began to worry and hoped he wouldn't like her picture, lose interest and not call. Nevertheless, the call came, in the short time it had taken to get a letter from here to there. In those days, there was lots of mail. It was not called 'snail-mail' back then!

His picture showed that he had a nice friendly face. It showed the kindness she had read in his words. When she answered the phone and heard his voice, it made him real and not just nice words on a piece of writing paper with no face. 'Now what?' she thought, 'couldn't mind your business!' She scolded herself repeatedly.

'Maybe it wouldn't be so bad to meet him,' she thought. She could always give him the bums rush if she didn't like him. She finally relented and invited him to visit. She liked him as soon as they met, and he was not the scary person that she had conjured up in her head. They spent the afternoon at her house exchanging information and becoming acquainted.

The amazing part of his stories was when he told her he lived on his own Island. She became very intrigued and wanted to know all about it! He said that he and his wife had bought the small island as soon as he learned it had become available. They wanted to build a summer home on it because they spent their winters in Arizona. Gia wondered how great that would be to live on an island all summer and then winter in a warm country. He told her it was fun but a difficult job to begin the process of building the cottage. First, he had to build a raft large enough to carry the planks and other types of wood. The building materials were floated across the water on the raft, as needed for each step, to actually build the cottage. He had also built a rowboat to get across which was their only access. They would leave their car on the mainland and row across the lake.

After visiting several times, he asked if she would like to see his place. The thought of going to an island was thrilling, but when she factored in that she would be on an island, alone with a man, it was terrifying.

"Can I bring my dog?" she asked. Teaka was a longish haired mix of yellow Lab and Collie from what she could gather. She had picked her out from a litter of about half a dozen puppies. A family had them in a box at the mall, and she could not resist.

"Of course," he assured her, "she is a part of your family! So how about if we plan it for next week and I will come and get you and Teaka, and you will be my guests for the weekend?"

"I'd love that." Which was her response, but her stomach knotted so badly, she just wanted to throw up.

He was such a nice fellow. If it had been anyone other than Zack, she was certain she'd been given an instructional map on how to get there and left her to her own devices. The week passed quickly, and soon he was there to pick her up. She was ready when he arrived, and Teaka jumped into the back seat of his Volkswagen Fox, her bag was in the trunk, and away they went. Gia had settled down considerably as her trust in Zack grew. They'd stopped at a quaint little seafood restaurant for lunch, got a doggie bag for Teaka and a pit stop then continued. It was a two-hour drive, and they were almost there. When he turned the car facing a waterfront, she sucked in her breath. It was such a beautiful spot. Getting out, he opened the back door for Teaka, and Gia got out as Zack lifted the trunk for her bag.

"I apologize for the hair in the back seat."

"Not to worry, I used to have a dog, too."

As they walked, Zack began to explain that after the cottage was finished, he wanted a better and safer route to the cottage rather than having to depend on a row boat. He came up with a plan for a footbridge.

"Really?" she asked, "it must be a long bridge, I can't see the cottage from here." This statement had multiple meanings only to her. 'How long is this bridge, how far away is the cottage and how the hell do I get out of here if the need arises?' There she was with the 'what if' again!

"It is a long bridge, and it had to be done in sections and then be connected in parts," he told her just as they arrived at the mouth of the bridge. The bridge was not quite wide enough for two people to walk side by side comfortably, so she followed him. There were rope handrails all along the footbridge, and beautifully designed. She thought about what a great mind this guy had. When they reached the cottage side, they stepped onto a forest floor. The ground was covered with leaves, mushrooms, moss and all kinds of different things that we don't normally see in our everyday travels. It felt like they were stepping onto a plush carpet into another world. There was a beaten down path from the bridge to the cottage and looking through the trees was like something out of a fairytale. 'This was an experience she would likely not forget.'

It was still a good walk to the cottage when they got across the bridge. It didn't seem long because there was so much to see, and the cottage was breathtaking. She was amazed at all the beautiful work his hands had provided. He showed her around and then took her bags into the bedroom. When he saw the look on her face, he eased her mind.

"Yes, there is only one bedroom, I will sleep in the living room, and you and Teaka can have the bed."

"You mean she can sleep on the bed with me?"

"Does she sleep with you at home?" he asked.

"Yes, she does."

"Well then, she can here, too."

Once they were comfortably relaxing before the fire, he asked her questions about her quest on the 'want ads.' It was a bit embarrassing to talk about, but she did. She told him about Beau and her three years with him and this 'want ads' thing was probably just a release from her loneliness and a diversion from her thoughts. She also told him about the other letters she'd gotten, along with his, and he kindly reminded her to be aware and cautious. It was a nice beginning. As their new friendship advanced, they began to open up to each other. He knew her heart belonged to someone else and that she was not ready to jump into another serious relationship. Honesty had drawn them closer as friends, but doubt had begun to enter. It came out, in one of their conversations, that she reminded him of his deceased wife. He referred to some of her actions, looks and behavior. She began to think that he was only interested in her because of the similarities he saw between her and his wife. It caused her to keep her feelings intact. She certainly didn't want to disappoint him, nor did she want to be disappointed in herself. She didn't want to behave differently in order to hold his interest. It annoyed her a little, when he admitted that he thought of his wife when he was with her, and it made her feel like a replacement. It had also made her feel honored that she could give a person back some of what he was missing. According to him, he'd had a great marriage that had lasted for twenty-five years. How then, could she compete with that, when she couldn't hold on to a relationship for longer than four years, at best?

When he had written that he was recently widowed that bothered her, too. What were his reasons for answering ads? Had enough time passed for him, had he grieved long enough and was he ready to begin again? She worried that he might be jumping into something for which he was not ready. She decided she would rather have him as a friend than risk losing him altogether. When they discussed it, he totally understood her reasoning, and they agreed that he should continue his pursuit for a mate while maintaining their friendship. That let her off the hook as well because she was not ready to move on with anyone, not yet anyway.

When she got home from the island and was alone with her thoughts, she reached for a pad and pencil and began to write a poem for Zack.

A Piece of Paradise

While crossing the footbridge, my thoughts ran free
What is here in this forest, for you and for me
I thought, 'should I stay here, or go home instead
The mystery began of what lies ahead.
What lies beyond this forest so rare
In my wildest dreams, did I know what was there
I stepped onto the moss, so soft beneath my feet
The mushroom and ferns made this picture complete.
The plants, the shrubs, and the leaves from the trees
What kind of forest would it be without these?
This beautiful Paradise could be Eden I thought
I could be happy here, more likely than not.
I entered the cottage through a door at the rear
This place is so lovely, I have nothing to fear.
I browsed in amazement to what my eyes took in
Between these walls, there is beauty within.
The view from the water, nothing else could transcend.
From the patio on one side to the balcony on the end
Exuberance overtook me, to say the least
My eyes saw everything, like the hungry at a feast.
We walked in the forest with nature all around
What a feeling of freedom, in this Paradise you found
Through the forest, to the hilltop, to a wide-open space
We came out in sunshine splashing our face.
We made our way back to the raft that you made
Soon the warmth of the sun on my body would fade
It was a little piece of Heaven afloat on the lake

To verify reality, I had to give myself a shake.
You showed me your Island from end to end
The dog at our feet, playing 'man's best friend'
It was a wonderful twenty-four hours we spent
Perfectly relaxed, at ease and content
I saw all the things that grew on the forest-bed floor
I must have missed something, this I am sure
I saw a loon dive into the water for food
We stood there and stared at a squirrel being rude
Your little piece of Paradise is a great place to be
A little piece of Heaven that you showed to me
You gave me peace and tranquility that I never knew
Thank you, my friend, for just being you.

She'd dated it September 24, 1991 and realized that Beau had been gone for three months.

Folding the poem into an envelope, she mailed it off to Zack. He was thrilled upon receiving it. It meant a lot to him knowing her visit impressed her enough to put it to poetry. He told her he'd had it framed and would keep it on his mantle. She had to believed him since that was her one and only trip there.

Zack would call and give her details of the dinner table conversations and the good and bad results of his dates. He would then tell her whether or not he would see them again. It was a joy being his confidante, and he cracked her up with his dry sense of humor. He had been out of the dating scene for years so when he asked for her advice, she echoed his advice to her... to be careful. They shared a special friendship and the kind of love, trust and respect that only comes with true friendship. He never let her down, and he never lied to her. She had a particular disdain for liars, and he knew it. He was always just a phone call away or a letter away and later on, just an email away. He was always there for her to talk to and bounce ideas off or just to listen. If she ever needed advice from him, he would write it out in detail, in words she could understand, and the information was always clear and precise. He never used his education to flatter or confuse her.

He was a great conversationalist, and he had many interesting stories to tell. She loved to hear about his adventures and accomplishments. She would listen to him tell about the period in his life when he had built his own plane. Since he was a teacher, he had the summers off. When the plane was finished, he learned to fly and got his pilot's license. Then he and his wife would plan out their itinerary, using the Stanley Airport to fly in and out of throughout the summer and then return to school in the fall. How exciting that must have been to have such a carefree sense of adventure. Up until the time that Gia began to write, he had already built, sailed and sold a small yacht. He simply amazed her with his talents. They were best friends.

Somewhere down the road of life, he met the one who eventually became his wife. Gia was happy for him and a little envious that he'd found something that she could not... happiness and a partner for life.

The Forgettable One

Another person answered her ad. He was so forgettable that she could put a name to him. He was from the city and asked if they could meet. They had spoken on the phone a few times, but she was reluctant to commit to a meeting. She'd discussed it with her friend, Elaine, and she said that to ease her mind she would go along to keep her company. When he called again, she agreed to meet at the halfway point. She and Elaine waited for him in the restaurant at the truck stop. They sat at a window seat watching for the car that he had described to her. They sat on the same side of the table so that when he showed up, he would be facing them from the other side. Gia could not believe her eyes when he slid out from his car seat. With the same look on their faces, the friends looked at each other.

"Please, don't let that be him," Gia said.

"It can't be," Elaine responded.

"Oh my! It is!" Gia said through clenched teeth, so he could not see her lips moving. He was all smiles as he walked up to their table. 'Lordy, Lordy.'

He introduced himself to her, she, in return, introduced Elaine to him and then he sat down. 'Where do these clowns come from?' she thought. She was sure she had 'Loser' stamped across her forehead. This guy was of average height, probably five foot seven or eight at the most, and as ugly as a hedgehog. He had a mullet hairdo, and of all things, it looked as if he had a set of plastic teeth. They weren't veneers or ceramic dentures, but they looked similar to plastic. 'This would be a good time to run,' she thought.'

After a brief, 'let's get to know each other,' awkward session, the waitress came to take their orders. She could not recall what she and Elaine ordered. She probably blocked it out anyway. She did recall, however, that he'd ordered vegetable beef soup which will likely be indelibly imprinted in her brain for all of eternity. When their lunches arrived, she was sure he had not eaten for a few days. He hoed into that soup as if it were his lifeline. Halfway through the lunch, he took time to pick his head up to breathe. Looking up, he gave them a big open smile. He had strings of roast beef sticking out from almost every one of those plastic teeth. Pressing her lips together, Gia was about to lose it. Kicking Elaine under the table, they could barely contain themselves! The meal could not end fast enough for her, so she could get out of there. They finally said their goodbyes in the parking lot and went their separate ways.

"Well, that was different," Elaine said.

"What? I thought he was cute!" Gia said.

Elaine looked at her with squinted eyes and Gia burst out laughing. It broke the mood of disbelief, and they both laughed. They were very happy to be on the road for home.

The Fireman

The letter was signed,

Best Regards,
Dan Smythe

Describing himself as 'recently' separated, actively working as a firefighter, he was looking for a gal who shared his interests. Neglecting to mention his interests, gave her no idea what they were nor, did she know what 'recently' meant. Did it mean a year, a month or five minutes?

She was going by her own experiences because Beau had only been gone a few months when she placed her own ad. She certainly hadn't revealed, in her ad, that she had just been dumped. So how was she to know if these letter writers were not in the same 'desperate' boat that she was and that it was slowly sinking.

She agreed to meet with him at her sister's house. She didn't have a picture of him prior to their meeting either. He drove a new

Nissan Maxima, that he leased, which was not too shabby. Dan was bald with a grey, almost white, wreath around his head. He had nice blue eyes and a gentle spirit. She noticed that he smelled better than she did. There was a mixture of deodorant, aftershave, baby powder, foot talc and some sort of fragrance from his laundry soap. He was definitely a hazard to the ozone layer. 'This would be a good time to run!'

He freaked her out when he began to verbally, move her in with him within the first hour they were together. When he began to figure out, on paper, the cost of a moving van and a storage unit for her stuff, she just sat there in disbelief.

"You do know that we just met today?" she asked.

"We only have the weekend," he said, "I have to be back for my twenty-four-hour shift on Monday."

"This is Saturday, we met this afternoon!" she said, again, furrowing her brow.

"Yes, I know that's why we don't have long to plan this out. If we don't get started, we'll run out of time."

He was as cool as a cucumber and totally serious. Suddenly, she realized that this guy must have OCD (Obsessive Compulsive Disorder) or ADD (Attention Deficit Disorder) He paid no attention to what she was saying. He had driven for four hours to meet her and was planning a lifetime together in five minutes!

"This is not happening," she said determinedly.

"What's wrong?" he asked turning from his notes.

"Seriously?"

"Ya, seriously, what's wrong?"

"Do you hear yourself? We don't even know each other, and you are planning our lives out for us!"

"I thought from our letters that you wanted this too," he said.

"Um, I agreed to meet you, I did not say, 'come and get me!' Where, in my letters, did I ever say I wanted a serious relationship? Especially, given the fact that we have only just met today!" Without skipping a beat, she continued. "How long have you been separated from your wife and are you even divorced?"

"We separated about three weeks ago. We haven't started divorce proceedings yet."

Gia was relieved that her sister was in the next room because this guy was scary.

"I think it's time for you to leave," she said, not wanting to be alone with him for one more minute.

"I just got here!"

"I know, but I want you to leave. You did get a hotel room before you came here?"

"Yes, I did, but I thought you'd come to the hotel with me."

"Seriously?" she said widening her eyes and nodding her head, "please, just leave."

Her sister walked into the room when Gia raised her voice, and she was never so glad for an interruption in her life.

Dan packed up his notebook with his 'cost of move' figures and pushed his pencil into the coils. Putting his jacket on, in a huff, he shoved the pad into his inside breast pocket and walked to the door.

"Can I call you when I get back to the city?"

"I don't think that would be a good idea, I'm sorry."

He pulled his collar up around his ears, looked back once and left.

"What was that?" her sister asked with a frown.

"A big mistake," she said rolling her eyes, "you don't even want to know. Where do these people come from?" she said, shaking her head. "Thanks for coming in when you did."

"What are sisters for, if not to interrupt?" she patted her on the back, and they headed to the kitchen for a cup of tea.

The Quarry Worker

Randal Malone wrote that he'd seen her ad and wanted to arrange a meeting. He described himself as six foot two, healthy, a homeowner and ready for a serious relationship. There were two words that frightened her right off the bat, 'serious' and 'relationship.' She already wanted to run.

She opened the door, and Tcaka leaped into the front seat of the car and Gia headed out to the halfway point. The same place where they had agreed to meet with 'The Forgettable One.' It was a busy truck stop, which set her at ease as much as she would allow. Arriving first, she waited with a feeling of dread as she asked herself again, 'What are you doing?'

He roared into the parking lot, in a Durango truck, with an enormous matching cap on the back. He pulled up next to her car and flashed a smile with a 'lucky you!' smirk on his face. She already hated him. She could tell that he was a big feeling ape who thought he was all that! Whipping off his sunglasses, he recklessly tossed them on the dash over the steering wheel. When he turned to look at her, she thought, 'Oh my God, he looks just like Lurch from The Addams Family!' She wanted to do a face plant into her palm but resisted the temptation. He jumped out of his truck and into her car so fast that her dog even growled at him.

Once they got through the niceties, she had already lost interest. The first thing she noticed about him was that he had a sinus problem. His voice sounded nasally as if he had cotton stuffed up his nostrils, and he was constantly wiping at the end of his nose. He breathed open-mouthed since his nose was plugged up. The conversation consisted of him bragging about all his toys and personal items he had accumulated. He said he had a 'Grand National' sitting in his garage. Looking puzzled, she asked herself, 'Am I supposed to know what that is?' When he saw the 'I don't know what the hell you're talking about,' look on her face, he told her it was a rare edition car and a twin to the Buick Regal. She wanted so badly to roll her eyes and give him her 'do I look like I care' look. 'Somebody please, just, kill me now!'

It was Thanksgiving Day, and he'd invited her to have dinner with him. She didn't know if she could sit across the table from him or not. 'Why hadn't she asked for a picture first?' There would have been no way in hell that she would have shown up for this meeting. To pass some time she agreed to eat with him. They had the traditional turkey dinner, and she tried very hard to involve herself in conversation. It was difficult to look at him and not stare at the Rudolf-like nose staring back at her. Breathing heavily, he tried to chew with his mouth closed while wiping at his nose every few minutes. She knew it was shallow of her to dislike a person who obviously had a serious sinus problem, but it was what it was. She declined dessert and said she had to get back home. She lied and said it was nice to meet him, but it wasn't. She just wanted to get the hell out of there and go home! He asked if he could see her again and she thought about it for a few minutes and said yes, then wondered why she'd said it.

He suggested that he would pick her up the next weekend and he would take her to his home. As much as she hated the thought, she still agreed.

He picked her up on time, and they began the three-hour trip. She insisted on taking her dog, and he insisted that the dog ride in the back of the truck. Not a good start on impressions. She wanted her dog with her, so she reluctantly agreed. Not liking him all that much, treating her dog like that, was not helping.

Before arriving at his house, he was already bragging about how beautiful it was. It would have been nice if he had allowed her to form her own opinion. It was a single level with an attached garage and true to his word; there was a Grand National inside. She still was not impressed. A light snow began to fall. Just what she needed. To make matters even worse, he insisted that Teaka stay in the basement so as not to get dog hair in his house.

Bedtime came, and she curled up on his couch with a blanket and to watch TV. Randal was in his bedroom, in the ensuite bathroom, getting ready for bed. Appearing in the living room doorway, he asked if she was ready for bed.

"I am in bed, I'm sleeping here," she said.

"Here?" he asked, looking puzzled.

"Well yes, you didn't think I was going to sleep in there?" she asked, pointing towards his bedroom.

Turning on his heels, he stomped back down the hall, and she settled back into the program. Only a few minutes had passed, and she heard him coming down the hall again.

"I can't believe you are sleeping out here!" he said raising his voice a little. Teaka barked at his loudness. "How are we supposed to get to know each other if we are going to sleep in separate rooms?"

Her thoughts went askew as she heard his voice raise. 'OK, I'm three hours from home, my dog is confined to the basement, and I have no way out of here.' Panic set in but only briefly. Suddenly she felt a little brave, or at least pretended she was. The last thing she wanted was for him to think he could intimidate or scare her.

"I'm not sleeping in the bedroom, I'm sleeping here," she said patting the arm of the couch. "I think you'd better go back to bed."

"Why are you being so difficult?" he said, still sounding annoyed.

"Am I missing something?" she asked. "Did I ever tell you, or indicate in any way, that I was ready to sleep with you? I didn't come up here expecting a sexual relationship with you; I agreed to it, so we could become better acquainted. This is not going to work if you are expecting anything more." She spoke rationally and firmly, but he was getting angrier by the minute. She began to panic even though she was trying to show otherwise.

"I want you to come to bed! Shut the TV off and come to bed!" he shouted.

Now she was angry! He had pushed the wrong buttons by trying to bully her. Throwing her blanket off, she rolled herself off the couch and stood up. "I am not going to your bed! Now back off and get the hell out of my face!" she said, standing her guard.

"What!? How dare you speak to me that way!" he shouted with a look of disbelief on his face.

"How dare you come out here and insist I go to bed with you!" she roared back at him. "If I had known you were such a bully I would never have agreed to come here. I want to go home!!!"

"I'm not taking you home at this time of night! We just drove for three hours, and I'm not getting dressed at this time of night to drive you back."

"Then I suggest you get out of my face and go back to bed... alone!" She turned her back on him and went into the bathroom. She knew he had a phone in there, so she went in to make a call.

By the time Elaine answered the phone she was in tears.

"Gia? What's wrong?" she asked.

She sputtered out her dilemma as best she could and asked her to please come and get her.

"It's storming here, Gia, I can't get my car out."

Gia pulled the curtain aside on the bathroom window, and it was next to a blizzard out there!

"Wait until morning when the plow is out, and I'll call you. Give me that creeps number." Just as she asked for the number, she heard a click and realized Randal had been listening to their conversation.

She gave her his number, and a feeling of defeat hit her in the stomach. 'What now? We are in the middle of a storm! What am I going to do?' She paced a little and thanked God that he had a spacious bathroom. She felt trapped. 'Why did this always happen to her? Why couldn't she ever mind her own business?' The house was as silent as a tomb and she thought he must have gone back to bed. The thought was not even out of her head when he banged on the bathroom door. A shot of adrenalin rushed through her from the interrupted silence. He must have imagined she was in there and up to no good.

"Come out of the bathroom, please," he said with less force this time. "What are you doing in there? Why are you so quiet? Gia, come out of there, please!"

"Leave me alone! I'm not coming out!" She could almost hear a sigh of relief coming from the other side of the door. "Tsk!" she clucked, "did you think I was going to kill myself to impress you?"

"The first thing in the morning we'll arrange to get you home," he said through the door. "I'm sorry I lost my temper with you, please come out and try to get some rest. Unlock the door, please."

She unlocked the door and glared at him as she found her way back to the couch. She heard him turn his light out and she breathed a sigh of relief. Sleep was not even a concept for her. Her mind would not shut down after being agitated, and all she wanted, was go home.

She quietly got up off the couch and made her way down to the basement. Teaka's tail wagged with excitement when she saw her. Sitting on the bottom step, she cuddled her and cried into her fur. Teaka licked her chin to acknowledge that she knew how she felt. When she got herself together, she began to whisper in low tones.

"Poor baby," she said, "he could sure take a lesson from Zack and at least allow you to come upstairs. We're going home soon, baby girl." When Teaka heard the word 'home,' she cocked her head sideways and began to wag her tail and licked Gia's face again. "Mommy will see you in a few hours, you go back to bed." She did as Gia asked and whispered, 'good girl,' and crept back up the stairs to the couch.

Morning, blessed morning had arrived, and the sun was shining. The plows had been out, and the roads were clear. She heard the phone ring, and Randal appeared. "It's for you," he said and walked to the kitchen.

"Hello?"

"Hi Gia, it's Elaine, are you OK?"

"Yes, it was a long night, and it's good to hear a friendly voice."

"I'll be about another hour, and then I'll have my car shoveled out. Do you think Randal could drive you down as far as the truck stop at the halfway point? She told her that he likely would, and if anything changed within the hour, she would call her.

"Thanks so much for doing this for me, Elaine."

"No problem, I know there is a lesson in this somewhere."

"Yes, there is, and I had all night to learn it."

"Good for you," she said, "see you soon."

Elaine was never one to place blame. She saw the good and the bad side in every situation and was always there as a good friend.

Randal had coffee on and offered her a cup. He tilted his head in a non-verbal apology and put on the hound dog eyes. She accepted the coffee, but that was all. She made her way downstairs to let the dog out for a breath of fresh air and her morning pee.

"I'm ready to go when you are," Randal said.

"Let's go then," she replied, "I'll get the dog." She barely spoke a word on the drive.

"Do you think we could start this over again?" he asked.

She said the first thing that came into her head. She told him she did not think a long-distance relationship would work for her, but it was nice to have met him... she lied again. He told her he was willing to travel if that would work for her. It seemed as if he was putting her on the spot, but she held firm knowing she did not ever want to see him again. He reached out to touch her arm, but she moved before he could make contact.

They finally got to the truck stop, and before the truck was stopped, she already had her hand on the door handle. As soon as it stopped, she was out of the seatbelt and out the door. Lifting the hatch on the cap, she let Teaka out. Teaka ran, played and jumped in the snow, relieved to be set free. Gia stayed out in the snow with her dog while Randal sat in the truck. Seeing Elaine pull in, relief swept over her as she got out of her car. She went over to Elaine, hugged her tightly and then walked back to the truck. Elaine was like a bear with a new cub as she waited by her car for Gia to get her stuff from the truck. She opened the side door and took her suitcase out. She walked up to his window and said, "Thank you for bringing me down this far."

Getting out of the truck, he reached out to hug her goodbye. Cringing at his touch, she shook off the urge to knee him in the crotch. Her dog was eyeing him up as they stood in the parking lot. He lowered his head to swoop in for a kiss, but she moved to pick up her bag. Teaka growled at him and he backed off. 'Good girl,' she said under her breath. She walked over to Elaine's car, let Teaka in the back seat, and she got in the front. 'Blessed safety.'

Elaine put the car in gear and spun out of the parking lot. Gia knew he was still standing there, but she did not care. Passed by, she never looked sideways at him.

"Thank you so much for coming to get me," she said looking over at Elaine. Teaka tilted her head sideways in response to her voice.

"That's it! I am so done with this crap! No more ads, no more meetings... notta!!!"

"I knew there was a lesson in there somewhere, good for you Gia. Remember the time you went with me to meet the cop? I got that creep's number before he hardly opened his mouth! Later I agreed to meet someone in the city while I was there on business. I think he was just trying to drum up business for his signage company! We both have been down this road. We are still alone; it doesn't not work ... not for us anyway."

Gia finally realized that the Lonely-Hearts Club was not for her. She could never replace Beau with just anyone, and there was no one out there who could measure up to him anyway.

The Users

Colin Richards

Gia was at a dance with several friends, when, close to closing time a tall, fairly attractive man walked in the door. She couldn't quite call him handsome, but there was something about him. From the time he entered the room, did a scan around, and got her in his sites, he only had eyes for her. He watched her from time to time, and a friend pointed out that it looked as if he was closing in on her. Finding courage, he strolled over to her when the 'last dance' was announced.

Giving her his full attention, he rarely lost eye contact. He asked her questions about herself and listened with interest. Gia thought, 'this is rare, allowing her to speak for a change.' She had always been the one listening. No one ever made her feel as if they cared what she had to say. When their dance ended, he asked if he could walk her to her car and she agreed. After telling him she had her own business, he asked if she had a card and she rummaged through her wallet for one. He asked if he could sit for a few minutes, which freaked her out a bit, but she agreed. He seemed harmless enough to her.

He asked if he could kiss her goodnight and after a few seconds of thought, she agreed. She could tell he was trying to impress her when he put both hands on the side of her face and drew her in toward him. The second his lips touched hers, her first thought was, 'no wonder this guy is single.' He rolled his lips around hers for a few seconds, and it was like kissing a hollow log. There was no emotion, no feelings of excitement, nothing. She just wanted to scream, 'get away from me and go learn something!' Pulling away from her, he grinned from ear to ear. His expression was, as if he had done a fantastic job while Gia wanted so badly to roll her eyes. They said goodnight and parted ways. When he got out of her car, she heard him flick her card with his index finger as if he'd hit the jackpot.

If she hadn't already had 'loser' stamped on her forehead, she would have seen the two red flags that were more than obvious to a 'normal' person. First off, he was too cheap to pay admission fees to get into the dance, so he arrived last minute, then he was far too inquisitive about her financial status, which Gia mistook for 'interest.' Yes, he was interested, but not so much in her.

They met up a few more times at dances (once she paid her own admission fee) and each time he gave her his full attention. They saw each other for several months, and most of that was either taking short drives in his mother's car (and her gas) or sitting around in Gia's living room talking about nothing in particular while eating her food and snacks. During their time together, there were no invitations to dinner in a restaurant, but he did ask his mother to cook a meal for them a few times. He would not take her out to a dance or to parties. Unless Gia invited him and paid for the reservations or tickets, they went nowhere.

Colin arrived, unannounced, one afternoon and during their conversation, he told her he had recently retired from the police force and had moved home, with his mother. He told her that he had been born and brought up in Kanyon Cove. He explained that the section he had worked in had been disbanded causing an early retirement and a buyout package. The lady he had lived with during his career had retired from her job and was living off her work pension, so he moved out and left her behind. If the money was not flowing, in a full-fledged pay cheque, he wanted to find a new interest. Living off her pension was not his style.

He was at her house so much of the time, that all of a sudden, he was living there. They shared a bed, but that was it. There was no relationship per se, just a friendship. There was no sex, but there were cuddles here and there. She bought groceries, and he ate them. She paid her phone bill, and he used her phone. He never offered to pay for anything. She soon realized what a cheapskate he really was. The friendship remained even though she began to resent his freeloading. He was not a bad roommate, and he kept her house spotlessly clean, which was when she noticed that he was very anal. There was never anything left lying around. Items had to be where they belonged, and at first, she thought it was sweet that he was so neat and tidy. It felt a little bit like the movie,

Cape Fear. Along with the obsessive-compulsive behavior, she began to notice mood swings.

At times, he was quite moody and withdrawn, and Gia took it as a sign that maybe he had something on his mind. On those days, he would not speak to her at all or barely spoke a single word. Then there were days when he wouldn't shut up for five minutes. He would ramble on and on until she wanted to scream, 'shut up!' Other times he would go from being moody and sullen to dancing around the living room with a broom pretending it was his dance partner. On these days, he was quite a show-off, and everything was funny to him. She soon learned to rely on his actions the first thing in the morning. It determined what mood he was in and whether he would speak to her or raise hell all day. It was like having an untrained cat around the house where you wouldn't know if it would be hanging off the drapes or hiding under a bed.

Shortly after Colin moved in, he got a letter from a lawyer. His former live-in was asking for a settlement for their time together. She was insisting on a one-time payment of ten thousand dollars. Needless to say, he went into panic mode. This spelled out 'dollars' to him, and he was not willing to part with any of his money. He had invited Gia to the appointment he had set up with his lawyer. She figured he had invited her only because he needed a ride to the city. He also invited her to sit in on the meeting. It was there that she'd learned about his finances. He had investments of a quarter of a million dollars plus a sizeable balance in his bank account, and he lived on that. She reminded herself that he'd worked hard and saved his pennies and deserved what he had. His lawyer suggested the ten-thousand-dollar settlement was reasonable and it would be cheaper than fighting it out in court. He relented and took the lawyer's advice.

Gia's work began to slow down, and soon she was taking money from her savings in order to take care of her house, lease her car, and put food on the table. With no money coming in, her funds had dwindled to no savings, the RRSP's were cashed in, and her bank account was empty.

They were driving home from the grocery store on yet another day that he'd watched her bring out her Visa card to pay for the groceries. Pulling over to the side of the road, he pointed out a few cans and bottles that were lying around and suggested she go and get them.

"They are worth five cents for deposit," he said, "they add up you know."

With a sinking heart, she realized she had no choices left. With a lump in her throat and tears nipping at her eyelids, she got out of the car and picked up the empty beer, pop and liquor bottles and cans that were lying around in the ditches and roadsides. She got so used to watching the roadsides, as she drove, that it became a habit. She found that she could not pass by an empty bottle or can without stopping. She knew that the more she found, the more coins she would have. When they took them to the recycle depot, there would be only a few dollars. It was disheartening, but she had no choice. It was all she had between her, starvation and the necessities of life. She soon learned that Sundays were a perfect time to go looking for recyclables. It was just after the weekend partiers and those who still believed in drinking and driving. The roadsides were littered with pop cans, beer bottles and cans, liquor and wine bottles, and everything else that was returnable and worth five cents.

One day on her travels, she noticed a dumpster on the side of a road. It was near a lake where summer and year around residents used for their garbage. Gia stopped, looked both ways to be certain no one was watching her and lifted the lid of the dumpster. It was as if she had hit a jackpot! It was almost full of recyclables! There were blue bags galore! The residents, who came from other places, did not recycle and couldn't be bothered to do it. So, everything went into the dumpster. She hurriedly put the bags in her trunk and closed the lid. She kept a bottle of hand sanitizer in her car and cleaned her hands before starting the car. Gia was more than grateful for the donations to her grocery and gas money.

Colin still had not offered to help her even in a small way. She still bought groceries, paid the bills and lived from day to day using her Visa card and no money to make even a minimum payment. When life as he knew it at Gia's changed, he moved back in with his mother. She had come home one day and found him waiting for her. He was drinking a glass of her wine and sitting at her table with his jacket on. His mother's car was sitting in the driveway with everything he owned, piled in the back seat.

Colin was a bipolar, gold digging, bastard who thought about no one except himself, and as soon as he figured that she was of no use to him, he moved on leaving her flat broke. He still had his fortune safely stored and accruing interest.

When Gia finally accepted that her company was finished, she didn't have the luxury of time to sit around and mourn or feel sorry for herself. She had to come up with some sort of plan to get herself going again. Speaking with a few senior family friends, she came up with a plan to create another business. She began to do light housekeeping duties for seniors and families who wanted and needed her services. She had planned a weekly schedule that filled her weekdays, and she soon had money coming in on a regular basis. She was once again making regular trips to the bank to deposit small amounts into her account. She finally had her independence back.

She found out that Colin was already in a relationship within weeks of moving out. He had met someone at the same place where he had met Gia. She was certain he had been on the lookout for someone before he left Gia broke and alone. She silently wished his new 'sugar mama' good luck, and hoped she had a healthier bank account than she did.

Shortly after Colin left, she had an email from Beau. Little did she know that he had been keeping up with Gia's life through a friend. He knew what had happened between her and Colin. He asked for her phone number and then he called her from somewhere across the world. It was great to hear his voice after so much time had passed. After the pleasantries were over, he came right out and asked if he could deposit a few bucks into her account to help her out. Relenting, she knew she couldn't refuse. He told her he would deposit enough in her account to pay off her Visa balance and enough to tide her over. Thanking him, he listened to her cry and feel sorry for herself but before the call was over, his kind, loving words helped her to face life and move on. The tears were mostly those of relief to have someone on her side that cared for her. He continued to deposit money into her account every few weeks until she was stable enough to be completely on her own.

Gino Bordaro

A friend of Gia's was going out of town and asked Gia to house sit for her. The house was situated directly across the street from a golf course, and it was up for sale. The friend needed someone in the house in case of an unexpected viewing.

The realtor called to make an appointment for the afternoon. The doorbell rang right on time, and when Gia answered the door, the realtor introduced her to Gino Bordaro. He had become interested in the location since he was an avid golfer and he played every day, weather permitting.

When they were introduced, she thought she must have said 'hello' the wrong way, because for some unknown reason he thought she had the hots for him. He took the tour through the house with the realtor, all the while showing more and more interest in Gia. At first, though, he thought the house belonged to her.

After the showing, he asked if she would join him for dinner. Sensing that he was a decent older man, she agreed. During the meal, he told her that he was an American summer resident. He came across the border from April to October and wintered in Fort Lauderdale, Florida. Gia guessed he was a man in his early to mid-seventies. He made it plain, but non-verbal, that he was rich, hoping she'd be impressed. This gave her the impression that he was a womanizer. She made her own money she was not looking for a rich sugar daddy. He had many interesting stories to tell, and she enjoyed his company, but she knew it would never go beyond that. Gino had opposing thoughts to hers and began to act as if he owned her. Besides being an 'old fart,' he enjoyed having her at his side in restaurants. After a few dinner dates Gia saw a pattern forming, and she didn't like it. He telephoned her relentlessly, and he showed up on her doorstep unannounced and soon became a real pest, so she refused to answer his calls, thanks to call display. When fall rolled around, and he went back to the States, she was relieved.

~

One day when Gia was at the bank waiting to be served, she saw Gino come in and go directly to the ATM. Ignoring him, she acted as if she hadn't noticed him at all. She went about her business and lo and behold when she finished at the counter; there he was waiting for her. She thought 'this is not going to be good,' but he was friendly enough, and so was she. It was not long before he started asking questions. He'd heard through the grapevine that her first business had failed. He was under the impression she was desperate and needed him. They were back to square one. He offered to buy her lunch, so they could catch up, and she accepted. After a few dinners, he began knocking on her door again.

When he'd realized that his charms weren't working on her and that she still only wanted his friendship, he began to proposition her. He asked her if she would do certain things for money! She got her feathers up over it, he asked her what the big deal was. She told him she had no interest in him, in that way. He then told her how she could benefit from his money. He thought if he could talk her into them using each other they would both benefit from it, and that she could rebuild her bank account faster. She told him, in no uncertain terms, that she would not become anyone's whore.

Rumor had it that he had been a gigolo in his younger days, but clearly, he had not changed. Having her own cleaning business and earning her own money with a broom, mop and cleaning rags was looking pretty damned good compared to what he was offering her!

The Visit

During a Christmas holiday, she got a call from Beau. She could count on one hand the calls she'd received from him since his job had taken him on assignments around the world. Christmastime had brought him to the town where his parents had bought a summer home. Even though it was winter, to be nearer Gia, he had decided to come there for the holidays. Somewhere in the conversation, the possibility of getting together came up. A suggestion was made for her to visit after the New Year. He could sense her excitement, and in the voice that she knew and loved, he cautiously said, "Are you OK with this?"

She read between the lines as he was telling her that it was just a visit and that nothing had changed.

"Yes, I'm sure, don't worry about me Beau, I'll be fine."

She knew what he was getting at, that he had broken her heart before and he did not want any further heartache for her. She knew he was going to be home for only a few weeks and would be gone again sometime into the New Year. She had made up her mind long ago that if she ever were to get a chance to see him again, she would accept whatever terms were offered. Knowing there was no commitment, and never would be, she still wanted to be with him. She could not, and would not, pass up this opportunity.

Plans were arranged, and a ticket for her to travel was waiting at the station and he'd asked her to bring along her passport.

The waiting was the hardest part. Christmas... after Christmas... New Year's Eve passed quietly... and finally, the day arrived for her to leave. She had taken the Shuttle to the train station, and she talked to herself the entire ride. Hoping to be nonchalant, there'd be no way he wouldn't be convinced that she could handle seeing him and leave without a scene. He would see a different side of her, a more 'grown-up' version of her than before he left. Still, those memories crept in just the same, and she had to really think about what she was doing. 'Is it a good idea? Should I put myself through it again?' She may as well have been talking to a stump because all caution had been thrown to the wind as soon as she heard his voice on the phone. She was going to be with Beau no matter what.

Remembering again... the morning they had packed up his car, and she stood brokenheartedly watching him leave. Memories kept creeping in to haunt her just a little bit. Her heart still ached when she went back too deeply into those moments, so she tried not to, but it still felt like it was yesterday.

Finally, when the time had come for her to board the train, she was ecstatic to be on her last leg of the journey before seeing him again. The trip would take seven hours, and she had lots of time to talk herself down and remind herself once again that this was only a visit and nothing else. Absolutely nothing else. She had to keep control over her thoughts, her wants and wishes, her desires and most of all, her heart. She had to fasten herself together, mentally so that she wouldn't fall apart, and she had seven hours in which to practice. She could not allow her fantasy world to creep in and make this more than it actually was. Every possible scenario went through her mind during the train ride. Her mind wanted to picture him as realizing what a mistake he'd made by leaving her behind and the 'happily ever after' was finally here. The White Knight was finally riding in to rescue her. No!! She had to let those fantasies go, and believe they were gone, forever.

Darkness had already set in when the train finally pulled into the station. Excitement took over as the train rolled slowly to a stop. Her heart began to beat faster and faster. She felt as if she were a teenager awaiting her first date for the prom. From her compartment window, she searched for a glimpse of Beau among the people waiting to greet other passengers, but she didn't see him. Her heart sank immediately in disappointment, and a whole lot of fear gathered. She hated darkness, 'what if he changed his mind and didn't come for her! Where was he?' It was dark, she was in a strange place, and there was no one to meet her! The station lights showed only the front of the platform. For a few minutes, her thoughts ran wild as she stepped out of her compartment and into the aisle to disembark. A uniformed station worker was standing on the platform at the exit, offering to take her suitcase and help her off the train.

"Is there someone here to meet you, ma'am?"

"I hope so," she replied as she searched the platform for Beau.

"I'll take your suitcase inside for you ma'am; it's cold out here."

The thoughts of having to wait at a train station alone weighed heavily on her mind. Just as she turned to follow him inside the station, she saw Beau waving his arm and running as fast as he could down the platform. When he approached her, he picked her up off her feet, swung her around in a circle, then set her back on the ground and kissed her. "I'll take that sir," Beau said, taking the suitcase. He turned and explained to Gia that he had been down at the front where he thought she'd get off, but instead she got off at the middle of the train. When he realized he had made a mistake, he ran down to find her.

On the way to the cottage, they stopped at a restaurant for a bite to eat. They both ordered soup and a sandwich. Of course, the first couple sips of soup opened the sinuses, and Gia searched her pockets and handbag for a tissue but to no avail. 'Now what?' she thought, as she tried to silently sniff and use her napkin to dab at her mouth and nonchalantly touch the tip of her nose at the same time. She was so disgusted with herself for not having a tissue and feared she would embarrass both herself and Beau. 'What a way to make a good impression, snot in your soup!' She was horrified and did not want to eat. She kept pressing the napkin to her mouth and touching her nose when she thought no one was looking.

When Beau came to her rescue, it was just like old times and time had stood still. He could see that she was in distress, so he laid his spoon down on the edge of the bowl. He leaned back in his chair with his face toward the ceiling, laid his paper napkin over his entire face, put two fingers next to his nose and blew out in a loud 'toot.' Gia got the giggles and said, "Oh thank, God!" As she blew her nose, too, they both laughed over the incident. Beau was still able to make her feel like she could be herself around him; that part of him had not changed.

It was snowing lightly as they approached the cottage. He loved the waterfront property his parents had purchased, and as they pulled up in the driveway, the headlights made it look like a winter wonderland. There was snow on the trees, the Bay was frozen over, and it was white for miles, even in the darkness. This place was not like the log cabin they had spent a Christmas in; it was more like a small two-bedroom cottage.

Walking in, she recognized many of the items he'd had when he lived in Hartley's Cove. Same stuff, different time, different house, same feelings.

Her heart swelled, and her eyes welled up as she wondered again, 'is it a good idea to be here?' Beau realized, seeing so many familiar things, was really affecting her. He was quick to explain that when he was leaving to go overseas, he needed a place to store his things. He didn't want to leave his stuff in storage for years. It made the cottage homier than just the bedding and dishes his parents had brought.

Beau made sure she was comfortable. He put her bag in the spare bedroom where she would have more room to maneuver. The bedrooms were small, and in the master, there was no room for her suitcase. She just unzipped it, flipped the top open and used what she needed when she needed it. It was perfect.

She had not been there very long when Beau scooped her up in his arms and carried her to the bedroom and laid her down gently on the bed. When they got their fill of each other, they spent the rest of evening talking and laughing about old times, and it was as if time had stood still. The only difference was, he had longer hair and Gia guessed it must be for an undercover job.

The next day he took her on a tour of the area where he now lived whenever he was home. He also showed her around another property he planned to build on someday. She guessed he must really love Canada! When they returned home, he had made several calls and then asked her to pack a few clothes because they were taking a trip the next day.

They crossed the border into Houlton, Maine, found the beginning of I-95 and travelled each day until they saw the sign that said, 'End of I-95.' They had reached Miami. Beau got them a quaint little place with a kitchenette, living room, bedroom and a balcony with a view of South Beach. The weather was gorgeous, and Beau took Gia to buy a pair of shorts, sandals and a hat so they could walk in the sunshine. It was a wintery January back home, and it was as if they were on another planet. They walked along South Beach on white sands and browsed small shops looking for nothing in particular. It was all so surreal to her she had to pinch herself to be sure she was actually there. That evening they strolled hand in hand along a boardwalk and came across an elegant outdoor restaurant. Perfect for what they were looking for, a place to sit down to dine, and a tropical breeze.

After spending a few days at South Beach, they decided it was time to head northward. During the drive, they came upon a roadside sign offering helicopter rides. Beau didn't even ask her if she wanted to go up for a ride because he knew what her first response would be. He left her in the car, sauntered over to a small building and disappeared inside. Gia looked around from the car window at the scary surroundings and prayed that he would hurry up. When he appeared, he just opened her door and said, "Come on, let's go."

"Let's go where?" she answered in surprise. For a brief instant, she thought he was planning to feed her to the alligators.

"We are going on a helicopter ride."

"What! Shut up! I don't like heights!"

"Aw, come on, stop being a Wuss, it'll be fun," he said as he led her by the elbow to the helicopter."

She wondered if people felt like this when they were being led to an execution. Fear gripped her as soon as she saw the inside of the helicopter.

"Let me help you up," Beau said, smiling at her, "it'll be fun."

'Fun!' she thought, 'fun?' And then all the 'what if's' started up in her head. 'What if it crashes on take-off? When they were up a little higher, what if we crash, what if we don't make the turn and the blades fall off? What if the pilot has a heart attack? How fast will this thing fall?' There were so many 'what if's' that she had all she could do to try and enjoy what sights the pilot pointed out. It was thrilling to be up in the sky, but it was mixed with the feeling of something dreadful happening while they were flying. She had the knee of Beau's pant leg wadded up in her fist, and if anything were to happen to her, he was going with her!

The view was breathtaking as they passed over magnificent waterfront mansions, resorts, popular food companies and properties belonging to the rich and famous. It had only been a fifteen or twenty-minute ride, but to Gia, it felt more like two hours. The control factor was stronger than her willingness to sit there as a free spirit and enjoy the ride. Once they got back to the helicopter pad and she had her feet back on solid ground, it did not seem so bad and Beau laughed at her for being such a chicken.

"Look at my pant leg," he said, "I have a permanent knot on my knee."

"No more surprises then and you won't have any more knots," she joked as they walked back to the car. Both were glad they had taken the ride.

They got back in the car and headed north again. Gia never knew what Beau was going to do, and since she was surprised with a helicopter ride, she doubted they were going straight home. Another sign appeared on the side of the road, and Beau slowed down so he could read it. Gia's heart dropped as he put the signal light on and made the turn. Getting off the highway, she turned her head to get a glimpse of the sign, 'Tour the Everglades.' She sat up poker straight toward the windshield.

"Beau! Are you insane?" she said as he pulled the car into the parking lot.

"We'll be on a boat; you'll be fine."

"I won't be fine; I'll wait for you here in the car! Remember the pant leg?"

He had that smile on his face that told her she was defeated as he tilted his head and said, "I don't think so." He went around and helped her out of the car, by the elbow again. Now she really felt like he was leading her to an alligator pit!

Beau was such a free spirit; and she loved that about him. He was willing to try anything at least once, including food. The only food that she was aware of that he didn't like, was celery. He hated celery!

He still had hold of her elbow as they approached the fellow who was obviously in charge of the tours. He greeted them and told them there was a seating area where a fellow was putting on a sideshow until the craft was ready for the next tour. Beau led her around the corner, and they found a seat to watch the show. A man came out with a baby alligator, and its jaws were wrapped with grey duct tape. People, in the audience, were encouraged to come down and hold the critter and have pictures taken with a live alligator. Beau took her by the elbow again, and, just like that, like it or not, they were standing next to the alligator. The man laid the gator carefully in her open hands. He knew she was afraid, so he stood close beside her. Beau took a picture of her, and she gladly handed the reptile back.

Stepping onto the airboat, they found a seat at the outside edge for a full view. Gia forced away the urge to get back on solid ground where she felt she had full control of herself. 'Now there's an understatement,' she thought, as the airboat roared off into the Everglades. Beau took her hand, squeezed it and non-verbally told her to relax and enjoy the experience. It helped a little. 'We could be eaten alive by gators out here,' she mumbled to herself. Beau just smiled and squeezed her hand. As the boat skimmed across the Everglades, they could see alligators slipping into the water from the riverbanks. Some were enormous as they wound their way across the muddy banks and disappeared under water. They were close enough to the riverbanks for Gia to take photos of the exotic and colorful birds that were perched on tree branches that hung over the water. Birds of all colors, in brilliant blues and yellows, were magnificent looking creatures.

Somewhere in the middle of the Everglades, the boat came to a stop. Gia's first instinct was that it had run out of gas or had broken down. The owner of the airboat turned his seat around to face the group and told them it was a safe place to stop. He began to encourage the passengers to go out and stand in the water to have their picture taken. Beau jumped right on that.

"All you have to do is step over the rail and down several steps and stand in the water for a few seconds, just long enough to have a picture taken," the owner said. Gia was having none of it, but Beau began to encourage her to go, and she finally relented. Taking off her sandals, she stepped over the rail and onto the ladder. She was searching the Everglades for any sign of movement. She slowly went down the few steps and into the water and then onto the soft and mushy bottom of the 'glades.'

There she was! Standing knee deep in the alligator-infested swamp in the middle of the Florida Everglades! She let go of the railings and raised her arms straight up into the air in triumph as Beau snapped a picture. She climbed back into the boat and Beau wrapped his arms around her with pride. "You did it!" he boasted as he passed back her sandals and camera. Life was so much fun with him, and although he knew about her fears, he never degraded her for having them, he just tried tenderly to help her overcome them.

The next stop was Disney World. The weather had cooled off considerably, so their first stop inside the gates was at a booth for something warmer to wear. He bought matching Mickey Mouse sweatshirts and then they began their day. They did Space Mountain, where she had put a bottle of water in the front pouch pocket of her sweatshirt, and when she got off the ride, the bottle was gone. On to, It's a Small World, Cinderella's Castle, Magic Kingdom, and The Hall of Presidents. They saw The Swiss Family Robinson's Tree House; they took the train ride and finally ended it off at Splash Mountain where Beau nearly lost his cookies during the five and a half story drop at the end of the ride.

They'd had a long day and what they both wanted was a hot shower to get the chill of the day, off them. They found a room just outside of Orlando with room service and spent a pleasant night inside.

During the ride back, she was trying to absorb all that she had accomplished in the last few days. The standoffish wallflower with the 'nobody loves me; nobody cares' self-absorbing attitude she carried, suddenly seemed to peel away a little as an exhilarating feeling of freedom flowed through her body.

The happy-sad mood began to creep in again as she realized the exhilaration was due to Beau's free spirit. She knew, and allowed herself to remember, that it was coming to an end. The end was always front and center for her and Beau. It was always in the foreground. People usually didn't anticipate the ending; they just enjoyed the moments as they came, but not Gia. She never wanted her time with Beau to end. The only time her life made sense, was when it was shared with him. Gia knew her ending, and she lived it moment for moment, not with anticipation but mostly with the inevitable.

With all the excitement and sunshine behind them, they continued northward. They brought out their layers of winter apparel as they drove farther north. They spent a few days on the road and checked into motels at night. Finally, in the middle of the afternoon on the third day of travel, they reached New York City. When Beau told her they were staying a night or two in New York, she was ecstatic. They stayed at the Sheridan on Park Avenue in downtown Manhattan. They were just around the corner from Central Park and the few blocks from the Lincoln Centre.

The room was beautifully decorated, with English country décor; nine-foot beamed ceilings, cherry wood furnishings and an oversized desk. The bed had an extra thick, plush top mattress. It was made up with three sheets, fleece blankets, plump down duvets and six or more feather pillows. The bathroom was finished in marble with a pedestal sink. Included, were bathrobes, a hair dryer and just about every amenity one would need for a few nights stay. It was the height of elegance to Gia, but it was just another room to Beau because, in his travels, he had stayed in many hotels and likely fancier places. As soon as they were settled in their room, they were off on a foot tour to see what was in the area.

It was only a few blocks to Grand Central Station. As they stood on the sidewalk, looking at the magnificent building, Beau grabbed her hand and ran inside just so they could say they were inside of Grand Central Station! The entire inside was made of wood. It was massive, and people were scurrying around the station, like rats, going in all directions.

They came upon Toys-R-Us and went inside to stand and look around, just because they could. They made their way to the theatre district to see what was playing. Patti Duke was starring in 'Oklahoma!' so, Beau went up to the ticket booth and bought tickets for the early performance. It would give them time to go back to the hotel, eat and walk back down for the show. It was the first live play that Gia had ever seen. The play was very entertaining, and they both enjoyed it, besides, who didn't adore Patty Duke? Beau had taken her the see Cats and Les Misérables, while they were dating, but this was New York City!

When the play ended, they went outside and found a waiting car. A chauffeur was standing beside it and he smiled and tipped his hat at them as they came out. Opening the back door, the chauffeur smiled at Gia and invited her in. Her jaw dropped almost to the sidewalk. Helping her in, Beau had already given the driver instructions as to where to go. He had surprised her by having reserved a Lincoln Towne car to pick them up outside the theatre. The chauffeur had instructions to give them a tour of New York City's most popular spots. While they were driving, Beau put his arm around her, picked up her hand with his free one and put it to his lips. He told her he had wanted to reserve a limo, but there were none available. She was touched that he would do such a sweet thing for her.

It was nighttime as they drove, but New York City is never really in darkness. The city lights were a multitude of brilliant colors. There were flashing billboards, twinkling lights and no matter where you looked; there were people. It was, 'the city that never sleeps.'

They could still see certain things that the driver pointed out to them. Times Square was amazing as they passed by on their way to Central Park. Although they could not see into the park, it was familiar from what they would have seen on TV. He showed them 'Ground Zero,' and at that time it had fences all around it and dirt, dust and rubble was still visible. They came upon the triangle-shaped building that Gia had often seen on TV, and she recognized it immediately. Driving into Soho, they saw Madison Square Gardens, Lincoln Center, Carnegie Hall, Broadway theatre district and then down the famous shopping district of Fifth Avenue. They drove over to see where the Staten Island ferry terminal was. There were too many places on the tour for her to remember, but it felt as if it were all a dream. Gia, being toured around New York City in a Lincoln Towne car, was the absolute height of her life.

The next day Beau had a business meeting regarding his upcoming assignment. Gia spent a lazy day in their room. She took a long, leisurely bath in the enormous tub, and afterwards she wrapped up in the thick fluffy bathrobe and spread herself out on the bed surrounded by pillows. She felt like she was making snow angels. 'So, this is what they call, The Life of Riley,' she thought, as she stretched out on the bed with a grin. She took pictures, from the hotel window, of the many Yellow Cabs that were scattered all over the streets. If she had to come up with a color for New York City, she would have to say yellow. There were literally hundreds of Yellow Cabs outside their hotel window.

She was dressed by the time Beau got back, and they watched TV for a short time and then decided it was time to go out for a meal. They ate at a Greek restaurant not far from the hotel, and afterwards, they strolled along Park Avenue. There was everything to see without looking for other streets for window shopping.

Their stay in New York City was over. The next morning, Beau called to have his car brought around to the front door, and they were off again. They spent the next fourteen hours on the road to make it to Beau's place. The days had flown by quickly, mile after mile passed under them and soon, they were back in Beau's driveway. It had been a whirlwind trip. They had lots of fun, and experiences that Gia would remember forever. They had both managed a nice tan with all the outdoor activities, but sadness was setting in for Gia. She tried her very best not to show it.

They were back from their trip for only a few days when reality set in, and Gia knew it was time for her to go home. She was aware that she had to give Beau time to get his life ready for his trip back to 'God knows where.'

"I think I should leave tomorrow," she said walking up to him as he lay on the couch reading a book. She felt a sense of pride at that moment, and she sensed that Beau was proud of her, too. His face showed that he had never expected her to leave until she absolutely had to. She seemed to have taken him, quite literally, by surprise because his head shot up as her words sank in.

"Geez, I guess it is that time, isn't it? I should be getting my travel plans in order as well."

So, the words were said, a plan was made, and time was ticking. She knew he had lots to do for his own trip, which is why she took it upon herself to act responsively and pretend she had accepted the terms of this trip. After all, she had told him she had accepted the terms of the visit, so she had to keep up the ruse. This way, she could leave on her terms and not his, this time. She certainly didn't want to be embarrassed, by him asking her when she was going to start packing.

The Ride Home

They were standing on the platform in front of her compartment door. Her heart was heavy heart, but she smiled as if her world was perfect. Tears were stinging the backs of her eyes as she stood beside Beau knowing she'd have to let him go, again. 'Don't you dare cry!' she scolded herself.

All Aboard! She nearly came unglued when she heard those words. Wrapping her arms around Beau's neck, he squeezed her tightly. They both admitted they had a great time and he promised to call when he got back to his destination. He kissed her and gave her one more squeeze before helping her on the train. She went into her compartment and stood at the window to wave at him.

Slowly, the train began to move away from the station, and Beau walked alongside the train. Gia pressed her forehead and her palms against the window and against her better judgment; she mouthed the words, 'I love you,' as she waved back at him. It was no surprise to him since he knew how she felt. As the train gathered speed, he blew her a kiss as he ran alongside of the train. As it picked up more steam, she saw him stop as he ran out of platform. She waved until he was out of sight and at her last glimpse; his arm was flying in the air and still blowing kisses. She knew he enjoyed spending time with her, but his life got in the way.

Slowly, she sat down in the chair and dropped her face into her palms to finally allow the tears to run free. She had been holding them back for the past few days, and now there was nothing from which to hide. She was in a compartment by herself, and there was no one to tell her how to feel, think or act. She was in control of her life again, and she would cry until she felt better. She had a seven-hour trip to feel sorry for herself, and she made good use of the time. The feeling in the pit of her stomach felt worse than having an ulcer. She was hurting so badly knowing she was going in one direction and he would be going in another.

Sadness set in as she thought about the possibility of not ever seeing Beau again. She was glad to have Patti to confide in when she returned. She had not seen Patti in a year, and she was excited to share her good news about seeing Beau again.

Gia had cried and bawled over Beau for weeks after he'd left, and Patti took it all in stride and stayed by her side saying all the right things or nothing at all. She felt exactly the same way as when he drove away from her all those years ago, only this time she was leaving him.

The train rolled on, and as the hours passed, it gave her time to think. She would return from her trip, a little sadder but very grateful for the opportunity to have seen Beau again. It had been four years, with only random calls in-between, since she had seen him. In her heart of hearts, she knew she would never see him again and once again she was torn between happy to have had the adventure and sad that it was over.

Patti Stevens

Since the train station was in the city, Gia wanted to visit with Patti before she made her final journey back to Kanyon Cove. She had so much to tell her, and she could barely contain herself. Taking a cab to Patti's address, she rang her doorbell. Surprise had slapped her in the face when Patti opened the door. It had been a while since they had seen each other, but Gia knew as soon as she saw her, that something definitely was wrong.

"Gia! Come in!" she said, holding her arms open for a hug.

"Patti, I wanted to see you before I leave the city."

"Where have you been?"

"I just got back from visiting with Beau."

"What!? Do tell!"

"We'll get to that, but first, Patti, how are you? You don't look well."

"Oh God, is it that bad? I have been feeling like a slug lately, but I didn't think it was that noticeable."

"Have you seen a doctor?"

She assured her that she had and that she was sure they were missing something in her tests even though they all came back with no abnormalities. She said she had told her doctor about the pain she was having in her stomach, especially when her cycle came around. He took tests including a pap test, blood work and an internal exam but everything came back normal. Patti still continued to have severe pain from time to time and considered getting a second opinion.

"I'm worried though, Gia, I'm almost certain something is wrong."

If Patti was admitting fear to Gia, then there was definitely a reason to worry.

"If you are still concerned, Patti, you must ask your doctor for a referral to a specialist, you need a second opinion. Would you consider coming home with me for a while and we'll do this together? We have a few good specialists in Kanyon Cove. We'll get to the bottom of this one way or the other."

Patti agreed and was relieved that someone cared enough to be as concerned as she was. They had talked long into the night about Gia's trip to see Beau and Patti's trips to see doctors.

The next day they had loaded up Patti's car and Gia drove them home. She was relieved that she didn't have to call the shuttle.

Gia got Patti settled into her spare room and insisted that she lay down for a rest. She was worried about her friend and felt responsible to care for her since there was no one else to do it. She knew that Patti would always be there for her no matter what and she was glad to have her there, with her. She closed the door to Patti's room and made her way to her bedroom.

As she unpacked her suitcase, she noticed her Christmas gifts piled neatly on the dresser and among the gifts sat a teddy bear. Gia smiled as she remembered receiving the teddy bear for Christmas just a few weeks ago. Picking it up, she pressed its head into her neck and hugged it. As if consoling a baby, she rocked back and forth, holding it in her arms. As she closed her eyes, she remembered Beau running beside the train waving goodbye. She knew that what she was going through was her own fault, but she didn't care. She would rather feel sad than feel nothing at all. She clung to the little teddy bear as if it were the last shred of Beau she would ever have. An attachment grew between 'Bo Bear' and Gia that day. She certainly understood how children could become attached to an inanimate object.

Bo Bear lived on her bed. It sat there all day, but at night, she wrapped it in her arms and held it close. When she woke up in the morning, it was still there. She never lost it in the bed sheets nor did it fall out onto the floor. It was always with her.

It did not bother her when people saw it on her bed and commented on it.

"Nice teddy bear. Is it yours?"

She always replied, "Yes, it's mine, it was a gift."

"At your age?" came the response.

"I didn't know there was an age limit on teddy bears," was her defensive comeback. By the tone she used, the conversation about teddy bears was over. She was like a defensive child, nothing and no one was going to separate her from her bear. She would not put herself in a position to be intimidated by anyone and hadn't for many years. It was something she'd learned in therapy.

The Big 'C'

Hearing about several new doctors in town, Gia took it upon herself to call the hospital for their phone numbers and gave them to Patti. By squeezing her in, Patti got an appointment for the following day, and Gia insisted on going with her. As they sat in the waiting room, Gia could sense that Patti was extremely anxious. She watched as she wrung her hands and moved her hair around unnecessarily. Reaching over, Gia touch her hand and Patti laid hers on top and gave a 'thank you' squeeze.

When Patti's name was called, Gia went into instant flashback mode to that scary place so long ago at the abortion clinic. Patti had been only seventeen, and here they were years later, and Gia was reliving that horrible time all over again.

"No, I'm sorry Ms. Lake," the nurse insisted, "you'll have to wait here." Hearing the words, she wrapped Patti in her arms trying to erase nurse Ratchette's voice from her memory. Déjà vu, all over again.

"I'll be right here, girlfriend, just like before."

"Thanks, my friend," Patti whispered and sadly nodded her head as if the same memory was haunting her. Gia could feel Patti's body tremble as she hugged her.

When Patti disappeared into the doctor's office, Gia sat down and looked around at faces that made no sense to her. Her eyes filling with tears, she put her an elbow on the arm of the chair and cupped her forehead with her fingertips. She was lost for words and prayer as she sat and waited and waited.

Gia jumped promptly to her feet when Patti finally appeared from the office. Reading her expression, they walked wordlessly outside arm in arm until they reached the sidewalk.

"There's a café just down the street," Gia said, "we can talk there."

"What happened in there?" Gia asked softly while cupping her drink.

"He ran different tests this time, Gia. Several tests I had done before, but I think this doctor is looking for something else. I mentioned the abdominal discomfort, cramps and bloating, which could be related to my periods and likely menopause. I should be finished with these damned periods anyway! How long does it take to get through menopause? Seriously Gia, this feels different. I don't usually feel this useless and worn out."

"How long before you get some results?"

"Sometime this week, a few days, I guess, they'll call when they're ready. Oh Gia, I'm not feeling good about this. It's making me really nervous."

"Then I'm going with you when the tests come in."

"Thanks, Gia, I was hoping you'd offer."

A few days passed at a snail's pace, and finally, Patti got the call she was waiting for.

"One o'clock this afternoon," she said, wringing her hands.

"We'll go together."

"Thanks, Gia, I really need you."

They were back in the waiting room at twelve fifty-five and were already being herded into a small room to await the doctor. They were both nervous, and even small talk seemed useless, so they didn't try. Patti habitually fluffed her hair, nibbled on her nails and watched the clock on the wall. Watching Patti, Gia became more aware and anxious with each tick of the second hand.

A turn of the doorknob startled them. They both looked up at the doctor's face trying to read his expression, but there was none.

Sitting down, he opened Patti's file, read for a few seconds, flipped a few sheets of paper, cleared his throat and began.

"Ms. Stevens," he said rolling his eyes up to look at her over the rims of his glasses.

Gia's first thought was, 'the sod doesn't have the decency to pick up his head,' and she already didn't like him. Patti was only a name on a page to him and nothing more, an office visit paid for by our government, that's all that mattered. He had seen her only once on the initial visit for tests and she may as well have been a specimen in a Petri dish, in a lab.

"I'm afraid I don't have very good news for you," he paused only briefly then continued. "The tests show late stages of ovarian cancer."

Air escaped Patti's lung as if she had just been unplugged and deflating.

Gia looked at Patti the moment she heard the word 'cancer,' and time seemed to stop. Patti reached out for Gia's hand while slowly turning to look at her with furrowed eyebrows as if to say, 'What did he just say?'

"Gia?" Patti whispered. Turning back to the doctor, one word fell off her lips, "What?"

"The symptoms you have been experiencing in recent months should have been diagnosed sooner. You were correct in asking for a second opinion, but I am afraid it was caught too late.

"What do you mean, too late?" Gia snapped.

"It is far too advanced for treatment. I'm sorry to have to tell you this but I've done all I can."

'You cold-hearted bastard!' was on the tip of Gia's tongue. She began to bristle now in her friend's defense knowing Patti had gone into shock at his words.

"Really? That's all you can do. Are you serious, right now? There are no recommendations for treatments or therapy of any kind?" Gia blurted out. "It's 'over,' that's all you've got?" Gia had a sudden urge to reach across his desk and rip his face off.

"She can certainly consider chemo and radiation treatments, but I wouldn't recommend it, not for this late stage of ovarian cancer. It certainly will not prolong the inevitable and will only add to the deterioration of her quality of life."

"Deteriorate her quality of life? What are you saying? How much time are we talking about here?" Gia spoke with annoyance as her dislike, for this ignorant man, grew. He was saying horrible things about her friend as if she wasn't even in the room!

"I'd say a year at best," he said as he handed her several pamphlets, all of which had 'dealing with cancer' written on the front of them. Gia was livid! She, too, had momentarily forgotten that Patti was still in the room, as she was blinded by hatred toward this dog they called a doctor as she fiercely defended Patti.

"Patti?" Gia whispered, "I'm so sorry honey, are you ready to go?" She glared at the doctor as she touched Patti's elbow for her to stand up.

She allowed Gia to maneuver her out of the building as if she were a child. Getting her to the sidewalk, she helped her in the passenger side of the car and fastened her seatbelt as if she were, indeed, a child. In the short amount of time it took for Gia to close one door and opened the other, screams could be heard a block wide. Jumping into the car, she pulled Patti into her arms, and they cried together.

"Gia," she sobbed, "I'm only fifty-one years old! I'm not prepared for this."

"I know Patti, I'm so sorry!" That was all Gia was able to say. Patti needed time to process and all Gia could do was to be there for her.

Patti had decided that she wanted to do the treatments. She wanted to do as much as possible to prolong her life. The nature of the beast.

~

Going through the rounds of chemo, she experienced no complications of any kind. She was not sick or weak afterwards. Gia wondered if they actually gave her chemo treatments or just placated her. She felt very fortunate and was sure the treatments were working. Gia was so proud of her, and the fact that she was fighting desperately for her life. Patti had a completely new outlook on life and felt she had beaten the odds. She looked forward to a future now and hoped she had overcome the impossible.

Then devastation struck again. The treatments had not been successful and actually, they had not touched the cancer at all. Radiation was offered and with little hope left, Patti agreed to take it. The doctor advised that radiation therapy is often given with palliative intent. Palliative treatments are not intended to cure but instead were meant to reduce the suffering caused by cancer. Although she had lost her hair through these treatments, she was still positive.

Patti's diagnoses of the treatments, for ovarian cancer, had devastated Gia. When Patti admitted to her, they hadn't worked, they cried together tried to come to terms with the horrible news.

Going back again to that scary place, where Patti had had her abortion, the same questions haunted her. Health class had taught them that too many sexual partners could likely cause problems down the road. She often wondered if Patti had completely skipped those classes on purpose, so she could continue her lifestyle guilt free by living in denial. Now she was dying from ignorance. Although haunted her, she never once brought it up to Patti. She didn't need the guilt.

~

When she'd returned from the visit with Beau; she had developed a completely new relationship with her TV. CSI (Crime Scene Investigation) was an interesting new show that held her attention because of the newness and graphics of it, but it was not something she cared about if she missed an episode. Then, along came the spin-offs, CSI Miami and CSI NY, and they had quickly become her favorites. Her first mistake was watching them in the first place. They continued to remind her of her trip with Beau, and she continued to go back there in her mind while keeping Beau close to her heart. The location scenes were all very familiar to her, and each one took her back again and again. She, alone, was responsible for her loneliness by constantly reliving the trip and living in her fantasy world where only she and Beau existed. She put herself through hell, only to relive the moments she'd shared with him. It made her feel close to him, and in her world, her TV set could take her back to where she had spent precious time with the love of her life. Sometimes she just wanted to scream at herself to move on, let it go and get a life already, other than the one she was stuck with inside herself.

Finally, the day came when she turned off the TV when those shows appeared on screen. She had finally come to realize that the White Knight was not going to ride in on a steed! He had never planned to and he was never coming back. After all these years the armor was likely cracked, and the damned horse was undoubtedly dead anyway!

She had read something once that made a lot of sense. Not that she took advice well, but she needed to start somewhere.

'The best way to make your dreams come true is to wake up.' In other words, get over it and move on!

There is no sadder love than that which is lost, especially the crippling kind when you refuse to get over it and move forward. A love so deep, that holding on, even by a thread, is better than no love at all. The mind tells you to let go but the heart refuses to listen, and the battle forges on. Heart over mind. Two very powerful forces pulling in each direction. The heart wants to win, if it gives up the fantasy, then that love is gone, and all hope is lost of it ever returning. The mind wants to let it go, give it up, move on, and concentrate on things that are more real and productive. That makes the heart even more determined! Letting go doesn't mean that you care any less about the person. It's realizing that the only person you really have control over, is yourself.

It took her a while but slowly she allowed herself to become open to the thought of another relationship. She reminded herself to call Lane.

~

Gia and Patti spent as much time together as they could during her final year, and Gia watched as her beautiful, young friend deteriorate practically before her eyes. She'd lost her hair to chemotherapy and radiation which was all for nothing because the cancer was too far advanced. However, when she was well enough, they went shopping for the perfect wig.

Patti was in and out of the hospital in the following months and then inevitably into palliative care. Gia was at her bedside almost constantly. There was no other place she'd rather be, than at her friend's side.

It was one year, from the doctor's prediction, late into the evening. Patti had been drifting in and out of consciousness all day. She would be in the middle of a conversation and she'd fall asleep and then come to, just as quickly. She was on a constant drip for the pain, but it was not helping at this stage. Still, it was there, at the push of a button, whenever it was needed.

She was bone thin and too frail to wear her wig at this point. It was too large for her head, and the cap made her head itch. It sat on the wig stand, on her night table, as a reminder. Gia replaced it with a soft microfiber toque that Patti insisted on wearing whenever she had a visitor.

Gia was sitting at her bedside reading a magazine when Patti came back around.

"Hi there," Gia cooed when her eyes opened.

"I guess I faded again, huh?"

"Yes, you did Hon, but that's fine."

"Can you lay with me, Gia?"

"Yes, of course, I can."

Patti was in too weak to move over, so Gia slid her arm under her pillow and laid on the edge of the bed. Patti inched her head close to Gia's chest as Gia cuddled up next to her. Resting her cheek on the top of her bald head, she rubbed her forehead, ever so lightly, with her free hand.

"That feels so good, Gia."

"I'm glad it does, my friend."

"Do you have enough room?" Patti asked.

"I'm OK," she whispered.

"I'm glad you're here with me."

"So am I, girlfriend, I wouldn't be anywhere else, I love you," Gia said as she gently kissed the top of her head. Her skin was sensitive from the treatments and any skin contact aggravated her, so Gia was careful to touch only lightly.

"Thank you for being my friend, Gia," Patti whispered.

Her voice was weak, and Gia had to strain to hear her words.

"It has been my honor to be your friend, Patti."

Patti reached up with the last bit of strength she had left and touched Gia's arm.

"It's been my honor, I love you too, my friend," she whispered.

Gia felt Patti's hand slide slowly off her arm. Life had slipped away from her friend as she held her in her arms. She thought she was prepared, but how does one prepared when losing your best friend. Gia still had her cheek on Patti's head when a nurse came in and saw her tears cascading down onto her friend. The nurse detached the hoses from Patti's machines and turned them off. She tenderly touched Gia's arm and left the room without a word. The room was deathly quiet. No beeping machines, no blinking lights, just ugly silence. Death had tried hard to take Patti so many times, but her will-to-live held out longer than anyone expected. Her battle was over and so was thirty-five years of friendship.

The following days were a blur, and she didn't know how she was ever going to move on from this, but she knew she must. It's what Patti would have wanted and expected her to do. At the end, Patti had no one, except Gia. Patti had burned her bridges with Tony, and they had long been divorced, and there were no children, so Patti had been alone.

As Gia made funeral arrangements, she thought back to how strong Patti had been when she had made all the arrangements for Tommy's funeral. She would not have gotten through that difficult time without her.

After the funeral, Gia decided to go away for a while. She booked a flight to the Bahamas for a couple of weeks and she left without telling anyone about her plans. She just wanted to feel alive again after all those months sitting at Patti's bedside with little or no fresh air. It was time for a change. She had done all she could.

Resting her head against the window of the plane, tears slipped down her cheeks as she watched Kanyon Cove slip away as the plane climbed higher.

Feeling a tug on her heart, she felt Patti's presence for a brief moment.

'Goodbye, my friend.'

Anna

Returning from a ten-day vacation of sunshine and relaxation, Gia barely had time to deal with Patti's death when an incident at another hospital needed her upmost attention. A situation was brewing at the hospital, where their mother was, and needed her immediate attention.

A family meeting was called by Anna's doctor. It was her daughters who'd showed up in the boardroom of the hospital. He told them that Anna had been refusing dialysis, and it was up to the family to decide on what to do next.

"If she refuses treatment," he explained, "then there is nothing the hospital can do."

"But..." Gia began.

"There are no 'buts, in these cases," he interrupted, "it is her right, and without her consent there is nothing we can do."

Leaving the doctor's eye contact, she looked towards her sisters and they too were as dumfounded as she was.

"It seems that my sisters and I were unaware of our mother's inability to make decisions," she explained.

"How can you refuse her dialysis in her state of mind?"

"She was very clear when she made the decision, which is why I have called this meeting. We can't proceed with treatment if she won't agree to go to the renal unit."

Holding firmly to his statement, he reiterated that she had the right to refuse treatment.

After the meeting, the sisters went to their mother's room to talk to her. Since Gia was the youngest and the closest to her, she agreed to talk to her. Pulling a chair up close to the side of the bed, she watched as her mother slept. Searching her mother's face, there was a look of sadness on her own. She knew her mother was in agony and had been since her kidneys failed. 'This must have been a difficult decision for her to make,' she thought.

Sensing someone was in the room, Anna opened her eyes.

"Is someone there?" she asked.

"Yes, Mom, it's Gia. How are you today?"

"Tired, Honey, I'm so very tired."

Gia touched her hand in sympathy. "Meagan and Molly are here with me too, Mom."

Gia took her hand and told her there was something they had to talk to her about.

"Oh? What's that?"

"Your doctor called us here for a meeting today to talk to us about your treatment. He told us you have refused dialysis, is this true, Mom?"

"Where are the other girls?"

"They are in the corridor talking to one of the nurses."

"Ask them to come in, would you, please."

Gia went to the door and signaled her sisters to come into the room.

"We're all here, Mom."

Anna opened her eyes briefly and looked at each one of the girls, one at a time; as best she could, with the eyesight she had left from cataracts.

"I'm glad you girls are here," Anna began. "Gia said that you were in a meeting with my doctor. I should have discussed this with you girls beforehand, but I am telling you now. I have refused dialysis; I don't want it any longer. I am sick, I am very, very tired, and I just want this to be over. I know you girls must understand how difficult this has been for me. I've been doing this for years, and my condition is only worsening. I knew what I was doing when I told them not to take me to the renal unit. This is my decision, and I'm not doing it to hurt anyone. My point is to stop the hurt and the pain."

Standing around her bed, they listened to their mother as tears rolled down their cheeks. They knew she had been in pain for the past several years and it was only selfishness, on their part, not to accept her decision. They knew it was hers to make though, and they would have to accept it. Gia pulled a tissue and passed the box to the others.

Hearing them all blowing at the same time, Anna took the opportunity to try and put their minds at peace.

"Girls, you know that I am not afraid to die. There is a better life for me on the other side, and it's where I want to be."

Gia and her sisters could not argue with her about that. They knew their mother had lived a Christian life for many years. They also knew there was a better place for her, in the great beyond rather than in this hospital wing, called a nursing home.

The sisters also knew it was not theirs, but their mother's decision to make. They were certain now, that she was rational, of sound mind, if not body and she had made up her mind.

Gia made her own plan. She had a staff member bring her a cot to sleep on, so she could stay in her mother's room. If this was going to happen, she certainly was not going to let her die alone. The doctor said the process could be as little as one day or as long as thirteen days, and Gia was prepared to stay.

With every visit, Meagan would bring Gia clean clothes, visit with Anna for a few minutes and go home. On Molly's visits, she'd stay with Gia for hours. They'd play scrabble, chat and sit with Anna.

Many mornings Molly got back home in time for a nap, a quick shower and go to work.

With each passing day, there were less and less signs of life in Anna's bed. She had no appetite, so she didn't eat; she slept and lost weight. They say the appetite is the first to go.

While Gia and Molly played scrabble, they noticed that something was different with their mom's breathing. It was loud, but not a snore-like sound, and it went on and on. They called a nurse in to ask about it. She explained that it was normal and believing in the nurse's knowledge, they continued with their scrabble game.

Suddenly, the room went deathly quiet, and they called the nurse back in again. They walked over to the bed together and watched as the nurse checked their mother. Looking at them, she nodded. Anna had passed away in the middle of the night on the thirteenth day. It was over. The nurse left them alone with their mother. Molly was uncomfortable with the way the nurse was so quick to point out that things were 'normal' in their mother's breathing. They soon realized that what they had heard was a death rattle. Both Gia and Molly figured that if the nurse had been honest with them and told them the end was near, they could have been at her bedside instead of passing time playing scrabble! Molly suggested they clean her room out before they left, as neither one wanted to go back later to do it. They packed up what few belongings she had along with photos and teddy bears, and at three o'clock in the morning, they kissed their mother's forehead one last time and left. They made a few calls along the way to family members, cried together in the car and sat in silence for miles. Gia had spent thirteen days at the hospital. She had not realized how tired she was until it was over.

Gia had buried her dearest friend, just a few short weeks before, and now she had to help her sisters prepare for their mother's funeral. Life was not fair, but then no one ever told her it was.

The days went by in the usual manner. Condolences came flooding in, food was accepted, and flowers arrived at the funeral home. Anna had wishes for the girls to fulfill, and the most important one was; there was to be no visitation. She'd always said that if people had wanted to see her, they should have visited while she was alive and so they certainly were not going to gawk at her after she was dead.

~

A memorial service was held at her church and family gathered for a private graveside service afterwards. Anna's wishes were followed to the letter and the family knew she would have been pleased.

It had been a matter of only six weeks since she had been at her friend's funeral. The pain from losing Patti had not subsided, and now she had to deal with the loss of her mother. She was thankful for the opportunity she'd had to spend with her mother during her remaining days. It had put things into prospective for her. Like the importance of forgiveness, the stupidity of holding grudges, resentments and the endless nonsense that she had carried around for years. 'And for what?' She had allowed herself to let go of her childhood grudges, and so, she buried them with her mother.

She would have given almost anything to have been able to talk to Patti. They had always been there for each other through all the trials life set before them, but she had to deal with this alone.

She found herself at Patti's graveside. Placing flowers near the headstone, she looked for a clean place to sit down. There was no grass to sit on yet because the grave was still new. Removing the scarf from her neck, she spread it out on the ground and sat down. She began to cry for both her friend and her mother and prayed that these things did not come in threes. Two deaths so close together was almost more than she could bear. Sitting in silence for more than an hour, she decided it was time to leave. Cemeteries are sad places to be in normal times for respectful visits, but right now she'd had enough of them for the time being.

The Runner

Gia wished she had not allowed herself to continue to think about her past. Whenever her mind went through one journey, it provoked another and brought more to the surface than what she'd bargained for. Sometimes it was difficult for her to deal with her past. For the most part, she'd rather live in her fantasy world than face the real one. It was safer there and easier to handle.

Being alone was safer, too, since it protected her heart. She'd had her heart bruised or broken almost her entire life. Not all of it was her fault, but most of it was. Although she could not give her whole heart to anyone, the part that she could give away was usually shattered in one way or another. If not by choice, then it was by chance. Sometimes it was her choice, and she'd walk into the situation, knowing full well, it would be doomed before it began, but it didn't stop her. Scott was only one example. She knew she couldn't trust him for five minutes, but she held on to prove a point. All she did was prolong the inevitable. It was the drive to prove she was right.

She got restless in relationships, very soon into them. It was the thrill of the hunt for her. Once she got them interested, and in love with her, the thrill was gone. Her 'work' was done, so she ran. It was then time to move on to the next hunt and something more interesting. No one held her interest for very long. A year or two and occasionally she held out for four. That was long enough. She called herself 'the runner,' because she ran, from not only bad relationships but good and decent ones as well. Most of her time spent in a relationship, she was planning how to get out of it. The plan was always there in the back of her mind, and she played around with it every now and then. Before the four years were up, the plan was in place, and she was more than ready to move on.

There is always, 'the one that got away,' and the same was true for her. She thought that Tommy had been the love of her life. She had met him at a very young age. Their time together was relatively short, when she counted their dating years, as kids, and their marriage; it added up to about a dozen years, altogether. She had spent so much time with him that she had to learn to live without him. Thinking back over her life she compared her feelings for Tommy, as opposed to Beau, it seemed more like a schoolgirl crush or puppy love. At the time though, it was 'love' to her, her first love. It was the only way she had known how to love anybody. Beau was different. He had stolen her heart at the first moment she looked into his eyes.

The one man that she wanted to be tied to forever, but couldn't have, was Beau. Every person after him was only a replacement. She compared everyone to him and tried to find, in them, what she had lost with Beau. When she couldn't find it, she lost interest, and she ran. He haunted her for more than twenty years, and she could not let him go, in order to move on with her life. He was always the third party in her relationships. She knew that the one reason she could never fully give her heart to anyone, was because it still belonged to him. She had given him her heart and had never taken it back.

It wouldn't have mattered, if she had been in a meaningful relationship, if he had come back for her, she knew, with all certainty she would go with him, no questions asked. If she were standing at the altar, preparing to say, 'I do,' she would still go if he'd asked her.

This is where she was the happiest, this was her fantasy world and she brought her misery onto herself. She knew he would never be back, but if she believed that he would, it was easier to deal with than the reality of him never returning. He was always there on the edge of her life, and all she had to do was push him over, and he would be gone forever, but she could not. From the time he'd left town, he never tried to physically stand in her way of happiness. Mentally though, she held on to him, as her White Knight. He had not exactly let her go either.

Present

While Lane was out doing errands, Gia went to the kitchen to make a snack. Opening the wooden breadbox, she found a mishmash of bread and with two of the least stale pieces, she made a sandwich. Pulling out the other bags of leftovers, she began to tear the bread apart to feed the birds. There was one hard Kaiser Roll, one crust of raisin bread and a couple of heels from the bag she'd found her slices in. Standing at the sink, so as not to make a mess with the crumbs, a memory of her mother flashed in her mind and caused her to smile.

It was from when she had visited her at her senior's apartment. She'd had a small flower gardens on both sides of the walkway and a couple of ornamental bushes on the lawn.

It was at the time when her mother was deeply involved in her church and living for God. Gia, however, was not at the same place, that her mom was, with God, but she had read her bible, and she knew about Him.

Tearing the bread apart and nibbling on her sandwich, she could not help but smile at the memory. They were sitting outside in a shaded area, when several types of small birds gathered on the grass. Anna went inside to get a few crusts of bread to toss out to them. Anna always wore dresses, (part of the church thing) crossing her ankles, she opened her knees a bit and laid the bread on her lap. Anna's angst for food had not changed much, and Gia watched as she broke the bread into the tiniest pieces and tossed them on the ground. They watched as the birds picked at the bread or carried it off to a safer place. Suddenly, a couple of crows appeared. Anna got possessive of the bread and she wanted only the smaller birds to have it. Leaping out of her chair, she waved her arms in the air. "Shoo! Shoo!" she shouted. Then mumbled how much she hated crows and what gluttons they were. Gia sat quietly watching her mother and thought, 'That is not very Christian-like,' so she decided to have a little fun.

"What do you think will happen," she said, "when you get to Heaven and Jesus says, 'I was hungry, and you did not feed me,' how would that make you feel?"

"What are you talking about?" Anna asked with a scowl.

"What if one of those crows had appeared here, disguised as Jesus, to test your faith in him? I think you just failed the test by refusing to feed the crows."

Gia smiled to herself again, at the memory, as she continued to tear the bread apart, she watched as Lane backed into the driveway. Before he got into the house though, she remembered her mother's reaction to her not so subtle statement.

Anna had leaped up from her chair and disappeared into the house only to return with a half bag of bread. Tearing it up, she tossed it out for the crows to feast on!

Gia smiled smugly remembering that visit. Lane came in and walked over to the sink, looked at the bag of torn up bread and right on cue, he said, "Are you going to feed the birds?"

Gia had another memory of her mother that often brought a smile. She remembered how, at family gatherings, Anna always told the story, as a joke.

Gia had been visiting her mother on another occasion. During the conversation, Gia would hear her mother sniff, as if her nose was running, but she never used a tissue. On and on it went, sniff... pause... sniff, until Gia, more or less, had snapped. The constant sniffing had gotten on her nerves so bad that she had to say something.

"My God Mom!" she hissed, "would you blow your nose!?"

"It's not my nose Honey," she said calmly, "it's my nerves."

"Well then, for Pete's sake, blow your nerves!"

It was then that Anna started to laugh when the gist of their conversation sunk in. She told that story many times, and it always made her laugh.

Gia quietly sipped on her steaming hot cup of coffee and allowed the memories of her mother to linger briefly before she carried on.

Going back in thought, to where her mind had taken her the night before, she silently regretted allowing the past to creep in again. Dragging up past history that should have remained in the past but still, there it was, in the raw. She remembered, again the day forgiveness came.

Forgiveness

Years before, she had been watching an episode of Oprah. Something told her to watch that day, and she was glad she had listened to that voice. It was before Dr. Phil had his own show and he was Oprah's weekly guest.

Tommy's last words flew across her mind, in a flash, as a voice inside her head spoke. 'Pay attention to this,' the voice said.

The guest on the show was a woman who had been molested as a child. She could not forgive her abuser, nor did she know how. This episode was about forgiveness, and it opened up a whole different perspective to Gia as she listened. This was something that she had struggled with for most of her life.

Dr. Phil had reassured the woman that what had happened to her, as a child, was not her fault and that she was not in any way responsible for her abuser's behavior. She was the child and he was the adult, and she was, in no way, responsible for any part of it. He then told the woman that it was up to her to decide, whether or not, she wanted to wake up every day, wrap her pain and guilt around her shoulders, like a heavy shawl and carry it around with her all day, every day, for the rest of her life. If she chose that, then she was giving her power to the one who had hurt her. "Take back your power," he told her, "you can do this by forgiving and letting it go."

Gia sat with her mind open and listened to Dr. Phil as he spoke to the guest, and he may as well have been talking directly to her. It was as if Tommy had appeared in the room and sat with her. A veil seemed to lift from her eyes, and she began to understand that she was not to blame for her father's behavior toward her. She also realized what Tommy had been trying to tell her, all those years ago, as he lay dying. He had wanted her to let go of the pain she felt, live her life and be free of the demons she carried around.

"Forgiveness is freedom, and you need to be free to move forward," he had told her. Making the decision at that moment, she let it all go. Silently she forgave her father for what he had done to her and refused to give him the power to control her any longer. She realized she had allowed him to control her for decades, even from his grave, and that was all he was getting from her. Gia had allowed her father's behavior to ruin every relationship she ever had. She wouldn't allow herself to trust anybody, males especially, and she compared them all, to him. He totally controlled her thoughts and her life, and she allowed it because she didn't know about forgiveness, at least that kind of forgiveness. She knew it would be impossible to forget about it, but she refused to wear it any longer.

Whenever sex had entered her relationships, it all turned sour from there. She thought they only wanted her for sex. Her father should have been a role model by providing her with a father's love that she needed and wanted. A role model who would teach her what love was about, and that men were not all creeps. All she saw was sick and twisted behavior, and when she saw that same behavior in the men she chose, they too appeared to be using her, the same way that he had. In her mind, he was supposed to have loved her and that was how he showed it, so why would she think other men would be any different.

From then on, she associated sex with love or love with sex. She never believed that any man could truly love her for her and that all they wanted was sex and she could not think about it any other way. She'd spent a lifetime searching for something she would never find.

Her very close friend, Zack Glendon, once introduced her to the term 'Arrested Emotional Development.' She looked into it only briefly, but she really didn't want to know a whole lot about it. Ignorance is bliss sometimes. Just the sound of it, 'Arrested Emotional Development,' sounded scary. She knew that any childhood traumatic experience stunted normal emotional growth. Many times, over the years, she felt herself reverting to an eight-year-old child, and she had to fight her way back to adulthood. She could certainly understand why so many abused children, eventually turned to drugs and alcohol to escape the pain caused by their abuser.

She'd always felt she didn't have the right to say 'no' to anybody and she was never told that she had that right until years down the road and many sessions with a therapist. 'It's OK to say no.' It had been a long hard road for Gia.

She had always given the impression that she was tough as nails with a 'don't mess with me' attitude that most women would kill for. That was the side she wanted people to see, not the side that showed she was as soft as pudding. She wanted to portray an air that screamed, 'you can't hurt me, I won't let it happen.' The steel trap that she pretended was around her heart, made her seem heartless, fearless and dangerously cruel. But she really was just like everyone else. She bled when she was cut, she ached when she was sad, and if you were to look closely, you would almost see her heart on her sleeve.

Just like everybody, she also had a side that hurt when she was lied to, snubbed or disappointed, by someone she cared about.

Even though she was crying on the inside, she held a smile that non-verbally said, 'go pound sand.' It was a difficult ruse that she had perfected since childhood. No one would ever know her true feelings. Something else she could thank her father for. It was not her fault; life made her that way. She didn't want anyone to see her vulnerable side, because the few times she had shown vulnerability, she had been taken advantage of. So now people saw her as rough and tough and that is exactly what she wanted them to see.

This was the side that reared on that dark and scary night, so long ago. This is where she learned to lock people out. She had her reasons. Gia had developed a sense of perfection for herself even though she knew perfection did not exist in her world. It was a made-up fantasy in her head that only she was aware of. She felt she had to be perfect, perfectly dressed, not a hair out of place and make-up had to be applied daily.

She had no sense of adventure since fear had taken over her life. She could not allow herself to make mistakes in front of others, and she lived with 'what ifs.' What if they laughed or thought she was stupid, or an idiot? She would never be caught dead doing something just plain silly, in case people would think she was simple-minded. She would not participate in sports because she might not get it right the first time. God forbid that she might strike out at a ballgame! As if it had never happened to the best ballplayers in the world. If she felt she couldn't do it, she wouldn't try. She could not take the chance of being laughed at by anyone.

She could not enjoy herself at parties, good girls didn't go to parties and she didn't touch liquor because good girls didn't drink. Isn't that what her daddy told her all those years ago? He had called her his 'good girl,' his 'perfect girl,' and did she not have to live up to those words he'd whispered in her ear so long ago?

Gia had a knack for keeping others from stressing out, yet she stressed over everything. From her sessions, with a therapist, she learned that her issues stemmed from not having control over the experience she'd had with her father. She had developed feelings of helplessness, fear, mistrust and sadness of a little girl lost forever. She also learned that childhood abuse, of any kind, can keep that child forever hanging in the balance because the emotional trauma will never go away. She'd learned they have difficulty moving on, letting go and even fully growing up emotionally. Sure, the body grows and develops but that inner child, in all of us, will be forever stunted unless therapy is insisted upon.

Forgiveness is one of the first steps, and to acknowledge that the child is not to blame for an adult's behavior, is the second step. Acceptance is essential. Some will never accept, nor will they learn to forgive, which leaves no room to move on. Some people never fully recover from abusive situations, and, are lost forever.

The Wedding (in the present)

As Gia entered the room, Lane was standing in front of the fireplace, waiting for her. He was tall and handsome in his dark suit that offset his well-groomed head of white hair. Pausing only slightly, she continued her walk toward him. He smiled and reached for her hand when she stepped in front of him. Talking his hand, they turned toward the Justice of the Peace. As their families and friends looked on, the JP welcomed everyone and told them that Gia and Lane had written their own vows to each other and asked Lane to begin. Beginning his vows, he hadn't gotten far into them when his voice began to crack. He proclaimed his love for Gia and when he finished, Gia squeezed his hand to indicate she was ready to proceed with hers.

Beginning her speech, she looked into Lane's eyes. He was trying to contain himself as he listened to every word that she spoke.

Gia was used to hiding her feelings, and she went through her vows without even a quiver in her voice or a sign of nervousness. She'd had many years of practice and actually, it was easier now not to show emotion. She was the only one who knew what was going on in her heart and mind and no one could tell exactly how well she'd hidden her feelings. She always smiled when she needed to smile, and she laughed at jokes that she didn't find the least bit funny. If the person telling the joke thought it was funny, then who was she not to laugh, if it was expected of her to do so. Most of the time, as she smiled on the outside, she was usually crying on the inside. She felt lonely in a crowd, and when she was in a crowd, she felt invisible and could most likely be found standing alone waiting to go home. She was a loner, from way back, and even as she stood there facing Lane, she had the feeling of déjà vu all over again. That brief moment crept in, as she once again wished she was not getting married.

She really wanted this relationship with Lane to be her last one, but according to her track record she was already overdue for a change, and she struggled with the conflict between opposite needs of stability and change.

'What was wrong with her anyway? Why did she have to feel like she didn't belong anywhere and yet she didn't want to belong to anybody?' She was once again beginning to feel alone even though hers and Lane's families were there with her. It was something she could not explain, not even to herself.

Gia had been single for more than thirty years, which was a long time with total independence. With relationships popping in and out of her life it was no wonder she had a padlock on her heart. She knew what she wanted in a relationship but what she didn't know was, if she was able to give it back. When other relationships ended, and the tears were dried up, it was over, and she'd moved on. She knew it was a heartless way to feel but most of the time she didn't feel as though she had a heart, so in a way she was heartless.

Other relationships, she was usually glad to be rid of, and a few others she had cried, as they walked out the door, but she didn't think it was for them, it was the fact that she had failed again. Generally, she would make it impossible for them to stay, and it was her way of non-verbally saying, 'get the hell out.'

She couldn't remember ever having that heart-stopping, pulse-pounding feeling of overwhelming love with anyone, except Beau. There was never anybody that she felt she absolutely could not live without, until Beau. 'Beau...' it made her heart beat faster just breathing his name. When she met Beau, she knew exactly what it was like to actually have emotions, and she allowed herself to feel them. In their relationship, she knew what love was, what love meant, how love felt, and how love was supposed to be. She knew what it was like to want to hold him so tightly, that she couldn't get close enough to him, or get to the point where their kisses were never long enough or deep enough. She also knew what it was like to want to crawl inside his skin, just to get closer to him... Beau... the love of her life.

~

"Gia?" She heard a voice in the distance. "Gia?" There it was again.

'Tsk, can I ever catch a break?' she thought.

"Yes?" she answered.

"Do you want me to repeat the question?" the JP asked.

"Yes, I'm sorry, I didn't hear you." 'Oh, Thank God for small mercies,' she thought, as she was brought back from that part of her past, that she'd longed to forget.

"Do you take Lane to be your lawfully wedded husband?" the JP repeated. She looked around, a little embarrassed while the guests stared at her, with furrowed brows, as if she had a milk mustache.

She looked up at Lane and said, "I will." She was sure she could hear air escaping from his lungs. He'd been standing there holding his breath waiting for her to answer the JP. The JP had one ring laying on her bible, and she passed it to Gia to put it on Lane's finger. She had not even noticed that he had already placed hers on her ring finger.

"Repeat after me, Gia, with this ring I thee wed."

She repeated the words as she slipped his ring on and wondered, 'where the hell was I during my wedding!' She'd missed most of her ceremony. The entire thing was a blur. She wanted to kick her own ass for allowing thoughts of Beau to creep in on her wedding day!

"Lane, you may kiss your bride."

"Gladly," he said with a smile as he cupped her face and kissed her. They held each other for a few seconds, and they parted when they heard the JP speak.

"Ladies and Gentlemen, I present to you, Mr. and Mrs. Lane Walters."

The guests clapped for them, and they walked over to their family and friends, for congratulations, hugs and cheek kisses, and the usual wedding sentiments.

As Gia walked around the room to chat with her guests, she had difficulty concentrating on anything they were saying. Her mind kept creeping back to her first wedding, and she fought with herself to stay in the moment. She tried to shake off the urge to go back in time, yet she didn't know why she wanted to go back there. It was the same as this one. That was her first wedding, and this was her second, but they were very similar. There was no big to-do at either one, she did not wear a fancy expensive gown back then either and she didn't have to feed a multitude of hungry guests at either occasion. They were both small and intimate, and she didn't want to be present at either one. So, what was her problem anyway? Why did she do these things? No one had dragged her to either one of her weddings; she got there under her own steam, and no one had held a gun to her head. She asked herself again why she did the things she did. She could never come up with an answer to her own questions.

Their guests were invited to stay after the meal for as long as they wanted. There was still finger food and drinks for everyone. They had all booked rooms, so there was no reason to close up shop yet.

Lane had been at the bar on more than one occasion, and Gia could recognize the signs from past experiences. He was a happy camper when he drank, but still, Gia was nervous. She had never been comfortable around people who drank. This was something that had only worsened over the years. She could remember always being uncomfortable with it, but as the years passed, and experiences happened, she had developed a real phobia about it. Lane was not a big drinker by any stretch of the imagination, and he was not into anything stronger than beer, but to Gia, it was all the same. It enhanced and changed personalities and some not for the better.

She didn't have to worry about all these things when she was alone, which was part of the reason why she enjoyed being single and alone. Not only did she not have to worry about cigarettes, booze or just men in general, she didn't have to wash their dirty socks and underwear! What was she thinking anyway? What was she doing?

When it was time for the party to end, Gia had to help Lane to their room. Rolling her eyes at him more than once, she silently kicked her ass for showing up for the ceremony. Her list of his 'things that pissed her off,' grew longer by the minute.

Helping him to sit down on one of the beds, he instantly toppled over. Pulling him up again, she tried to get his jacket off, but managed to get one arm out before he fell over again. Clenching her teeth, she yanked him up with the empty sleeve and got the other arm out as his head bobbed around. When she got the jacket off, she tried to get him out of his shirt, but it was useless. He had flopped over again, and she left him right where he landed, with his upper body on the bed, and his feet on the floor. 'Dumb Ass,' she grumbled under her breath. She went into the bathroom and ran a tub of water. Stripping off her clothes, she got in, sank to her neck and closed her eyes. She was still steaming mad at herself, as well as him when tears began to sting at her eyelids.

Getting out of the tub, she dried herself off, and didn't bother to unpack the beautiful wedding ensemble she'd bought for this damned night. The room had two queen size beds, and he was on top of one. Although she thought about it for maybe five seconds, she decided not to put a cover over him. Instead, she walked by him as if he was not even there. Going to her bed, she dropped her towel onto the floor, and got in under the covers. All she wanted to do was to go home and forget this day ever happened.

She still missed Beau, and she knew she always would, but she refused to go back there especially on this night and in this mood. She rolled over with her back to him and cried herself to sleep.

~

There was no sense in Lane trying to apologize to Gia; she would have no part of it. He had ruined their wedding night, and she was in no mood for excuses. He tried to placate her, but Gia was having none of that either. There was no excuse for what he'd done, and she was in no mood to even be around him. She was disgusted with him, and he knew it, so he gave her a wide berth and hoped she'd forgive him. She absolutely hated acts of 'stupid' and 'dumb.' It was OK if she was dumb or stupid at times, but she could not tolerate it from others if it involved her. They could be dumb on their own time, but not hers, and to her, what he had done was both dumb and stupid. You only have one wedding night, and if he wanted to spend it drunk and asleep, then that was dumb. If you wanted to drink until you pass out, then that is stupid.

She hated 'stupid' just as much she hated dumb... dumb questions in particular. When you hear someone running a tub of bathwater, the last question you should ask is, 'Are you having a bath?' When Gia heard Lane ask that, she stood in her bathroom and wondered if she should answer a stupid question with a stupid answer. So, she did not.

Once when she was making a peanut butter sandwich, Lane walked into the kitchen, and saw what she was doing and still asked, "Are you making a sandwich?"

"Are you being serious right now?" she asked in disbelief.

"Yes, I guess that was a dumb question."

Again, once when their phone rang, she picked it up and said, "Hello? No, you must have the wrong number." She barely had time to replace the receiver, when Lane said, "Who was that?" If it was a wrong number, then who cared? Another time they were at the door ready to go out, and he looked at her and said, "Are you wearing that?" She just shook her head and opened the door, but not before cutting her eyes at him. She really hated 'dumb.'

The Journey

Gia felt it was time she put her past to rest. She had a few things that needed taking care of, and she wasn't looking forward doing them. In order for her to heal, they had to be done. She planned to be away for several days, and if it took longer than that, then so be it.

Lane was hoping Gia's journey would help her get through whatever she felt she had to do and hoped she'd come out on the other side a happier person. He knew that she had to walk through it step by step, and he also knew she had to go through it alone. He sometimes wished he could push her along to help get her to the other side a bit quicker. She had a lot of years, a lot of time and a lot of baggage, not to mention the damage, to drag along with her so it'll take her some time to get to the other end. Worrying, too, that she might not make it to the other side, and still be the woman she was after finishing her odyssey. He would rather have her as she is now, than find a stranger at the end of the tunnel.

Kissing Lane good-bye at the door, she said, "Wish me luck."

"I do wish you luck Gia and I also wish you'd allow me tag along. I may not be much good to you, but I would at least be there for you."

"Thank you, Lane, but no thanks; this is something I must do alone. See you in a couple of days!"

Getting into her car, she started her long, and much needed, journey. Along the way, she passed the old house that had belonged to her grandparents. Several times her parents had lived in the ell on the end of a once grand old house. Actually, she had been born in the upstairs bedroom, where her grandparents had once slept.

Just a short trip down the road was the old house where her childhood trauma had taken place. Passing by, she glanced up at the bedroom window, and she felt her stomach muscles tense up.

She got the same feeling every time she drove past. Many times, on her way by, she would deliberately turn her head, to avoid looking in that direction, until she was well passed the house. She was not in denial; it was deliberate avoidance. The house had always made her skin crawl. 'Out of sight, out of mind,' did not apply here.

Continuing on her way, she tried to put speeches together in her head, but nothing seemed appropriate. Her stomach knotted as she reached her first stop. She made a right-hand turn in the driveway and climbed carefully up the steep, narrow hill, past the old church, around a sharp turn and past some old headstones. Driving slowly over the one lane grassy path, she stopped next to her mother's grave. Turning the engine off, she rolled her window down, and felt the gentle breeze, from the river, blow on her face. Laying her head back against the seat, she thought back to how her mother ended up here.

~

Back when Anna was in her late sixties, she had experienced chest pains. Taking no chances, she made an appointment to see her doctor because she thought it could be a sign of a heart attack. The doctor had told her there was a possibility of blockages and as a precautionary measure, he ordered a dye test. Hindsight, as they say, is great, but she should never have agreed to have the test done. Being a diabetic, she was taking a drug called Metformin, taking that particular drug, she should not have had a dye test done before going off the drug for several days prior. The doctor should have known the risk was high. Giving the dye tests to Anna, being on Metformin, caused the dye to settle in her kidneys, causing kidney damage and inevitably, kidney failure. As a result, she needed dialysis several times a week.

Anna, no longer able to look after herself, had closed up her house, and moved into a senior's home, for independent living. It was considered more of a senior's room and board than a nursing home.

For several years, three times a week, she travelled an hour each way to an out of town hospital for dialysis. Suffering terribly with back pain, she was forced to spend hours sitting in the renal unit, then another hour in a car for an agonizing ride back home.

Finally, the time came when she just could not bear the trips any longer. At the hospital, where her dialysis was given, they had a wing that was used for a nursing home. She had her name on a list for a bed and finally, her travel time was over. After moving in, someone was there to wheel her to the renal unit, have dialysis, and then back to her room.

Anna, being on dialysis, became inactive since her kidneys failed. As a result, of the inactivity, poor circulation caused her to lose part of her leg. Soon signs of dementia surfaced and she slept most of the time. She recognized her family only by their voices but was unable to see them very well since cataracts had formed on her eyes.

Eventually, she had no quality of life, and her family began to worry when she had aggressively refused dialysis.

~

Once the dialysis stopped and Gia was alone with her mother, she'd sit quietly by her bed, hold her hand and talk softly to her. She wanted to make peace with her mom before she died. Gia wasn't sure if Anna had ever known about the resentments, she'd held toward her from her childhood. She explained that she held her partly responsible for some of the hang-ups she'd had to deal with. Saying that she'd felt she had not protected her when she was a little girl and that she had never forgiven her for that. She told her, that all was forgiven, and she was sorry she had not let go of it sooner. Releasing the relief of forgiveness, tears rolled down her cheeks as she watched her mother, so tiny, thin and frail. Suddenly, and ever so softly, she felt a tiny squeeze on her hand. It was her mother's way of telling her everything was OK. Gia brought her mom's hand up to her lips, kissed it, and then pressed it against her cheek in acknowledgement of what she was trying to tell her.

~

Being at the gravesite, with a gentle breeze blowing, she got out of her car and stepped out onto the grass. She had been here more than once. It was the family gravesite and everyone in her past generations, on her mother's side, were there also. Everyone except her father and she had no idea where he was buried, but she had to find out.

There were fresh flowers placed on the grave, so she knew someone had been visiting recently.

"Hi Mom," Gia said as she looked down at the headstone. "It's been a while and I know I should have been here long before now, but even though I didn't come, I still think about you every day. I see you in my dreams, too, Mom, and when I do, it's like we are having a real visit. It's nice to be able to see you in my dreams, because you are always young, active, smiling and happy. Watching you wither away in the hospital, wasn't easy for any of us, but seeing you, in my dreams, as the vibrant woman I remember, was very comforting."

Mom, I'm going to visit Dad, too. I don't know where he is buried because, as you know, I didn't attend his funeral, so I don't know the location of his resting place. I know it is several counties from here, and he is in the same cemetery as his sister, so I will have to do a search of the area. Other family members attended the funeral, so perhaps one of them can help me. It has been a long time since he's died, and I'm certain, as I stand here, that nobody has ever visited him since his funeral."

Gia walked around the gravesite and read the names of her other family members. There were four generations there, and she remembered them all. Her great-grandfather, her grandparents, her mother and two of her brothers, all there together. Her youngest brother had been cremated, and his urn was buried in their mother's grave. Since he had been placed there, less than two years ago, the wound was still fresh. Gia had not been there since his burial. It was difficult being there alone, and she decided to leave. She walked back around to face the headstone and gently swiped her hand slowly across her mother's name carved out on her stone.

"I'm leaving now, Mom, but I promise not to take so long between visits, rest in peace mother, I'll be back soon." Putting her fingertips to her lips, she touched the stone one last time before walking back to her car. It amazed her that she would go to the cemetery alone, but now that she did, it wasn't as bad as she thought it would be.

Driving slowly out of the cemetery, she didn't know if it was relief or sorrow that she was feeling. She did know, however, that she had some work to do now, in preparation to visit her father's grave. She was not looking forward to it, but it had to be done and the sooner, the better.

Back at the motel, she scribbled down a few notes, and spent an entire day contemplating, and basically getting her nerve up to meet with her family members. The older siblings, who had attended his funeral, gave her as much information as they remembered, or cared to remember, but no one had offered to go along with her for moral support. Then again... she really didn't want anyone with her. This was something she had to do for herself, by herself.

She did a Google search of the town and local area, wrote down as much information as she could find and set out on the long drive alone. It was at least a two-hour drive, and it was the hardest thing she ever had to do on her own. To pass some time, she went over what she would say if she did find him. 'If' being the operative word here since she was going, blindly, into a place she had never been.

After several wrong turns and backtracking, she finally found the cemetery, and slowly she brought her car to a stop. Sitting there for several minutes, she looked out over the huge cemetery and thought, 'He's in there somewhere... but where?' Gathering up what last bit of nerve she had left, she got out of her car and began her journey through the unfamiliar grounds and glancing at headstone as she strolled but didn't recognizing any names.

'He's been here for more than forty-five years,' she thought, and this will be her one and only trip since she had no intention of ever returning, so this was it. What she had to say, had to be said today, there were no second chances, or 'I shoulda said this, or, I shoulda said that.'

Since she was not present at his funeral, she had no idea where to begin to look, and she searched for what seemed like a long time. "This place is massive," she mumbled aloud. Other people were roaming around too, seemingly searching, touching and reading headstones, or kneeling quietly with a loved one. "Well, at least I'm not alone," she mumbled aloud, again through clenched teeth and knots in her stomach.

Something familiar caught her eye and air was involuntarily sucked into her lungs. Stopping in her tracks as if frozen in time, it took her a minute to recover. 'Bradley C. Lake.' Staring at the coldness of the surroundings, she realized she had been rooted to the same spot, similar to a deer in headlights. A car crept past, and the crunch of gravel against rubber, startled her and brought her back to the reason why she was there. Feeling her knees bend, she lowered herself down on the recently mown grass. This was the first time, in many years, that she'd been alone with him and panic clawed at her throat. Pulling it together, she straightened her shoulders and thought about the bigger and better person she'd become since those years when he'd had control, but she still couldn't escape getting in a couple snide remarks.

"Well now, who do we have here? Bradley C. Lake, my dear old dad. It took me a while to find you, but I knew you were here somewhere." Speaking the words, she brushed dead grass off the headstone, more from nervous fidgeting than wanting to tidy up his place. Looking at the dead grass, she thought, 'How appropriate!'

"What in Hell have you been up to? No pun intended, Dad. You know, the first eight years of my life were a living Hell, thanks to you, but since you left, I have not regretted one day without you in it. I can still remember the last time I saw you." Closing her eyes, she flashed back to the day she watched him walk away, "but

I must say, I'm glad you're here. I was deathly afraid of you as a child, but once I grew up and realized that the abused had rights, I know now that I would have put your ass in jail. But you were dead by the time I turned seventeen, but that's just like you, isn't it? Always taking the easy way out. You dropped dead at the age of forty-nine before any of us could stand up for ourselves. You bullied us into fearing the very sight of you, cringed at the sound of your footsteps, and we quaked at the rattle of your belt buckle. You were such a bully and a tormentor."

Standing up to stretch her legs, she turned her back on the stone for a few minutes just to breath in fresh air. Fresh, warm tears stung at her eyelids and slipped down her face. Realizing at that moment, her tears were not for him or what he had done to her, but they were cleansing her entire being. All the hurt, anger, resentment, disappointment and yes, even hatred, flowed from her body. Uncontrollable tears streamed from her eyes as she gulped for air. Shivering and shaking uncontrollably, she slowly went back to her knees.

Close to fifty years of pent-up feelings, and unshed tears were finally set free. The tormented little girl, who had gone through Hell, had come out on the other side right there, in the cemetery beside her tormenter's grave. In her mind's eye, she saw that little girl, her inner self, standing beside her for support. She looked at his name one final time and spoke her last words to him. "I forgave you many years ago so I wouldn't drag your crap around with me. I wasn't certain if the forgiveness was real or not, but as of today, I know it is and we are done."

"Goodbye, Daddy, I won't be back. Are you resting in peace?"

It was close to sunset before she turned her back on the headstone. Not having anything left to say, she just stared at his name and felt composed. A calming peace, that she couldn't remember having, engulfed her like a bear hug. Still on her knees, she envisioned her inner child. Gathering her up in her arms, she held her for all the lost hugs as a child. Looking toward the Heavens, she said, "Thank You, for being here with me today."

She could not remember being hugged as a child nor had she heard anyone say, 'I love you.'

Back then, there was no independence, no voice, no opinion, just incredible emptiness, and this invisible bear hug felt like going home, after many years absent. Her inner child stood beside her as if telling her that she would go through it with her.

Leaving the cemetery, it was nearly dark as she turned her car around and headed home. She knew she would have to pass her childhood house of torture. As she got closer to the house, she realized she didn't have the usual pangs of resentment in the pit of her stomach, no urge to turn her head in the opposite direction. It was gone!

Facing the Past

Pressing her foot slowly on the brake pedal, as if she were in a hypnotic state, or determined to meet that ghost that's been following her for decades, she knew what she had to do.

The left signal flashed, and she crept up the driveway. The same driveway from where she'd watched her father walk down and blessedly out of her life, all those many years ago. Turning off the ignition, she sat quietly in the driveway for a few minutes and her eight-year-old inner child sat with her. This time she was not full of rage and anxiety, just curiosity.

The front door opened, and a young man stood in the entrance, like a dark blob. She could not see his face, just his shape against the porch light. She knew she had to get out of the car now or leave. Leaving was not an option, since he was aware of her sitting there in his driveway.

"OK, little girl," she said, looking over at the eight-year-old, whom she had obviously been dragging around for years. "Let's go," she said. Opening the car door, she put her feet on the ground and stood up.

Closing her eyes briefly, 'Breathe!' she reminded herself and inhaled deeply.

"Can I help you miss?" he called from the porch.

"I'm not sure," she replied, "I hope so."

"What can I do for you then?" His voice seemed stern as if he were protecting his home from her.

"Well," she began, "for starters, please don't think I'm crazy, I'm just nervous.

"OK, let me be the judge of that, and tell me what you want."

"I don't know where to begin," she said as she walked up the front steps toward him.

"I'm Georgia Lake," she said holding out her hand in introduction.

"Hello, I'm Grant Parker," he said taking her hand, "would you like to come in?"

"Thank you," Gia said, stepping into the entry taking in a quick view of the inside of the house. It looked very different from what had been stuck in her mind for decades. It was a place she would not have recognized if she had been brought in blindfolded. Yet, here she was standing in the doorway of the childhood home, that her parents had rented until it sold. She didn't know who these new owners were and did not recognize their last name.

"This is my wife Carol," she barely heard Grant Parker say.

"Hello," she said shaking her hand.

They stared at her as if she were an escapee from the mental ward. The touch of a tiny hand slipping inside her palm brought her out of her trance.

"I'm sorry for intruding on your evening," she said as Grant glanced at his wife, and back at her.

"What can we do for you, Ms. Lake?"

"Gia, please, call me Gia," she paused only briefly and continued.

"I spent several years in this house as a child, and on an impulse, I wanted to come inside for reasons that would only make sense to me."

Relief crossed between the Parkers when they realized she was not a crazy person after all.

"Just standing here inside the door, I can see how very different it is from when I lived here," Gia said.

"Please come in, Gia," Grant said, waving his hand towards the kitchen.

"Thank you; it's so unlike me to do something like this."

They seemed to sense she was mesmerized by the surroundings.

"Would it be an imposition if I had a quick look around, while I'm here?"

"No, it wouldn't be, let us show you around and please take your time."

Gia mentally squeezed the hand of her inner child as her mind returned to the mid-1950's. Going into over-drive, she stepped into the kitchen. Thoughts were racing around her head in all direction. She had not been inside this house for over fifty years and the layout of it had not left her mind. Every time she passed by, that shabby old house was indelibly imprinted in her mind. The exterior had not changed its shape except for the color and a few new windows, so if the outside was the same, then why would the inside change?

She saw, in her mind, a shabby kitchen with an old sideboard sink with a hand pump. A drinking dipper hanging over the sink on a nail, for everyone to use. On the sideboard, a soap dish with a bar of yellow sunlight soap in it. Over the sink there was a shelf that held a comb that was stuck in the center of a hairbrush, a few toothbrushes stood in a glass along with a flat and badly bent tube of Pepsodent toothpaste. 'You'll wonder where the yellow went, when you brush your teeth with Pepsodent.' She could hear the ditty dancing around inside her head. Most of these objects were there for everyone to use including the toothbrushes. There was an old radio on the shelf that had one station. A mirror hung from a nail on the wall below the shelf so that everyone could see in it. She pictured kids on their tippy-toes and the taller ones bending to see in it. Below the sink, on the floor, and behind an old curtain were cleaning items such as a box of SOS pads, Gillet's lye, a bar of lye soap, Creolin and a box of Duz, 'Duz does everything,' she heard the ad clearly in her head. The box of Duz came with either a free glass or a hand towel tucked inside. On the back wall under the sink was another nail to hang the dishpan on to make room in the sink for the hand basin.

An Enterprise wood stove was across from the sink with a wood box behind it. She could still remember the big washtub in front of the stove with bathwater in it so each one could have a bath on Saturday night. Close to where she was standing, was where they had the table with several mismatched chairs with or without backs on them and there was usually worn out oilcloth on the floor. Gia could picture newspapers spread out on the floor after it had been scrubbed, and they stayed there until it was dry. That was the kitchen as she remembered it back then. This only took a few minutes of flashbacks, but Gia remembered an eight-year-old standing there waiting for her father to come roaring in.

'Oh well, so much for you, old man, I know where you are, and you don't frighten me anymore!' she thought.

She remembered there had been a back door next to the sink that lead to the porch, where the washtub hung on a spike, and the scrub board sat below it, waiting for washdays. The porch was more of a back shed attached to a rickety garage and at the end of the garage was an indoor outhouse. It was in that outhouse where she saw the blood from the morning after her abuse. The memory was as fresh as if it had happened yesterday. On the right of the back entry was a pantry where everything was kept because there were no cupboards or fridge. Beside the pantry was her parents' bedroom, (hence, the easy access to the pantry for nighttime snacking) when walking across the bedroom to the far wall, there was a door that led into the living room and then once in the living room it lead back out to the front entry and into the kitchen, in a circle. It was as vivid in her mind as if she still lived there.

Her mind suddenly left the past and opened to what was before her. She was standing in a gloriously updated, beautiful kitchen with all the built-ins you would ever want or need. There was absolutely no sign of the run-down kitchen from her youth.

They took Gia into the living room where she, and her eight-year-old inner self, stood looking around. She saw a sparsely furnished room with an old black and white TV in one corner and in another corner, she saw an old armchair that may or may not have matched the couch that was against another wall. There were step end tables at each end of the couch, worn oilcloth on the floor and plastic curtains hung at the windows.

Coming back to reality, she saw a huge bay window in the front, and beautiful hardwood floors, with imported scatter mats here and there. There was a plush sectional couch with a matching loveseat and ottoman, as well as floor lamps, wide screen TV, glass top tables and large potted plants throughout the room. She didn't remember a living plant in her youth. Where her parents' bedroom had been, off the living room, there was now a wall of brick and glass, made into a fireplace that could be seen and enjoyed from both rooms.

She could hear voices, but she was deeply absorbed in this beautiful room that seemed impossible, in her mind, to be in this house! How could all this beauty be in the ugly house that she had lived in as a child? There were no signs of the old place anywhere. All the ugliness had only been in her mind all these years. Gia's heart felt light and peaceful knowing it was a happy place filled with love, and not the rundown shack where she and her siblings had been abused, tormented and unloved.

"Would you like to see the rest of the house?" It was Carol's voice she heard now.

Thinking that maybe she didn't want to go any farther, and that she had seen enough, but she heard herself saying, "Yes, I would."

Across from the front door, where she came in, was an open stairway that curved into the living room. When she lived there, it was enclosed, with a door and walls on both sides, and no handrails.

In her mind, she turned the knob with one hand, took little Gia's hand with the other, opened the door and climbed up the stairs.

When she got to the top, there was the huge hallway that she so vividly remembered. The hall was a big, almost square room with a single light hanging from the ceiling on a cord and a pull chain to turn it on and off at night. She remembered getting up in the pitch dark and swinging her arms around in hopes of finding the chain. Over on the far side of the hall, she could see an old chamber pot sitting there for them to use in the middle of the night. That was all that was in the hall, in her time there, a chamber pot and a hanging light. Dread began creeping in, but she shook it off and returned to her inner journey.

Still with her back to the stairs, she took a step to her immediate left, to the room she'd slept in with her two sisters. She saw the double bed that she shared with Meagan and the single bed that was Molly's. She didn't remember dressers, just a single closet not even deep enough for a coat hanger. There were coat hooks screwed into a board, at the back of the closet, to hang things on which invariably left a bump at the back of neck in the shape of the hook.

Moving her eyes to the next room, she remembered it had always been off limits for them. Curiosity only made them want to go in there even more. It was a room that the landlord, at the time, used to store his belongings. He had chosen that particular room because it had not been completely finished on the inside. The walls were made of slats, falling plaster, rough boards on the floor, and the room was not usable for anything except for storage. They feared the odd ghost roamed around in there too.

Still rooted at the top of the stairs, she was still taking the journey in her mind. Directly across from the forbidden room was her brothers' bedroom. Off to her right was the room where the abuse had taken place. Her heart sank, and she briefly closed her eyes, took a deep breath, and forced her mind to go through the door. Mentally, she opened the door, and immediately saw the bed, one lone, cold, brown cast iron bed, stood under a slanted wall in a room barren of other furniture. Across the room, by the window, the infamous window, that she had to look at every time she passed this house, she saw the double bed that had been so indelibly imprinted in her mind since she was eight years old. It was as if her spirit was hovering over the bed watching what he had put her through. She mentally got a faint smell of stale tobacco and she could feel a choking sensation well up in her throat. A petrified little girl was being told to do things an eight-year-old should be oblivious to. Blood seemed to drain from her body as she felt Grant's arm catch her when she reeled.

"Are you OK, Gia?" he asked with concern.

Closing her eyes for a few seconds, she got her bearings, but her mouth was dry as she swallowed and whispered, "Yes I think I am, Grant, thank you.

Opening her eyes again, the images, as if by magic, had disappeared. She had absorbed copious images in just a few minutes, yet the past was moving in what seemed like slow motion. In reality, she had not been inside of the house for more than a few minutes and she was dizzy with remembrances.

Carol opened the door to their master bedroom, and Gia no longer saw a barren room or heard the whimpers of a child being molested, it was all gone. Replaced by a beautifully carpeted room, a king-size sleigh bed, matching dresser and highboy were the pieces of furniture. A huge side by side window with a window seat had replaced the old single paned one. Family pictures were everywhere, with happy people in them. Some were of picnics; some were beach outings, reunions and weddings. Nothing ugly remained in the room.

A door had been added for an ensuite bath where her brothers' bedroom wall had been. The door to the once bedroom had been left to gain access to the bathroom from the hall as well. In the 'forbidden room' was an office with a huge "L" shaped desk with computer equipment, printer, fax machine and accessories of all kinds which indicated it was set up for a home office. Her childhood bedroom was set up as a spare room that resembled an elegant motel room. She was in awe of the entire tour.

Turning around, Gia came back out into the hall to where both Grant and Carol were watching her closely, not knowing what to expect. Smiling broadly, they in return, breathed a sigh of relief, and smiled at Gia as if she were a prospective buyer, liked what she saw, and ready to make them an offer.

"Thank you both so much for giving me this opportunity. You will probably never know how much this means to me, but I can tell you, it has changed my life and I cannot thank you enough for what you have allowed me to do here tonight. This place is amazing, and you've done an awesome job renovating it."

"Thank you, we're glad we could help you," they said as they walked her to the door.

Gia walked down the steps of this one-time, run-down shack, which is now a beautiful, loving home and all the sadness lifted off her heart. She realized that this entire nightmare, that had been trapped inside her head, was finally over. Evil did not live in that house; her father had made it evil, in her mind. Reaching her car, she opened the door and slid herself inside. She could almost see her inner self, sitting in the passenger seat giving her a high five. Turning the key, she started the engine, and as she turned toward the center of the car to fasten her seatbelt, the passenger seat was empty. Sadly, but happily, she had to let her go.

Now was the time to look at what was ahead for her. She had spent so much of her life looking backwards, that she had forgotten about the future. Her life was nearly over, and it was time to look ahead and leave the ghost of the past behind her.

The End of Gia's Journey

Moving On

On her way back to the motel, Gia sort of compared her life to an automobile. She should not look at life though the rear-view mirror, with her father always in the back seat, but to keep her eyes forward. She decided to look through the windshield, and watch where she is going, not where she has been. She must remember, 'Do not look back; you are not going that way.'

By realizing these words, her life would no longer be viewed from the rear-view mirror. We all look back over our lives, when certain people, things, thoughts or events spur on flashbacks and memories. Good or bad, it doesn't hurt to remember them, but it will hurt if you stay there. She had come far enough now, that she didn't want to look back on her memories as 'all bad.' She wanted to focus on some of the 'good' times that she could recall and make new 'good' ones, as she headed back home to Lane. She would not forget her past, but she had learned forgiveness.

She remembered a quote that she had once read:

Life is not the way it's supposed to be... it's the way it is. How we cope with it is what makes the difference.

Ending a Friendship

On her way home, she decided to stop in to see Faith, unannounced. She had not seen her for what seemed like fifteen years, maybe even more. She pulled into the driveway and could not believe her eyes. The house looked as if it was falling apart. At one time, it was one of the prettiest homes on the street. Glancing up at the deck, she remembered sitting there drinking iced tea, but now it was rather dilapidated. All she could do was shake her head. She knocked on the back door and waited. When the door opened, Gia was taken aback for a few seconds as she devoured the sight of her. She searched for a resemblance to the beauty of years ago, but there was none. "Gia!" she said, "come in!"

Her voice was even deeper and raspier, and the room was filled with smoke in the background. A cigarette lay burning in an ashtray on the kitchen table. 'Some things never change,' she thought, 'this is like something out of a 1940's movie.' She felt pity, not for herself for a change, but for Faith. There before her, stood a haggard, deeply wrinkled, still 'blonde,' 70ish woman. Her once beautiful, bold, deep blue eyes were now hollow. The high-cheek bones were still there but her face was sagging and jowl-like. She was just a wrinkled up, humpbacked old woman. Her hair looked as if it had been in curlers or wrapped in a curling iron, but she had forgotten to comb it out. There was not a lot to say, and they both knew that too much time had passed. It was not the kind of friendship that could be picked up in one phone call and seem as if no time had passed since they last spoke. Gia had had that kind of friendship with Patti.

It wasn't until she married Lane, that she finally let go of Faith. She never gave her a reason why and there had never been a phone call from Faith to find out why she had not heard from her. Even in this day and age, with email, cell phones and long-distance packages, but still, there was not one word, not even out of curiosity. It was as if a weight had been lifted off her shoulders when she realized her work was done and her one-sided friendship was over. More than thirty years was wiped away with one last visit.

Going Home

Lane was waiting outside when Gia pulled into the driveway. Feeling a bit apprehensive, he watched her get out of the car. Worry had plagued him while she was away. If her trip had not gone as planned, then he had to wonder about their future. Seeing the smile on her face, he began to relax.

"Hi, you! How did it go?" he said with a half frown. He opened his arms for her, either way and wondered if she needed a hug for support, defeat or triumph?

"It went very well, Lane," she said closing the car door and walking up to his waiting arms.

"I'm so glad you're home, Gia."

"So am I Lane, so am I." Putting her hands on each side of his neck, she pulled him in for a quick kiss.

"It was worth the trip, Lane. I feel absolute freedom from all the baggage I've been dragging around my entire life. I truly didn't know what the outcome would be, but I'm glad I took the challenge. I won, Lane! I accomplished what I set out to do, and I won!" She was filled with so much joy that even Lane could feel it.

"Guess what I did?"

"Dare I ask?" he laughed.

"After I visited my parents' graves, I stopped to see Faith for a few minutes.

"Had you planned to see her?"

Walking arm in arm towards the edge of the lawn, they looked out over the serenity of the water.

"No, it was totally impromptu, but I'm glad I did, it helped me to tie up those loose ends with her, and I needed to go there."

"What else did you do; you were away for a few days?"

Turning to face him, she looked into his eyes and smiled. There were no tears in her eyes as she spoke. "Lane, I went through the house!"

"What house?" he asked.

"The old house, from my childhood."

"Gia, that's amazing, I'm so proud of you!" He hugged her tightly and when they pulled away, he waited for her to tell him about her trip back in time. Listening to her describe her journey, he saw a remarkable change in her attitude. She spoke without bitterness or tears. The smile on her face was one that he had never seen before, and it was beautiful. He loved her, baggage and all, but this was a wonderful transformation. He was extremely proud of her.

Looking out at the water and taking in the peaceful surroundings, they hadn't spoken for several minutes. They were both absorbing what had just transpired.

Finally, Lane turned to Gia and said, "Guess what I did?"

"What, Lane, what did you do?" She was being mischievous and playful, which he was not used to seeing.

"I quit smoking," he said quietly.

Wrapping her arms around his neck, she held him tight. "I'm so proud of you," she whispered into his neck.

"Actually, I had quit a few days before you left but you had so much on your plate to deal with, I decided to wait to surprise you with my news."

"It's a great surprise, thank you, Lane. You know how much I hated those things."

"Yes, I did, and you reminded me every time I lit one up!" he laughed. "I have another surprise for you."

"Oh? Do tell! She giggled as she tickled his ribs.

"I bought us tickets."

"Tickets! To where?" she asked wide-eyed.

"Paris, France. I want to take you to a few places I've seen while I was a commercial pilot. I planned it out with a travel agent. While you were away, I was busy too, Babe. I'm calling this your reward for daring to face your demons and live to come home and tell me about it!"

Picking her up, he swung her around once and put her down. "Good for you Sweetheart," he whispered into her hair. "By the way, we leave tomorrow at three o'clock."

Gia smiled at him and said, "Another journey!"

Other Titles by the Author

Gifted

Gifted in Kanyon Beach
Revised Edition

The Grand Manor

Timeless Love

Secrets in Kanyon Ridge

All books available online in either
eBook or paperback editions

Tidbits, Tips & Treasures
a Self-Help Book
Available Online as an eBook

Coming Soon

J O Y

**To remain in touch with Dee Cohoon-Madore, contact
her through her website at**
http://www.deelightfulreading.com/contact-dee

www.ingramcontent.com/pod-product-compliance
Lightning Source LLC
Chambersburg PA
CBHW051336020726
47501CB00007B/2116

* 9 7 8 0 9 8 6 9 5 0 7 3 5 *